TATOUINE

Jean-Christophe Réhel

TATOUINE

Translated by Katherine Hastings & Peter McCambridge

QC FICTION

Revision: Katherine Hastings, Peter McCambridge
Proofreading: David Warriner, Elizabeth West
Book design: Folio infographie
Cover & logo: Maison 1608 by Solisco
Fiction editor: Peter McCambridge

Originally published under the title *Ce qu'on respire sur Tatouine*
by Del Busso éditeur, 2018 (Montréal, Québec)
Translation copyright © Katherine Hastings, Peter McCambridge

ISBN 978-1-77186-228-8 pbk; 978-1-77186-235-6 epub; 978-1-77186-236-3 pdf

Legal Deposit, 3rd quarter 2020
Bibliothèque et Archives nationales du Québec
Library and Archives Canada

Published by QC Fiction, an imprint of Baraka Books
Printed and bound in Québec

TRADE DISTRIBUTION & RETURNS
Canada - UTP Distribution: UTPdistribution.com
United States & World - Independent Publishers Group: IPGbook.com

We acknowledge the financial support for translation and promotion of the Société de développement des entreprises culturelles (SODEC), the Government of Québec tax credit for book publishing administered by SODEC, the Government of Canada, and the Canada Council for the Arts.

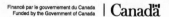

THE DAYS ARE LONG. By the end of my first shift, I considered committing seppuku between the hunting magazines and the Mauricie tourism guides. But I didn't. I've never had such a boring summer job. I never thought I'd get hired at a tourist office, but unfortunately for me, I was the only applicant. Nobody ever comes in. I arrange the brochures, I sweep the floor, I stare at the ceiling. Every now and again, Charles, the guy who works in the park, drops by for a chat. I can talk to him about *Star Wars* and my obsession with the planet Tatooine. I think about my life. Not very original, I know; everyone thinks about their life. I wonder what the hell I'm doing here. I've been learning Mandarin for the past couple of years. I watch Chinese TV every night. I started really getting into Asia after I saw *Crouching Tiger, Hidden Dragon* with Chow Yun-Fat. Now that I think about it, it's ridiculous to want to go work in Asia just because of a movie. I'd like to be an interpreter over there. Whatever. I'm thirty-one. I don't have a girlfriend. I've never really had a girlfriend. Sure, I've kissed a few girls. And a guy once, too. He was a really good kisser. No, that's not true: I had a girlfriend for two years. I even vacationed down south with her and her family once. I haven't been in love much. Once, maybe. And it wasn't with the girl I went on holiday with. I've fallen head over heels for thousands of glances, thousands of smiles, thousands of chins. I've had twinges of regret, disappointments, thoughts of death. Thoughts of death cause I'll never be able to know everyone. Cause I'll never be able to kiss everyone. I often feel like a ghost. A ghost who's learning Mandarin. A ghost who works in a tourist office. "Whoo-oo-oo-oo! Where's Trois-Rivières? Trois-Rivières is that way. Whoo-oo-oo-oo!" I try to find myself somewhere. I flick through the Gaspésie tourism guide. There I am. I'm the hole in Percé Rock.

It's sunny today. Blue sky, no clouds, no soul, no nothing. It's nine-thirty in the morning, and the heat is enough to burn your balls off. The air conditioning's not working. I open all the windows, but it's like being in a greenhouse. I'm a fucking Mandarin-speaking plant. I talked about Chewbacca with Charles, but he went off to mow the grass as soon as he saw a guy walk into the office. A man about fifty, wearing a bike helmet. I hate cyclists; they're always happy. He smiled when he saw me. "Phew, I just rode fifty clicks!" I replied, "Way to go, that's... that must be long." I didn't know what else to say. I have fifty clicks of skin wrapped around my heart. I don't feel much. I watch the flies buzzing around the office. There are tons of them. I try to kill them all with my cap. It takes me an hour to kill five flies. Where do flies go when they die? I picture ghost flies flitting around my head. I spot a cute girl walking up to the glass doors of the tourist office. There's something wrong with her; she's limping. I like girls who've got something wrong with them. She walks past my desk and heads to the washroom. She disappears. Another girl, another sorrow. It's incredible. Girls are like butterflies. They flutter, they dance when they walk, they appear like magic. They've barely come near me in months. I'm a very ugly flower, and the days are long. I've got a big, fat face. My face has gotten fatter. I've got fat cheeks. I try not to smile in photos, otherwise I look like I weigh about three hundred pounds. A three-hundred-pound flower. I look a little slimmer in the right pants. If my heart wore pants, it wouldn't even exist. The sunlight's done a one-eighty in the office. In the morning, the light's the right way up. In the evening, it's upside down. Like a bat.

The air conditioning's working again today, and I'm cold. I can't adjust the temperature. I'm wearing a sweatshirt. It hides my fat belly. My frozen, flowery potbelly. Everything's under control. Very early this morning, a man from Russia asked me how to get to Montreal. He'd come all this way to see the giant puppets. He lifted his arms in the air and repeated, "Big puppets! Five floors! Like that!" I didn't know what he was talking about. I looked it up online and the Russian got all excited: "Oh, yes, it's amazing, it's amazing!" He smelled like lilac. A scrawny Russian who smelled like lilac. I pretended they were really cool. I didn't want to hurt his feelings. The puppets creeped me out. There was something satanic about them. I would have burned them all one by one to save Montreal. The day went by slowly after that. A bunch of ladies walking their dogs. A man holding an ice cream cone, staring at the sun. It was pollen season. All the poplar trees were giving off sticky, floury flakes. In the sunlight, it looked like the trees were dropping dimes from their pockets. An old guy came into the office and said, "Where's the snow coming from?" I liked that. I told him it was coming from the trees. He didn't believe me. He laughed. I laughed, too, just to humour him.

It's raining. The place is empty. Charles didn't come to see me today. Too bad. I would have talked to him about R2-D2. I went outside to smoke on the porch. On the paths in the park, the pollen was dirty. It looked like wet poodle fur. It felt like I was smoking little waves of pollen, my lungs swaddled in a white cocoon. I don't think I'm much use in this life; I don't serve any purpose. I don't know, I would have liked to have been a wrench or something. I'd have known exactly what I was expected to do, and I'd never have questioned it. I think of useful things: the sun is useful, car tires are useful, a flowerpot's useful. I smoke a cigarette and watch the rain. I smoke nine cigarettes, one for each hour of work. Cats have nine lives, and I smoked nine cigarettes. A homeless guy came in. He looked at all the displays. He asked me how to get to Highway 20. He went to the washroom. He dried his socks under the hand dryer. The rain stopped. The sun came out. I would have liked to have been a hand dryer.

I like to choose random books at the library. Yesterday, I picked up a book by Thomas Hirschhorn, a Swiss artist. On the back cover it says, "There's nothing else to be done." And beneath that, a question, "When shall we light the fire?" Anytime, Thomas! I'd set fire to trees, flowers, houses. I'd set fire to anything that moves. I have a little volcano in each eye. At lunchtime, I had a nosebleed. I blow my nose too much. I blow my nose to pass the time. I saw the police drive by the tourist office. I'm glad the cops can't read my mind. They'd arrest me, for sure. In the afternoon, three women asked me if I had a brochure for an inn, the Auberge du Mange-Grenouille. They were wearing little crosses around their necks. If Jesus had had a belly, I might have been a Catholic. I just can't relate to such an athletic-looking guy. There's no way they'd let me into heaven. They'd probably tell me to go jogging. Fuck you, Jesus. Behind my counter, the silence is deafening. I saw a branch fall from a big poplar tree. I would have liked to bury that branch, to say a little prayer for it.

Charles arrives at the office. He's trembling a little. He's sweating. "A guy... a guy tried to kill himself in his car!" A man had put some propane tanks on the backseat of his car, had set fire to a jerrycan of gas, and had stumbled out of his car screaming, in panic, his head, his back, his arms badly burned, he was still conscious, sitting on the ground, the car a smouldering wreck, the fear, all four tires had exploded, he was screaming that he wanted to die. "It was a movie. It was like in a movie!" I scratched at my skin. I'm a hypochondriac. I invent my own invisible ailments. When someone has a cold, I have a cold. When someone's quadriplegic, I can't move my limbs anymore. When someone fucks up their suicide, I'm a car that won't burn. I try to lighten the mood and explain to Charles how the Ewoks managed to defeat the Empire in *Return of the Jedi*. The rest of the day goes by slowly. I think about the scorched guy and about the Ewoks. I brought a Cara Cara orange to work. Peeling an orange is like building a house or making love: it takes time. I look at the clock. I'm late closing up. I turn off the lights and lock the office door. On my way out, a butterfly flutters around my shoes. I'm afraid I'll step on it. I'm a green grape.

Summer is a Chinese ghost. It's September and it's stinking hot. That's life. To justify it all, I say, "That's life." My last day at work is done. I feel nothing. I get in my car and drive. A song by the Beatles comes on the radio. I'm crying. I'm not sad. I stop to eat at McDonald's.

It's full of people. I order two meals. I'm ashamed.
I sit down in a booth. I feel something touch my back.
A little girl is looking at me. She smiles. She's holding
a toy, a little ninja figurine. She pretends to give me a
few kicks. I pretend it hurts. She laughs. Her mother's
talking on her phone. I try to translate "little rascal"
into Mandarin, but I don't know how. I smoke a cigarette in the McDonald's parking lot. The smoke hides
my face. The smoke makes me disappear a little in the
McDonald's parking lot.

I dropped out of university. I started to hate Mandarin.
I started to hate Chow Yun-Fat. I'm at the bank. I don't
like banks. I feel like I'm sweating interest rates. I'm
depositing my royalty cheque for the last poetry collection I wrote. There's only one person behind the
counter. I'm stuck with Mrs. Nosy. She wants to know
where the money came from. "It fell from the sky." I'm
full of myself. Not in the mood to talk. I just want to
get paid. She knows me. Whenever I have a deposit
to make, I always go to the bank. I could deposit the
cheque at the ATM or even take a photo of it with my
phone, but I don't trust machines. I'm scared I'll mess
it up and lose my money, scared someone will say, "You
never deposited that money. You never wrote those
poems." I am a hundred and two years old. I'm out of
breath, always out of breath. I have cystic fibrosis. I'm
depositing a cheque for $702.69 because I wrote a few
poems, and I have a lung disease. I barely smoke at all

now. Instead I eat breakfast out every morning. Maybe I'll live a day longer. Maybe a year. Maybe I'll come back as a Big Mac. Anyway. Mrs. Nosy is pecking away at her computer. I applied to extend my line of credit, she says. I don't remember anymore. Oh, that's right, I did. A while ago now. I'd bought a bed and two bedside tables at Structube. I didn't have the money in my account. For two months, I had just the one bedside table. I was pissed. Then I wondered why I needed two anyway. I live by myself, don't have a girlfriend. "You have to have two," my sister said. "You just do." "I live by myself." "Doesn't change a thing." I leave my glasses on the table to the left and my phone on the table to the right. Mrs. Nosy asks if I still want a bigger line of credit. I'm hungry, don't really know, so I say yes. I end up in an office with a financial advisor. She looks at her screen. "It's been a while... 2015. The last time we saw each other was 2015." "Oh." She asks if I'm still sick. I don't remember telling her I was sick. "Yes, I'm still sick." I laugh. It's not funny, but I laugh. She laughs, too. I bump my line of credit up to $5,000. That makes her smile. At least now I'll be able to buy all the bedside tables I want. I'll be able to build a barricade with the bedside tables in my room. I'll be able to go to war against everyone who's not sick. After the bank, I go have breakfast at Chez Rémi. I eat there all the time. If I've written a good poem, I'm allowed to have eggs. I lie to myself. Most of the time my poems are bad, and I have eggs all the same. I pretend my writing's going well.

By the time I leave the restaurant, my cheque's down to $690.69. All the same, I can't help stopping by the Halloween store at the mall. I buy a scary rubber mask. A green monster with yellow eyes, its mouth closed. It looks a little like me, I think. My cheque shrinks to $610.69, and just like that I don't have enough money for my rent. I'm a green monster with yellow eyes who might end up sleeping on the streets next month. Beside the Halloween store, I see an ad in the window of a shoe store. They're looking for someone to work out the back. I go into the store. A young woman greets me with an enthusiastic smile. She seems happy, which makes me happy. "Good morning!" "Hi." "Can I help you, sir? Looking for anything in particular?" "Actually, I'm looking for a job." She bursts out laughing. I notice her nail extensions. They're long and blue. I'd like to have blue nails, too. I'd like to have one really long nail so I could switch off the light without having to get out of bed. She asks if I have a resumé. "Not on me, no." I pretend to be a little rueful. "We've been looking for someone to work in the back for three months. Write down your phone number and when you're available. I'm pretty sure the manager will call you." She hands me a pen and paper. I pretend to be pleased. I would rather it hadn't worked out. I could have walked away, disappeared forever. I set down my mask on the counter and write that I'm available anytime. The saleswoman lets out a little shriek. "Oh my God, I *love* Halloween!" She holds the green face in her hands and gives it a shake. It feels like

17

she's holding my face; it feels like I'm going to get the job. I wish I hadn't given them my real phone number. I should have put down the number of a funeral home. I should have run away or hidden in a shoe. That would solve all my problems. I should just go live in a shoe.

I've had the same routine for the past few days: I have breakfast at Chez Rémi, I work at the shoe store, skip lunch, finish shelving the boxes in the back of the store, stop by the convenience store, go home, heat up a frozen meal, and write poems. When I'm at work, I sort the shoes by size and colour. I stack the boxes. Every which way. They're never in the proper order. If there's a mistake, I have to move row after row of boxes on the shelves. They're all piled up on top of each other. I need a stepladder to do it. I have to go up and down and up and down and up again. All the boxes are white, and they form long, separate corridors. I feel like Jack Nicholson in *The Shining*, but without the axe, the kid, and the wife. When I walk down the rows, there's barely enough room for my shoulders. I have a hard time breathing. Maybe there are too many boxes of shoes in my lungs; maybe it's too much mucus. Once I'm at the top of the stepladder, I have a coughing fit and open a shoebox. The manager doesn't know I hork into the boxes. The manager doesn't like me. She asked me to initial the sticker on the sole of every shoe I shelve. She wanted to see my mistakes. After a while, every mistake could be traced back to me. Now, whenever the manager comes into the back of the store for a box, I pretend to be writing my initials, just like I pretended to be playing the recorder during music class at elementary school. And like I pretended to be playing the saxophone at high school. I hate playing instruments. I never figured out the tunes, the holes, the sounds. The reed of my saxophone—or the "fucking reed" as I always called it—would be too wet, or it wouldn't vibrate in the mouthpiece. I've always been a bit of a pretender. I've pretended to study, pretended to laugh, pretended to come, pretended to be happy. It's the same technique. I often wait for things to blow up in my face. I don't like working. I don't like much besides having breakfast at Chez Rémi and writing poems. I'm often depressed. I drink a glass of water and I get depressed. I drink something stronger and it goes away and comes back and I go back to water. I live in Repentigny. I found myself a little apartment by the mall. It's handy. For the longest time, I didn't have a car. "Why don't you buy a car?" people would keep asking. And I'd say that I didn't know where to go, that I didn't have any money. Now I have a car and I still don't know where to go. Now people say, "Get a new job, go back to school, earn more money." Just to change the subject, I tell them, "Yeah, I'll do that." I dropped my Mandarin classes and, this morning, my manager caught me horking into a box. She yelled at me and told me to never do that again. I didn't say anything. I don't do anything. I'm good at doing nothing. I'm good at having no plans. I just stand there in the living room and water the plants. I've got big plants and small plants. I don't ask myself too many questions. Listening to the radio makes my head spin. Too many ideas, too many words. The same thing, over and over. The news is a potted plant.

I get on my bike. How I manage to keep my balance is a mystery. Like all those hushed-up documents on JFK and the autumn leaves that fall quicker from one tree than from another. It's a conspiracy. I don't want to know the answers. The pumpkin on my balcony will be dead by Halloween. It's a conspiracy. If I were a tree, I'd still have leaves in February. People would say, "What the fuck?" I don't fall off my bike. What the fuck? Leaves. What the fuck? The wind that day in Dallas? What the fuck? I put on a pair of jeans. It's complicated; I'm risking my life here. My leaves still aren't falling. At Chez Rémi, I always order the same thing: two eggs over easy–bacon–white bread. I try to say it as fast as I can. The waitress is proud of me. It's a mystery. I walk along the sidewalk. A guy pulls up alongside me in his car, asks for directions. I repeat the directions several times over, wave my hand around so that he gets the idea. I put my heart into it: key information, left, left, right, left. He says thanks, then disappears. Hours later, I realize I sent him the wrong way. I'm balancing on a leaf. It's a conspiracy. I have spicy pad thai for lunch. After that, I head over to the Super C grocery store across from my apartment to pick up a twelve-pack of beer and a box of Lucky Charms. I eat a bowl of cereal, I drink seven bottles of beer. I go to the bar not far from where I live. I drink alone. I write a short poem at one of the tables. A friend asked me out for a drink. I stop writing when he gets there. I hide my poem in my pocket. He asks how I'm doing. "Great." Everything's always great. It's less complicated that way. "I'm selling my condo," he says. "Wow." He asks when I'm going to write a novel. "I can't," I say. "I only write poems. I finished another collection. It's going to be published next year." He won't drop the nonexistent novel. "Poetry doesn't sell," he says. He's not wrong there. I don't tell him that my poems paid for a Halloween mask and half the rent.

I never win anything. I've never won a prize. I make myself a tomato sandwich. I put lots of pepper on it. I notice they've cut down the tree behind my apartment building. Now, when I'm doing the dishes or making a sandwich, I can gaze at two streetlamps on Rue Iberville. I can see the grey apartment buildings across the road a little better now. They're not dirty; they're new. They're grey metal. My tongue is grey. I think that, beneath my skin, there's a grey metal apartment building. I smoke a cigarette. I can't stop. I have a smoke before doing my lung treatment. I prepare the medicine. I have to take three millilitres of sodium chloride solution using a syringe. I have to mix the chloride with Colomycin powder. I put the mixture in a nebulizer that's connected to a compressor. It sounds like a car engine. I breathe in the mist, I breathe in the medicine. I cough, I spit, I cry. I'm not sad. I'm congested. My lungs are stuck together. I'm trying to unstick them. I've always had sticky lungs. I started to smoke when I turned twenty-five. I got hooked on smoking after I was hospitalized for a different problem. I had a serious bout of anemia. I passed out in the Rona parking lot. I was this close to having a blood transfusion. I was kind of traumatized by the whole hospital experience. I thought I was going to die. I shared a room with a paraplegic called Louis. He kept repeating the same thing over and over, kept shouting that he wanted to kill himself. The nurses never managed to calm him down. I wore my headphones all day long. I had to wait until my hemoglobin count went back up before they'd release me from hospital. In the meantime, the doctors speculated, they were expecting the worst. They thought I had cancer. Then, thanks to the cortisone, my hemoglobin climbed back up. They let me go. For six months, I had to go to the hospital every week for blood tests. Then the visits grew fewer and farther apart. There was a risk my hemoglobin would drop again without warning. The doctor I saw regularly looked like Beetlejuice, and he didn't know why I'd contracted anemia. He said, "It's idiopathic, we don't know the exact cause. You've got autoimmune hemolytic anemia. It's idiopathic, that's all we know." That's when I started to smoke. So, then. I stare at the ceiling in my apartment. There's a little spider making its way across. I don't feel like killing it. I finish my cigarette.

I won't go to Chez Rémi tomorrow. I'd like to mingle with the trees on the other side of the street. I'd like to love a woman. I would rub her back. She'd say, "You're making a fire on my back." It's raining. I'd be able to make a fire on her back even if it's raining. I stare at the leaves stuck to the asphalt on my street. I feel sorry for dead leaves. I would take in all those sad-looking leaves in my apartment. I would dry them one by one by the patio door. It would take ages. I'd burn them on the back of the woman I love, just to watch them glow at night. Just so I wouldn't miss a single flicker at night.

I didn't drive my car to the hospital. I never take my car when I go to Montreal; I'm afraid I'd cause an accident. In the waiting room, I think again about the spit drying in shoeboxes, and I laugh to myself. I scan my health insurance card at the counter. A number pops out. I have to stay alert. There are plasma screens on the walls of the waiting room with numbers flashing across them. On the other side, big windows look out over Montreal, showing the city from another angle. I have to go for a spirometry test. It checks the amount of air in my lungs to see if I have a lung infection. I've never had good results. They call my number. I walk past a door, down a corridor, into a smaller room. The respiratory therapist appears in the doorway and asks me to weigh myself. The scale shows two hundred pounds. I say: "Wow." I'm only five foot nine. I feel swollen. My skin's swollen. My heart's swollen. I feel my belly. It's hard, it doesn't give, it doesn't deflate, it stays taut. It wants to leave, and so do I. Only I don't know where to go. I touch my cheeks. It feels like my cheeks are four times too big. But I'm not hiding any food in them. If I could, I would, for sure. I had a dwarf hamster once, for two years. His name was Paul. I used to stick him in a little plastic ball, and he would roam around the apartment on his own. Paul always went to the same places: the kitchen, near the microwave, or next to his cage in his room. I'd always wondered why the stupid thing always went to the same spots. Then I realized that I was exactly like my hamster. I don't travel. I always go to the same places in my apartment. I always sit at the same table at Chez Rémi. I always order the same thing. I always take the same route to work. I always sleep on the right side of my double bed. I feel empty. Paul died last year. He had an ear infection. I woke up one morning, and he was bleeding from one ear. I took him to the vet. They told me there wasn't much they could do. I had him put down. I still don't know if they actually gave him an injection or just stuck him in the garbage. I cried when I went to pay with my debit card. The lady at the desk tried to comfort me. "Are you alright, sir?" "Yeah, yeah, I'm fine." The respiratory therapist passes me the nose clip. I blow into a tube connected to a little computer. He says gently, "Blooooow" and tells me to take a breath and blow out into the machine for as long as I can. It shows 43%. The air that's getting into my lungs is a number. It's a lot like my math grades. I'm usually around 48%.

The respiratory therapist cracks a few jokes. He tries to lighten the mood. It's nice out. I don't want to be an asshole. I laugh at his jokes. I want to kill myself. I look at the window; I think about throwing myself out the window. Then I think what an idiot I am. I get three tries. Three chances to blow into the machine, I mean, not to jump out the window. I blow three times. I get 43% all three times. "OK." The doctor sees me in her office. She asks how I'm doing; she takes my blood pressure. It's a bit high. "Oh." She takes it again, but it's still high. "Let's try the other arm." The third time is even worse: 160 over I don't know what. "OK, we're going to stop there." To explain away my high blood pressure, I tell her, "I think I have white coat syndrome." But actually, I'm not sure. I'd like to be able to use white coat syndrome as an excuse to avoid going to work, or paying the rent. She says, "You're going to have to buy a little device at the drugstore and test yourself at home." The only thing I feel like doing is going to eat at A&W. She adds, "I think it could be a good idea to give you an intravenous treatment, too." "OK." I don't really have a choice; I've never really had the choice. I've already had a dozen IV treatments. I know the drill. When I leave the office, I already know when they'll be putting in my PICC line. I call my boss. I tell her I'm going to be off work for three weeks. She seems irritated, but resigned. I tell her I have cystic fibrosis. I never tell my employers I have a lung disease in case they decide not to hire me. I don't have insurance. My provincial health insurance covers part of my expenses while I'm on antibiotic treatments. It doesn't pay the rent, but it's better than nothing. When I was a kid, I loved to skateboard and I wanted to be a computer scientist. Now I eat at Chez Rémi and I write poems. The pay's lousy. I think about my friends' jobs: police officer, firefighter, accountant, carpenter. But in my case, I'm sick. I've never managed to get a good job. My eyesight's poor. I'm not good with my hands. I pretend to count when the cashier at the corner store gives me my change. I studied French literature. I quit university after three semesters. Then I went back to study Mandarin; I don't know why. On my way out of the hospital I write a poem about a volcano that has cold feet, and I think about all my friends who have kids or homes. I'm 43% volcano. I take the bus. I'm hot. I keep my coat zipped up the whole way. I get off the bus and go to the A&W next to the bus station. I order a Teen Burger, onion rings, and an iced tea. My blood pressure calls me a stupid asshole. Fuck off. My blood pressure changes with the wind. I notice the guy behind the cash has something wrong with his hands. His right hand has two fingers, and the other has only one. It reminds me of my lungs, and I think it's a good look. The cashier is nice. He asks how things are going. "Like the wind," I reply.

I get my line put in on Halloween. I got up super early to take the bus. I couldn't sleep anyway. PICC line mornings always do that to me. I'm not looking forward to what comes next. Injecting myself three times a day in my kitchen. Taking a shower with my arm stuck up in the air. Visits to the clinic to have my bandages and tubes changed. The drugstore delivery lady who brings me huge bags of meds I have to inject into myself. Yeah, whatever. I eat my Lucky Charms. The pumpkin on my balcony is black. I've got an hour to kill before I take the bus. I pull out the Halloween makeup kit I've had for ages. I want to be a vampire. I wish Halloween would last 365 days a year so I could spit in a shoebox, disguised as a vampire. I've only got white face paint left. I'll be a ghost instead. I cover my face with white makeup. Lots of it. I don't look much like a ghost. I look like a guy wearing a lot of face paint. I want to wipe off the makeup, but I realize I'm running late. I throw on my coat and my boots, and I leave the apartment. I manage to catch the bus on time. During the ride, I listen to *Consideration* by Rihanna seven times. In the song, she says when she looks outside her window, she can't get no peace of mind. Neither can I. Rihanna and me, we're made for each other. If I was going out with Rihanna, I could go to the hospital by helicopter. I still wouldn't have any peace of mind, but at least I'd get to fly in a helicopter. When I get on the metro, a little girl stares at me. She's sitting on her father's lap. I stare at my reflection in the metro car window. My makeup doesn't cover my black stubble or my eyebrows. I'm pale. I'm attached to a metal pole. I can't float through it. I'm not a ghost.

I walk through the main entrance and go wash my face in the hospital washroom, but I can't get rid of all the face paint. "Fuck it, I'll go as half a ghost." I remember buying a Halloween mask. That would've been simpler. I go up to the third floor and sign in. They call my name. A cute nurse comes to get me. She's wearing a little mask that covers her nose and mouth. She smiles at me with her eyes. "Take off your shirt, put on a hospital gown, and come join me just over there." I lie down on a table, stretch out my arm on a board that juts out. A man disinfects my bicep. Blue paper covers my shoulder and part of my face. I can smell the disinfectant. A surgeon comes over to me. He's in a good mood. He whistles as he looks inside my arm with a little camera that he presses against my bicep. He studies a little TV screen, looks for the right vein, freezes the vein with a needle. It stings, it smarts, it burns. "How do you feel?" he asks. "Like I'm on a water slide." Everyone laughs. I'm a comedian. The surgeon inserts the line. It goes in smoothly. I could really go for a smoke. Last time, the surgeon hit a nerve. My arm shot up all by itself. It was like an electric shock times a thousand, stabbing me in the armpit. I cried out; there was a long silence in the operating room. I think about the Ewoks. I go up to the sixth floor. They need to give me my meds before I leave. I sit there in a big armchair for two hours. An attractive black woman comes to see me every half hour and asks if I'm OK. "You're not gonna die on my shift, are you?" I laugh. She has a big gap between her front teeth. It makes her even cuter. A man in a hunting shirt is sitting in the same waiting room as me, reading the paper. His left foot is wrapped in a huge bandage. When the nurse takes it off to give him a new dressing, I see that he's missing two toes and has a hole in the sole of his foot. I stare at the hole in my bicep where the line enters my arm. We're both full of holes. We could be brothers. I'm still the hole in Percé Rock.

I leave the hospital and walk to the closest McDonald's. I'm hungry, and feeling a bit woozy. I buy four cheeseburgers, a poutine, and six chicken nuggets, careful all the while not to look the cashier in the eye. I eat everything, feel funny. I shouldn't really be wandering around. I have meds to take at set times. I check my bank account balance on my phone. Counting my last pay and my royalty cheque, there's somewhere around $200. Call it $241.25, before I take the metro and the bus home. I'm going to have to go to the food bank or buy my groceries at Dollarama this month. In the classes on offer at school, I've never seen "Tips and Tricks for Eating at the Dollar Store." It's already dark by the time I get home. I spend an hour looking for a movie to watch. I can't find anything. I throw my pumpkin out. I make myself some Lipton soup. My phone pings at ten o'clock. I inject my meds. I haven't seen a single kid walk by in a Halloween costume. It would have been nice to see a little witch or two. I wish I'd seen a ghost, at least.

This morning, my landlord called and asked if I wanted to shovel the sidewalks outside the apartment building this winter. I don't, but I said yes. Twenty bucks a snowstorm. The apartment's cold. I turn up the heat for the first time since the fall. It smells like something's burning. I'm going to have to move out. I can't afford a two-bedroom place, even if I shovel all the snow in the world. I inject myself with the first dose of the morning at eight o'clock and make two slices of cheese on toast. I tuck the line into the little white mesh cover that runs around my bicep. I take a nap. A half hour later, I wake with a jump. My ass is on fire. It's unbelievable. I go take a cold shower. I lather up my butt for ages and gently pat myself dry. Nothing doing. It itches like hell, all the way down to below my butt cheeks. I try hard not to scratch, but I can't help it. I claw at my skin. I manage to sleep for forty-five minutes on the couch. I inject my afternoon dose at two o'clock. I walk around the apartment naked. It's cold out, so I turn up the heat. Maybe that's why my ass is on fire. I study the second little bottle that holds my meds. Little bubbles float down the tube and disappear into my arm. I'd like to be a bubble, to disappear into an arm. My bottle looks like a baby's bottle. There's a little balloon of drugs inside. When I connect the two lines together, it creates a suction effect, and the liquid pours into my body. I know I'm done when the balloon has gone from inside the bottle. I'm laid out on the sofa, and to pass the time I read the directions on one of the bottles: "... every twelve hours." I leap to my feet and start freaking out. I've been taking it every eight hours for the past two days. I call the nurse. "Drink lots of water, stop taking it right away, and come see me tomorrow." I ask if it's dangerous and she says, "Yes, it can be dangerous." I don't feel like going into Montreal. I don't feel like dying. I'm naked in my kitchen, drinking twenty glasses of water. My stomach's all swollen; I need to pee every half hour. I'm gonna die, no doubt about it. I'm gonna die, butt naked in my kitchen. They'll find my body right after the first snow, when the landlord comes by the apartment block and sees I haven't been shovelling. To take my mind off things, I start looking online for a room to rent. There's one in a house not too far away. It's $400 for electricity, Internet, and rent: twenty snowstorms a month and that's before I've even eaten. I get dressed and go outside. I spend the rest of the day in a café. It rains. The sky is grey, the sky is white. I stay there all afternoon and part of the evening. I write a poem about a snowstorm that doesn't have a cent to its name. There's a row of reeds alongside the windows, all a little bent beneath the weight of the rain. Tiny drops of water are stuck to the end of each narrow stalk. I keep waiting for them to fall, but they stay like that all day. The fuckers.

While the dermatologist examines my butt, I remember once having really sore testicles when I was a teenager. I saw three different doctors about it. They'd all had a good feel, without ever figuring out where the pain was coming from. I'd bared my balls for absolutely nothing. I thought the same thing as they prodded at my butt: I'm going to have bared my ass for absolutely nothing. When I pull my pants back up, the dermatologist says, "May I take a photo?" I don't see why. He insists: "I'd like to take a photo. For my students." "No." He tells me that I have baboon syndrome. A condition that attacks the folds of the joints: the armpits, buttocks, knees, and arms. I'm having an allergic reaction to one of the intravenous drugs. "It's documented, but it's not especially common." The dermatologist looks like Viggo Mortensen in *Lord of the Rings*. Aragorn with grey hair, Aragorn out to destroy the Ring as he inspects my ass. He prescribes me a very strong cortisone cream to soothe the itching. He repeats, "Wash your hands well, give yourself a good rinse, watch your eyes." I spend the rest of the afternoon at the hospital. The nurse fills twelve vials with blood. They want to know if I'm going to die because I messed up the dose. It's the final countdown. I wait for the lab results. If I could swap every hour spent in a hospital for a pushup, I'd be all muscle by now. I go into the doctor's office. She's waiting for me with a smile. "Baboon syndrome?" I shrug my shoulders and close my eyes. She laughs. I'm a comedian. She tells me that's a new one on her, that the blood tests came back normal. I'm a baboon, a miraculously cured baboon.

I keep going with the intravenous treatments for a few more days. It still itches, but the super powerful cream helps me through it. I wish I could put the cream on all my problems. I could be normal, could live a normal life. I write some poems for a literary magazine, I make soup, don't drink any beer, don't smoke. I'm a good boy. I don't go out, except to get my dressing changed at the clinic a ten-minute drive away. My car's almost out of gas. I'm almost out of money. I'm a month behind in my rent. The landlord takes pity on me when he sees my arm. He gives me more time. The days fly by. I get my line taken out. The nurse tells me to take a deep breath. She yanks the line out of my arm at lightning speed. I keep the dressing for another twenty-four hours, long enough for the hole in my bicep to heal. I'm not to pick at the scab. I take a shower, lather up my bicep around the scab. I haven't washed my right arm in weeks. "My bicep isn't big enough to light me up," I tell myself again and again in the shower. I've nothing left to eat in the fridge. Nothing but a tub of margarine that's almost brand new. I go to Chez Rémi. Breakfast costs me $10 with tip. Not too bad. At the restaurant, a guy walks past me with an old woman on his arm. She's wearing a bandana on her head. I hear her talking to the waitress. They know each other. I only make out a few words: "Chemotherapy... lungs... it's long... the weather could be better... the potatoes are good." I recognize the guy holding her arm. I worked with him a couple of years ago selling lawn-care estimates over the phone. It was the middle of winter. I didn't even understand what I was selling. There were snowbanks everywhere, and I was telling people that a team would "come round to estimate how much it would cost to look after your lawn." There were maybe eight of us in that tiny office. I would stuff a finger in one ear so that I could hear. I had my text with all the keywords in front of me. I remember the pressure, the big whiteboard, the boss, an asshole in his thirties who'd keep shouting that there were targets to meet if we wanted to keep our jobs. There was always a zero beside my name. We'd call random numbers when people were having supper. Half the time, they'd tell me where to go or just hang up. I might have managed to rip two people off. I remember feeling proud of myself. I worked there for two weeks before they showed me the door. It was a real shit job now that I look back on it. I chuckle out loud in the restaurant. The guy whose grandmother is in chemo catches my eye, but he doesn't seem to recognize me. We didn't talk much. I don't know what I might even have said. "Hey. I write poems and I have baboon syndrome." I wonder if I'll get cancer one day. I wonder if I'll go through chemotherapy some day. I grin like a dumbass on my way home. My heart is a lawn with a snowbank on top.

I don't go back to work at the shoe store; I don't return my boss's calls. I'm a bastard. So sue me. Since I decided not to go back, one of my wisdom teeth has started to hurt. I think she cast a spell on me. I feel the glimmer of a massive fire in my mouth. I decide to go visit the room I saw advertised the other day. When I get to the front door, there's not a single light on inside. It looks like there's no one home. I ring the doorbell anyway. Someone comes to open the door; it's the landlord, I'm sure. He stares at me. It smells like ground meat frying. I say, "I'm here about the ad." He invites me in. He reminds me of Joe Pesci in *Goodfellas*. He shows me to the basement. I can't see a thing; it's pitch black. As we go down the stairs, he tells me his name is Norm. I feel a little less scared. The windows are tiny. The basement's not very big. There's a leather sofa with a Ninja Turtles blanket rolled into a ball. The TV's on, but the sound's off. The ceiling is low. "There's a bathroom over there, and another bedroom, but it's even smaller." The mood's a bit strained. Norm turns left just past the sofa. We enter a small, dark room. He spreads his arms. "Voilà... There's room for a single bed, a desk, a small dresser." "I've got a double bed and two bedside tables." I realize from his expression that I'm going to have to kiss goodbye to my bedside tables. Goddammit. I walk around the room. It doesn't take long. Norm watches me. "Take your time. I've got a pot on the stove. I'll be back." I look out the window. Even though the shed at the end of the yard is in the way, I can still see a sliver of sky. It's a brilliant blue. There are a few bus-shaped clouds blocking the view a bit. Maybe it's nicer that way, I dunno.

I'm the eldest, but next to my sister Cammy I feel retarded. She's travelled all over the place. She lived for a year in Australia. She met her boyfriend in Bali. He's American. He was living on an island, working as an underwater photographer for tourists. Now she and Aaron live in New York City. I call Cammy. I only ever call her when something's wrong. She says, "What's wrong?" "Oh, nothing. I just wanted to see how you're doing." There's a moment of silence, then, "C'mon... What's wrong?" I tell her about the rent, the room, the furniture I'm going to have to move, the job I lost. She sounds disappointed. I can't see her, but I can picture her in my mind's eye: a small, svelte blonde. Then there's me: the retarded, brown-haired alien brother. I've always wondered whether we're really brother and sister. Cammy got her life in order very early on. Whereas I've always let myself go a bit. When people talk to me, I let myself go. When I make my breakfast, I let myself go. When I write poetry, I let myself go, only a bit less. My sister's never judged me. She's always been there when I needed help. I hear a dog barking in the background. "You've got a dog?" She tells me they got it yesterday. It pisses all over the place, but she loves it. There's a silence. I get the feeling it's my turn to talk. "I could use your help, just for a day... We could go get our shots together. I bet you haven't had your shot this year." She laughs. The next day, Cammy shows up in Repentigny with her dog and her boyfriend. Aaron has never really liked me. I don't think he dislikes me; it's just, you know. I struggle to find the right words. I can't find anything intelligent to say. I pour a glass of orange juice for Aaron, but he's not thirsty. "Oh, no thanks, man." I drink it instead. "I made up a bed for you guys. That extra room's gonna come in handy." Aaron goes off to the bathroom. Cammy sits there in the kitchen and strokes her little dog. She gives me a strained smile. "We were actually thinking of staying at a hotel." "Oh, alright, OK then." She asks me if I can look after Elliott Smith. "Elliott Smith?" She laughs. "It was Aaron's idea. He loves the song, *Angeles*." "Oh, OK." I say yes, even though I don't like dogs. I don't really have a choice. I have nothing in common with them. I'm always afraid they'll bite me. When I was about eleven, I went on holiday to Guadeloupe with my dad and my sister. A big German Shepherd jumped on me, baring its fangs. A French guy who was passing by ran over and gave the dog a whack. The whole time we were on holiday I kept seeing that dog prowling the beach. I was terrified it'd find me and gobble me up. Sometimes I imagine it walking down my street in Repentigny. Other times, I get this feeling it's hiding behind my shower curtain. It jumps on me, trying to rip my throat open. There's blood everywhere, but I don't die. To calm it down, I tell it I'm sorry. I give it a bowl of Lucky Charms. And we make peace.

We went to get our shots, then Cammy went off to the hotel with Aaron, promising they'd be back early in the morning to help me move. I don't have much in the way of furniture. I'm giving practically everything to my landlord. We made a deal to cover the two months of rent that I can't pay. I'm leaving him my stove, fridge, washer, dryer, sofa, and kitchen table. The hardest things to move are going to be the books on my shelf. I've got too many novels and comic books. I bring Elliott into my room and I lie down on the bed. As soon as they left, Elliott Smith started whining by the front door. I gave him some dog biscuits my sister had left me. He wasn't having any of it. I tried giving him some baloney. He just gave me a "What the fuck?" look and barked even louder. I heard someone knocking at the door. I remembered there was a no-animals rule in my apartment building. It was my neighbour. She looked a bit like Annie Wilkes in *Misery*. When I moved in, I'd promised myself to never break a leg in the stairwell. She was not happy. "Can't a person get a little sleep around here? What's that?" She pointed to the dog. "That's Elliott Smith." She was pissed. She went back to her apartment and slammed the door. Too bad for her. I'm out of here tomorrow anyway. Elliott Smith keeps barking. I google his breed. After a little searching, I decide he must be a Boston Terrier. I put him on his leash and take him for a walk. I ask him if it sucks to live in New York, seeing as he's from Boston and all. He looks at me in silence. We turn right on Richelieu, then right again on Iberville. Elliott Smith tries to run off. He pulls with all his might on the leash. My arm is weak after my flu shot. I'm afraid he'll take off. I knot the leash around my wrist. We walk for a long time. I think about my sister. She's healthy. She doesn't have cystic fibrosis. I've always wondered what kind of person I would have been if she'd had the disease instead. I would've been different for sure. Maybe I would have been an accountant with lots of money. Maybe I'd have played golf. I'm sure I would have played golf if I didn't have cystic fibrosis. Or maybe I'd already be dead. Maybe my sister saved me again without me realizing it.

I'm shaped by the wind. I'm standing in front of my apartment with my living-room floor lamp when a gust of wind pushes me from behind. The wind tries to carve a hole out of my back and I think, "I'm shaped by the wind." My sister's boyfriend's car seems incredibly far away. My arm still feels weak. After four boxes of books, I say to my sister, "My arm's a bit sore." She replies, "Brilliant idea to get your flu shot the day before you move." I don't answer. Aaron is looking grumpy. I didn't dare offer him another glass of orange juice. I get it. If I were him, I wouldn't feel like helping out a thirty-one-year-old retard who didn't ask his friends to help him move cause he was afraid they'd knock his new apartment. A big retard who has to get his little sister to help, and who can't even stand up to a gust of wind. Well, at least I was smart to get rid of the big pieces of furniture and to solve my rent problem. I see Cammy come out carrying a kitchen chair. "Oh no, that stays there." She doesn't get it. "Aren't you taking Mom and Dad's kitchen table?" "No." She looks sad. I tell her, "It's only a table." But I'm sad, too. I'm nostalgic. I get attached to things, maybe even more than I do to people. One time, a girl said to me, "You're a Taurus," and ever since, I've been using my star sign to explain away my actions. I don't believe a word of it, but it makes things easier. Everything in my life has a story. Take, for example, my magenta sofa with the flowers on it. It's ugly, but I like it. It reminds me of my dad and table hockey and wrestling. When I was little, my dad used to hold me up in the air and throw me onto that sofa. Now, I'm giving it to my landlord. Actually, I'm giving it to his brother. When we made our deal, my landlord said, "My brother's moving in here." He's going to take all my furniture. He's going to live my life a little. I wonder if he writes poetry. I wonder if he's a Taurus. I wonder if he, too, is shaped by the wind.

I realize that lots of things are touched by the sun. I realize there's no running away from it. I have to face the light that gets in my hair, that gets in my eyes. Sometimes, I have eyes. Sometimes, I feel as though they've gone off to Florida somewhere and I'll have to get to the store without them. I told Aaron how to get to my new place. We made five trips, filling my car and his each time. Cammy gave me some money. I was able to buy gas and give Norm a month's rent. Now I have to find a new job. I know I should get on with it, but I'm not stressed. I never am. I'm a mucus factory. My horks are as heavy as trucks. Little trucks with no wheels; sticky, driverless little trucks. The drivers are tired; the drivers have gone to bed. I spit up clumps of light. Once the last box has been set down on my bedroom floor, Cammy gives me a look that says, "What are you doing in this place?" It's dark, even with the lamp on. This room feels a bit like the inside of my head. I flash her a forced smile. "It's all good." Aaron is outside smoking. We go join him. His fair hair is perfect, combed to the side. He smells good, even though he's not wearing cologne. He has man's hands, big clean hands with just enough veins. Mine are tiny, fragile. My dad used to say I had the hands of a pianist. No, Dad: the hands of someone with lung disease. Elliott Smith is barking away in the car. I say, "Thanks, Sis. Thank you very much, Aaron." We kiss cheeks, we shake hands. "You're welcome, my friend." I watch the Volkswagen disappear. I'm alone again. I can still hear Elliott Smith barking, but that's impossible; it must be in my head. The wind gusts against my face. The wind hollows out my face and leaves a hole in my cheek. When I turn around, I see Norm sitting on the deck, smoking a cigarillo. He's wearing pyjama bottoms with different Hulk faces on them. "Want some rigatoni? It's a tradition of mine. I make a beef and rigatoni cake every time someone moves in." I've never seen a rigatoni cake before. I understand once Norm takes it out of the oven. It really does look like a cake, with melted cheese for icing and little rigatoni tubes all standing to attention. We tend to imagine things to be more spectacular than they really are. A rigatoni cake or someone with lung disease, same thing. As he stabs at his plateful of pasta, I can see that Norm is proud of himself. I enjoy seeing people feel proud of themselves. It makes me proud to see them proud. It's silly, I know. "You're not much of a talker," Norm says. He takes a swig of beer, then adds, "I saw you bring in two bedside tables... There won't be room for them with your double bed." "I put one of the tables in the closet for the time being." He laughs and takes another forkful of pasta. "You're really something." He's missing his front teeth; all he has are the ones at the bottom. A toothless Joe Pesci. His laugh is teasing, contagious. I laugh along with him. I ask him if he's had many tenants. "Not that many. I started last year. I've had two, so that makes you the third." He's very laid-back. I finish my plate and help Norm with the dishes, then I go hide in my room like a kid. A thirty-one-year-old man who hides in his room after supper. I unpack, put my bookshelf against the wall opposite the window. As I'm arranging the first half of my books, by publisher, on the shelves, I come across Hemingway's *The Old Man and the Sea*. I really got into fishing at one point because of that book. The story always made me want to head for the open water, to get lost at sea. I'd like to feel far from home, I'd like to leave for Pakistan and smoke in a tiny boat surrounded by mountains. I'd like to gaze at Pakistan's rivers all winter long, to compare the rivers there to the river near where I live. I'd like to live in the waters of a river with a Pakistani woman. I'd protect her, I'd build us a house underwater, I'd wear a veil instead of her.

My bed takes on the shape of my body. When I walk, I take on the shape of the sidewalk. When I speak, I take on the shape of all the garbage I spout. I run through my list of meds. There are so many, all of them keeping me alive. Good job, meds. But today I've run out of some. I call the lab at the drugstore. The pharmacist knows me well. She always opens with, "What can I do for you, love?" I reel off my list like it's a grocery order. Colistin bananas, Advair Diskus with lettuce, and a syringe loaf. Yes, thank you, that's very kind. I go up to the kitchen. It doesn't look like Norm is home. I peer out the window, take a look to see if there are any birds around, think of *Return of the Jedi*. I go read up about Jedi knights online. There are all kinds of books and parallel stories set before, during, and after the movies. I explore the hundreds and hundreds of made-up planets, species, spaceships, weapons, and types of food. I'd like to eat Lamta. I could be brushing up on socialism in postwar Germany or reading the philosophical works of Kierkegaard, but instead I'd rather know that the Jedi High Council sits on the planet Coruscant. I make myself two slices of toast with Norm's Cheez Whiz. I don't think of his teeth. I promise myself I'll go buy some groceries and drop by the pharmacy. I have another look for birds. There's got to be at least one. I don't see any. There are breadcrumbs around my plate. I perform a voodoo ritual. A voodoo ritual involving Cheez Whiz. I think about Tatooine: a sand planet where everyone is poor. I'd like to have a Gaderffii stick with a poisoned blade. I'd like to wear a breathing apparatus and live in a tent made from Bantha hide. I should invent the ideal planet, just for me. I'd call it Tatouine, almost the same as the real one, but just different enough. There, I'd be an out-of-work sandman, but I'd still be super rich; all my problems would disappear and life would be good. It crosses my mind that every fall I manage to miss absolutely every single book launch in Montreal. My thoughts turn to Darth Maul. I imagine a battle between Darth Vader and Darth Maul. By my calculations, Darth Maul would be in deep shit, that's for sure. I imagine Darth Maul tumbling off the deck. I imagine Darth Maul, his body cut in two on Rue Richelieu. I wish I had a little speeder so that I could go to all the book launches in Montreal. I wish people would tell me, "Your speeder's really cool!" I wash my plate, get dressed, put on my coat. I don't have a key yet. I leave a note in the kitchen to remind Norm. I don't want him to be annoyed that I left the door unlocked. It's freezing outside. The temperature has plummeted. There's frost on my car windows. I can't help but think of the Nelligan poem. I don't even like that poem. I wonder what Nelligan's writing would have been like if he'd had a car. I wonder if you can see blond skies disappearing from a beat-up, old Mazda. I wait until the heater has melted the frost away. I notice that my winter coat is losing its feathers. A small, white feather drifts above my parking brake. There are blond birds over my parking brake, Nelligan! Nelligan! Do you hear me, Nelligan? Dumbass.

I'm in the little waiting room at the pharmacy. I think Qui-Gon Jinn's my favourite Jedi. A guy the same age as me is holding a baby in his arms; it's screaming blue murder. It reminds me a little of Elliott Smith. I pull a face at the baby behind the father's back. I like pulling faces at babies behind people's backs. Weird, I know, but it is what it is. I watch the baby's eyes widen in surprise, which makes me laugh. It stops crying, forgets why it was sad. It stares at me. I pull another face. It can't believe it. I wish it worked for me, too. I wish people would pull faces at me on every block. I rummage around in my pockets. I've got fistfuls of Monopoly money from McDonald's. Maybe enough for a free cheeseburger. I'm happy and more than a little pleased with myself for saving up all those McDonald's coupons since the promotion started. The pharmacist calls me over to the counter. She gives me my bag of meds. She doesn't pull a face. It costs me $84.06. I don't have private insurance, just the public plan. I have to pay part of my meds, which works out to around a hundred bucks a month. The money my parents left me is long gone. It was enough to buy a car, some furniture, a few semesters at school, and two years' worth of meds. Now all I have left is McDonald's Monopoly money and a little something Cammy gave me. The girl at the cash asks if

45

I want to round it up to $85 and donate to a kids' charity. "No." Fuck the kids. I decide to go to McDonald's and eat my burger. The place is empty. I take out my phone and write myself a note: "Every Monopoly coupon from McDonald's is an Émile Nelligan poem/Every moment of sadness is a dog that lives in Boston." Three businessmen dressed in suits and ties are talking loudly beside me. "Buy this, sell that, hurry!" All I can buy is two bedside tables from Structube. I'm tempted to ask if they can help me sell the bedside table in my closet, but I don't. I decide to eat the rest of my burger in my car. I get an email from my publisher inviting me to the book fair in Montreal. I don't like the book fair; it makes me feel like a performing monkey. A ghostly, thirty-one-year-old monkey that no one can see. I pretend I didn't read the invite. I'm an invisible monkey in an old Mazda. I decide to go buy some groceries. I buy frozen veggies, potatoes, a big box of rice, bread, milk, meat sauce, spaghetti, and tomatoes. I feel like getting drunk tonight. The girl at the cash gives me a big smile, asks if I'd like a bag. "You just saved my life." She thinks I'm funny. I think I'm ugly. A notice behind her reads, "We're Hiring." I'm up for it. I'll bring my resumé tomorrow. I buy a bottle of Chemineaud from the liquor store across the street and don't look the cashier in the eye. It's already dark outside and the wind is ice-cold. I've only got one thing on my mind, and that's drinking. All I can think about is my little room and the bottle I'm holding. As I walk back to my car, I feel excited. I want to take a swig right away, but I fight the urge. I'll have to make myself supper first. Yep, I'll cook my pasta, warm the sauce, eat my spaghetti, chat to Norm, go hide in my room, listen to the soundtrack from *There Will Be Blood* with my headphones on, then drink Chemineaud. That's the reason I exist right now; I know that for a fact. That's the reason I am on this earth. As plans go, it seems huge, it seems dull, it makes me feel proud. I am Qui-Gon Jinn and I have a bottle of Chemineaud. There was a line from Agnès Varda that really struck a chord with me when I was young: "If we opened people up, we'd find landscapes. If we opened me up, we'd find beaches." I start the car, turn up the heat. If someone opened me up, they'd find bottles of Chemineaud and lightsabers. No trees, no mountains, no nothing.

My wisdom tooth still hurts. It's pumping like a heart. I wish I had a tooth instead of a heart, then I would feel something. I keep probing my tooth with my tongue and my fingers. I dunno, I think it's making it worse. They were calling for snow, but it's not snowing. I eat my Lucky Charms. I wish it would snow inside my tooth. Norm is stringing up Christmas lights in the only tree in the yard. I feel sorry for Norm all on his own outside. I help him decorate the tree, and he's happy. A toothless Joe Pesci and a two-hundred-pound Macaulay Culkin getting ready for Christmas together; it's so sweet. I've gotten used to how Norm's house smells. I've gotten used to Norm being around. I've gotten used to my little room in the basement. I feel like Luke Skywalker on Dagobah, and Norm is Yoda. When I go back inside, I google Dagobah: "a world of murky swamps, steaming bayous, and jungles." That's exactly it. That was my first impression of Norm's basement: a swamp. I bet it smells like fried ground beef on Dagobah. I'll soon be able to lift Norm's house right off the ground using my mental powers, just like an X-wing starfighter. From the kitchen window, our Christmas tree looks pathetic. There's a big black hole right in the middle of the lights.

Half the time, Norm smiles when he sees the tree lit up at night. The rest of the time he doesn't. I waffled about whether to drop my resumé off at the grocery store, but I finally decided I should. I filled out the form and said I was available anytime. While I was filling it out, an old guy came and tried to get a refund for a bottle of ketchup. It was complicated. When I left the Super C, I took a different route and walked along Rue L'Assomption so I could look at the houses along the waterfront. I like looking at houses. I often imagine I live in one of the houses I walk past, and I invent a life for myself. I say, "Dinner's ready, honey!" My wife smiles at me, fondles the back of my neck, tells me she's so happy here with me. During the day, I go upstairs to my office. I write novels; I make a living writing novels. My style is original, like no other. I'm often in the papers, and I'm asked my opinion on all kinds of news stories. During one of my many interviews, I say, "It's high time we invested in education. The future of our young people is hanging in the balance," and everyone claps. I don't live alone in a tiny basement room. I teach at the university, and my students find me funny and brilliant. I'm respected by my peers. I go on trips with my wife and children; that's right, I have two children—a girl and a boy. They're super smart. I travel the world. I speak Mandarin. Yeah, whatever. When I get home, it's dark out, and Norm is watching TV in the living room. I make myself a cup of Lipton soup. I notice Norm is wearing a strange expression. He confesses he doesn't like Christmas. "It reminds me of my kids and my ex-wife. Christmas is not for people who're alone." That makes me feel anxious. I try to reassure myself. I'm not alone. I don't live here for real. I live on Rue L'Assomption in a house with my wife; all this is just temporary. To change the subject, I say to Norm, "Well, your tree sure is nice, anyway." He laughs. "What about you? Where will you celebrate the holidays?" I shrug. "D'you have family?" "I never knew my mom, my dad died a while back, and my sister doesn't live here." I try to sound lighthearted. I'm not one for drama. Norm stays silent. "I'm gonna buy a turkey for Christmas. D'you like turkey?" I nod. He gives me a thumbs up, like Tom Cruise in *Top Gun*. "Okey-doke." He goes back into the living room and lets me drink my soup in peace. It's funny, my tooth doesn't hurt anymore. It looks like it's snowing out, but it's not. I bet if Yoda had had an oven on Dagobah, he'd have roasted a turkey for Luke.

I clear my throat all the time. I've always got something in my throat. I could use a mini vacuum cleaner to suck all the mucus out of there. I feel like I'm in *Alien*. Every time I spit, I wonder if some creature is going to come slithering out. I do my treatment in my bedroom and cover the compressor with a blanket, so Norm doesn't hear the motor and ask me what that noise is. I don't know why I haven't told him I have a lung disease. I check my emails. My publisher is disappointed I didn't go to the book fair. Vivian, a girl I know, sent me a message: "Hey, I've got some shitty questions for you." I skim through her message. She suspects her four-year-old daughter may have cystic fibrosis. I decide to answer all her questions at once. I don't tell her that I spit up aliens and that her daughter probably will, too. I reassure her. I tell her that life expectancy is high nowadays, and that the scientific progress has been amazing. I don't tell her that I don't have any RRSPs and that I prefer to spend every dollar of my retirement fund on McDonald's cheeseburgers. When you've got cystic fibrosis, a cheeseburger is a tangible thing. "If your daughter has cystic fibrosis, life goes on... Only now I'm going to have some competition in the 'Quebec Poets with Cystic Fibrosis' category. Damn!!" She writes back that I make her laugh, and that it feels good to laugh. I turn my computer off, go to the bathroom. I shave my beard off, but I keep my moustache. I want to look like Daniel Day-Lewis in *There Will Be Blood*. I wander around the basement, I poke around, I realize the only books Norm owns are the complete collection of Time-Life's The World's Wild Places: *Africa's Rift Valley, The Australian Outback, The Rocky Mountains, The Bayous of Louisiana, The Sahara*, etc. They're lined up on the TV stand. I halfheartedly pull out *Soviet Deserts and Mountains*. I'm amazed by the stunning photos. The landscapes are rich and varied: the Chatkal Nature Reserve, the huge Medvezhiy glacier, the snowy slopes of the Tian Shan, and more. I stare for a long time at a photo of Lake Issyk-Kul. I learn that it has forty-four tributaries. I have three PICC lines a year. The book could have been called *The Deserts and Mountains of Cystic Fibrosis*. Every mouthful of mucus I spit up is a different shape and colour than the one before. I'm a kaleidoscope of landscapes. I hork up spit all the time. I often have migraines. I try to recall that quote by Nazarov, "All it takes is to sit, even only for a moment, next to those beautiful dark blue flowers, to be struck by a violent headache." Everywhere I sit, the flowers are there. They follow me to the café and to the bar and to my car and to the toilet and to my bed, and I never get a moment's rest and I spit everywhere and I sow mucus but I don't grow it: I just let it dry on the sidewalks of Repentigny.

I wake up with a deep cough, short of breath. When I breathe in too deeply, I feel a throbbing pain just below my left collarbone. During the night, a mucus plug must have formed in my airways. People ask me, "Is it true

51

you breathe through a straw?" "No, I breathe through a cheese grater." This morning, there's snow everywhere. The lady who lives next door has already made a snowman in her yard. I make two slices of toast with Kraft Singles. I swallow my pills; I have about twenty pills to take every day. I'm an old man. The disease affects my digestive system, too. I have to take enzymes before every meal otherwise I get cramps. If I were a snowman, everything would be so complicated. It would be too much work to look after me. People would just destroy me and build a younger, healthier snowman. My hair's starting to go grey. I'm as ancient as old snow. I pluck out the grey hairs one by one with tweezers. I concentrate as hard as if I were working for NASA. I pluck out twelve hairs. It's appropriate, cause I'd like to drink a twelve-pack of beer this afternoon. It's been ages since I've been for breakfast at Chez Rémi. I haven't had a smoke for ages, either. I feel like I'm just waiting for someone to bring me two eggs over easy–bacon–white bread. I eat only one slice of toast with a Kraft Singles. I throw the other one away; I'm not hungry. I wish someone would eat for me. I wish someone would smoke for me. I wish someone would sleep for me. Outside, people are starting to be up and about, and going places. I should do like them. I should do something, take my mind off things, invent someplace I have to go. But I just do my treatment. The white smoke that comes out of the nebulizer is thick and heavy. The smoke hides my face. The smoke makes me disappear a little in my room. I've got another twenty minutes to go; there's still tons of smoke. I've made a mess of it. Fuck it. I turn off the compressor, get dressed, pull on my winter boots. They're hot as hell. It makes me feel proud. I go out for a walk. I head back to my old apartment. It takes me forty-five minutes cause I take tons of detours. I walk along streets I've never taken before. I look at the houses like I'm at Disney World, finding fault with those I don't like. I count the immaculate houses—those without a single footprint on the steps or leading to the garage. I count thirty-seven houses, thirty-seven solitudes who're away on vacation or who just don't leave the house. I walk up to each front door. I create thirty-seven ghosts wearing ski-doo boots and pretend to knock on each door. When I get to my old apartment, the curtains are drawn. They're red and ugly. The street is deserted; not a single car passes by in the space of five minutes. I'm a bit sad, nostalgic. When I was a kid, I cried for two weeks because I had to change bus stops. Two weeks' worth of tears for a bus stop. Ridiculous. I walk around the back of the apartment building, I take Rue Richelieu, I notice a mountain of empty boxes and a sofa-shaped object. As I get closer, I realize it's my old magenta sofa, the one that used to belong to my parents. I didn't recognize it right away beneath all the snow. I'm not sure how to react. I want to get even, but how? I go up to the front door and ring the buzzer of my old apartment. Once, then twice, then a third time holding my finger on the buzzer. I hear my heart pounding in my left ear. I don't know what I'm doing. It's stupid. I walk away from the building and cross the street. I hear someone shouting from the balcony, "Hey you, what's your fucking problem?" It's my old landlord's brother. They look alike: they're twins. He's in his underwear on the balcony, wearing a gold chain around his neck. He glares at me, and I notice he's pretty muscular and tough-looking. I turn my back and keep walking. He shouts, "Why're you ringing my doorbell, you stupid fucker?" "Wrong address." He doesn't hear me. "What d'you say, dickhead?" I lose my temper. What an asshole. I can't resist. "Fuck you!" I give him the finger and continue on my way. Behind me, I hear, "You little fuck!" When I look over my shoulder, he's no longer on the balcony. "Fuck." I start running, but my boots slow me down. What an idiot. I feel a tightness just beneath my collarbone. I'd forgotten I was short of breath. I'm fucked. I manage to make it to the end of Rue Richome, and when I glance behind me again, I see a guy in a brown coat running towards me. "Shit." I cut left where there are a bunch of stores. The dairy bar's closed, the jewellery store isn't open yet, neither's the old Italian restaurant. I run like crazy, even though I'm out of breath. An old lady comes out of the corner store carrying a bunch of plastic bags. I go in, and the guy behind the cash, an old Egyptian guy who always smells like cologne, and who always wears an Adidas jacket, recognizes me. I used to go there nearly every day to buy my Unibroue beer bombers and packets of popcorn. He smiles at me. "I haven't seen you around for a very long time." I pretend everything's just fine, struggle to catch my breath. I say, "You doin' okay?" He says yes, and continues to arrange the lottery tickets on his counter. I go to the walk-in beer fridge at the back of the store, and I stay there. I stare at a case of Pabst Blue Ribbon and pray the bastard doesn't find me. I stay there for at least ten minutes. I know there's a security camera in the fridge. I pretend to be having trouble deciding which beer to get. I pace back and forth. I'm a snowman in a beer fridge, waiting to get the shit kicked out of me. Someone opens the fridge door and my heart stops. It's the cashier. He asks if I'm okay. "Yeah, I can't decide which kind to get." "OK, don't stay in there too long. You'll freeze. It's already very, very cold tonight." He laughs. I force myself to laugh, too. I grab a twelve-pack of Pabst and ease my way out of the fridge slowly, then I stay there for a long time, head down, examining the shelves of chips before I finally decide to pay and leave the store. I take all the back alleys I can to get back home, looking over my shoulder every thirty seconds in case I get attacked from behind. When I get inside, I put on my black sweatpants and an old Mickey Mouse t-shirt. Norm's not in. I realize I never asked him what he does for a living. I crack open a beer. He's probably retired. I'd like to be retired. I could do that all day long, I mean, leave early in the morning to ring people's doorbells and piss them off, one by one. The beer goes down nicely. I finish one can, then another, and another. I put on *White Blood Cells* by the White

Stripes in the living room upstairs, and I turn on the TV. I listen nine times to *Fell in Love With a Girl*. I yell and I dance and I laugh out loud. I spill beer on the floor, wipe up the puddle with my wool sock. I stand in the middle of the living room in front of the big window, and I pretend I'm holding a guitar and singing into a mike. I pretend I'm Jack White before an adoring, screaming crowd of fans. I'm hot; my forehead's clammy. I pretend to look over at Megan White on the drums, loving the beat she's thumping out with her drumsticks. I finish my ninth beer. I've lost track of time. I'm Jack White and I don't have cystic fibrosis anymore, bitch. I notice my phone screen lighting up; someone's trying to call me. I rush over and turn off the music. It's the manager from the Super C. She wants to know if I'm available for an interview tomorrow morning. I'm a bit drunk, but I reply, "Sure," like I'm stone sober. I end the call, empty the dregs from the beer cans into the sink, and stick the empties in a plastic bag I carry outside to dump in the recycling bin. The wind's wicked cold; my nostrils stick together. When I lift the lid of the plastic bin, I notice the neighbour's snowman no longer has a head. Snow does that to you: it makes you lose your head.

There's a humming in my ear. The sound washes up in dull waves in my left ear. I feel like a seashell, a brown-haired seashell who's off for an interview at Super C. I can't remember what I ate last night. I don't think I ate anything. No, I must have eaten something, since I'm not hungry. I'm losing my memory. I can never remember my postal code. I've been known to make one up. I live in Moscow, Shanghai, at a flower shop in Saskatchewan, at my old apartment with a crazy guy who walks around in nothing but a gold chain and his underpants. I live in New York with Elliott Smith. I feel fat. My sleeves are a little on the short side, and that worries me. Maybe they shrunk in the wash. Maybe it's me who's getting fatter with every load. Maybe my shirts are shrinking a little each day, just for the hell of it. I bought four shirts at Wal-Mart. They all look the same, and in each shirt I lose a little more of my memory. I wait for a miracle to happen. I wait minute by minute. I put my trust in each minute, but every last one of them betrays me. When I go upstairs to the kitchen, I bump into Norm, who's wearing his hat. He's been outside shovelling snow off the steps and the driveway. He still smells of the cold as he walks past. "You don't have winter tires," he says. "I drive slowly." "Smart," he deadpans. I read *Plumbing Something or Other* on his coat. Ah, so Norm's a plumber. I watch him go back outside and drive off in his car. Everything would be so much simpler if my lungs were made of pipes. I'm still not hungry. I forgot all about my treatment; I'll do it when I get back from the interview. I brush the snow off my car, turn up the heating, wait for my windows to come back to life. Driving to the grocery store, I listen to *Fell in Love With a Girl* again and drum my hands on the steering wheel. I can't get enough of that song. Once I arrive, it takes a good ten minutes before I can see the manager. I watch a young boy crying beside a grocery cart. His mom is doing up his laces. The manager appears wearing a broad smile. She says my name, I nod, and we shake hands. I wonder what I'm doing here. "I'm Mireille." I can still feel her hand in mine. Mireille has a firm handshake on her. She shows me into her office and asks me a ton of questions. I didn't think I'd have to answer so many questions to work in a grocery store. I'm a little stunned. I try to concentrate, to up my game until I'm as intense as she is. She asks what skills I have. I don't want to be here. I'd rather be listening to the White Stripes in my room. I'd rather be walking the snowy streets of Repentigny. I stop myself from telling her the only thing I'm good at is writing poems. I even tell her there's something wrong with my lungs, that I can't work in freezers, that I can't catch cold or else I'll end up in hospital on a drip. I don't want to work. I don't want her to hire me. It's the first time I've told an employer about my health problems. Usually, I wait to be hired, I work for a few weeks until I get sick, and then I say, "Hey, so I'm sick. I'll be off work for three weeks. Bye." Mireille doesn't say anything. She tells me those are just details, that she's all for social inclusion and equal opportunities. I'm taken aback. I don't know what to think. I'm spineless, a spineless shell of a man. Mireille says she likes my moustache. "Is it for Movember?" I say yes, even though that's not true. I'm just trying to look like Daniel Day-Lewis, that's all. She says her husband had prostate cancer. "I'm sorry." "He's not dead," she laughs. "He recovered." We shake hands again. I make more of an effort this time. She smiles, says she'll be in touch in a day or two. While I'm there, I buy some eggs, milk, raspberries, orange juice, bagels, and lots of Sidekicks. But just the packs that you make with water. I'm too poor to add milk. My ex didn't like me cooking Sidekicks in her apartment. She thought they smelled like garbage. I think back to her apartment. It was right across from the Édouard-Montpetit metro station. I was over there all the time. She'd often be out, off at her classes at school. I'd sleep and spend my days in her room or in the living room watching movies. I'd make her supper and sweep the floor. I'd jack off a lot when she wasn't there. In every room of her apartment. When she'd get home, I'd smile, kiss her, tell her I'd throw myself in the fire for her. Now I realize it was just as well I didn't. Now I barely masturbate at all. All my libido has been lost to packs of Sidekicks. On my way out, I decide to go to the liquor store. I buy two little bottles of Chemineaud. I'm happy. I want to shout, to tell anyone who'll listen that I'm someone deserving of social inclusion.

The pain below my collarbone went away by itself, but now I'm tired. I don't have the strength to get dressed or go to the bathroom. I watch the dust pile up on my bedroom floor. Everything's dirty. I haven't washed my sheets since moving in to Norm's place. Friends call, but I don't pick up. I don't feel like seeing them. I don't feel like socializing. I stay in my room for two days. I've stopped writing; I don't see the point anymore. Still no word from the publisher who wants to put out my poetry collection next year. I reread the book that I submitted and that they accepted, and I realize it's bad. The publisher called me a few months ago and was all excited. He congratulated me. I pretended to be thrilled. I open *The Deserts and Mountains of Cystic Fibrosis* and read a page at random. "Guided by its antennae, a scavenging scarab busily furrows the sand, searching for tiny bits of animal or plant matter." I don't have the strength to furrow anything at all. I don't have antennae; I have ten fingers that aren't much good to me, apart from making Sidekicks and going online to look up Jedi knights and planets that don't exist. I think about Tatouine. There would be no sandstorms there, so people wouldn't have to constantly seek shelter. In Repentigny, the storms are in my head, and the only thing I have is a tiny room where I can hide from myself. I'm not the bravest of Jedi; I'm not a Jedi at all. I get out of bed and, standing there by my bedside table, I see black spots. I stood up too quickly. I'd like to live in every black spot in my eyes. I'd look to run away into my eyes and hide behind a black spot, following its movements until I'm in time with it. I make my bed; the bedspread weighs five hundred pounds. All the strength has gone from my arms. I'm breathing heavily. My breathing makes bubbles, like someone blowing into a glass of water with a straw. I'm going to cough up blood. I can feel all the fluids build-

ing in my mouth. "Fuck." I spit up some blood. I always
know when I'm going to spit up blood. I'm always sure
to cough, to get it out. To expectorate it. That might be
my favourite word: expectorate. I'd like to expectorate
tiny bedrooms, cats, houses, streets, towns, entire planets. Expectorate! Expectorate! I take a Kleenex, spit, and
look down at the little pool of blood. It's sad and fascinating. The first time you cough up a good amount of
infected secretions, it's impressive. The first time I saw
all that blood, I was sure I was going to die. Then you get
used to it. You get used to the blood, get used to dying.
I'm no longer impressed. For years now, I've been blasé
about all the blood I can cough up. I could vomit blood
and make a mountain out of it. "Quick!" I'd tell people.
"Come climb this mountain of blood." I look over at my
narrow little window, all covered in snow. I want to get
out of here. I want to grow heirloom vegetables. I want
to grow vegetables on Tatouine. Sweetcorn, that kind of
thing. That would make me happy. I'm sure I could be
happy growing sweetcorn. My phone lights up on the
bedside table. It's Mireille calling to tell me I've been
hired at Super C. It takes an effort not to cough into the
phone. "Oh, wow, that's fantastic." I sound sincere, for
some reason. She asks if I can start tomorrow night. "Of
course." I hang up, go upstairs to the kitchen, and drink
a couple of glasses of orange juice. I drink orange juice
every time I spit up blood. It's psychological. It feels
like it helps me keep the flare-ups under control. Once
again, the absurd, grotesque nature of the bleeding hits

home. It can last anywhere from three days to a week. It can happen all the time; it might not happen again for months. It can strike at any time. If it won't stop bleeding, I need to go to the hospital and they'll stick something in my vein and fuck that, etc. etc. It's a routine I've mastered over the years until it's now part of my day-to-day. I've got a dog in my lungs. A dog that hates my guts and I don't know why.

I'm in a café. A new place that just opened in Repentigny called La Brûlerie. For the longest time I hung out at the Tim Hortons coffee shops around town to write my poems. It feels weird to go to a new place. I'm not big on change. I'd be perfectly happy to live in a cube with four pale-grey walls. A cube that smells good and that blocks out noise from the neighbours. A cube with a little kitchen, a bookshelf, and a TV to watch movies on. Yeah, anyway. I open a Word file, "Diabetes in the kitchen." Twelve pages of data on my glycemia. I'd forgotten about it. I'm such a hypochondriac. I remember when I used to prick my fingertips twenty times a day. I see in my file, it was two years ago on January 14, that I was hyperglycemic. I write a note next to the results: "I'm gonna die for sure... Fuck it, today I'm eating the whole pack of baloney. I hereby bequeath all my Gaston Lagaffe books to my hamster Paul. Farewell." I chuckle to myself. I think about the scene in *The Phantom Menace* with Qui-Gon Jinn and the young Anakin. Qui-Gon takes a drop of blood from the young Skywalker to check his midi-chlorian count. He wants to know if he's Force-sensitive. As for me, I'm the Anakin Skywalker of hyperglycemia. Anakin, who's sitting drinking coffee at La Brûlerie in Repentigny, waiting for his heart to explode. I'm trying to write a novel; I'm trying really hard. The servers float past me in the café. I write, "The days are long," and it really sucks. I think of my university prof who used to trash the style of today's young writers: "You need style, dammit, you need style... Proust and Céline had style, for God's sake!" Yesterday, I finished the bottle of Chemineaud in style. The prospect of my first day on the job is making me anxious. Yesterday, the only trick I found to calm myself was to drink too much and to puke my guts out during the night. I puked so much it made my nose bleed. I don't take good care of myself. I don't feel like taking good care of myself. I think about my dad. Every time I came home drunk, he would come stand in my doorway and mutter, "Omigod!" He'd say it in one breath, one damning breath. It would make me feel so small. Now, every time I throw up, I think of that *Omigod!* and I recite it like an ancient prayer. I'm an asshole, omigod; I'm dumb, omigod; I write poems, omigod; I'm Anakin Skywalker, omigod! I've got to work in a couple of hours, later in the afternoon. I got up super early, even though I was hungover. I did my treatment, and I even cooked myself some eggs. I stuffed my old laptop into a backpack and stole a few granola bars from Norm. I've been at the café for a while now and I've got my earbuds on. I'm listening to Jean-Michel Blais on the piano. It makes me want to cry. I cry without making a sound. I don't like attracting attention to myself. The tears run down into my moustache. I'm Daniel Day-Lewis crying into his moustache. It's taken me four hours to write "The days are long." That's a good reason to cry, too. I go online to pass the time. I come across an article that talks about "persistence hunting." I read, "A form of hunting in which the hunter uses endurance running in the heat of day to drive his prey to the point of hyperthermia and exhaustion so that it is easier to catch and kill." I feel like an animal that's suffering from hyperthermia but hasn't yet decided to make a run for it. I'm a ghost that's been shot and that's spitting up ghost's blood. Omigod!

At the Super C, I start seeing stars. Shit, you can't be serious. My eyes are watering. When I get stressed out and walk at the same time, I cough like crazy and feel like puking. I'm right in front of the store, but I can't go in like this. I try to calm down. I open A Soft Murmur on my phone. I love that app. It lets you mix sounds, with varying intensity. I select waves with a bit of thunder and I close my eyes. I'm a brown-haired seashell on the Super C shore. I'm leaning on a grocery cart, a little ways away from the automatic doors. I concentrate on the thunder as I look around me. It's cold out, but the sky is dazzling blue. It's cold, but beautiful. A perfect day for spitting up blood. I watch the old men and the old women pushing their grocery carts to the sound of

64

rain and thunder. They struggle to load their plastic bags full of groceries into the trunks of their cars. I crank up the thunder volume on my earbuds as far as it'll go. The apocalypse is here! It seems like people are more hurried and less patient. An old man wearing a Florida Panthers cap pushes his cart through the parking lot without looking where he's going. A man honks at him and calls him an asshole. A baby sitting in its mother's cart screams and cries. It doesn't want to leave the Super C. Not like me: I just want to get out of here. To each his agony. Someone taps me on the shoulder. It's a guy who works at the grocery store fetching the grocery carts scattered around the parking lot. He says something to me, but all I can hear is the thunder in his mouth. I take out one of my earbuds and give him a blank look. "I just need your cart, please." I realize I'm still leaning on the grocery cart. "Oh, sorry... Here you go." Thanks to my stupid, imaginary apocalypse scene, I'm ten minutes late. I go through the automatic doors. A young woman with really long hair is counting change. Her black hair nearly touches the quarters. I walk up to her and wait until she's done counting, so she doesn't lose track. When she's finished, she looks up and waits for me to say something. I ask her if Mireille is there. She points to an office. When I get there, it's empty. I stand there for at least five minutes wondering what the hell I'm doing there. It's always the same thing; always the same weird feeling. With every new job, I pretend to understand what I'm being told. I pretend I've been doing it my whole life. It doesn't take long for my bluff to be called. The employers realize soon enough that they've got an imposter on their hands. Take the time Michael Jackson died. I was working as a cook's assistant at Pacini's. I was supposed to make bunny-shaped pizzas using a rabbit mould. I had to use olives for the eyes and a piece of pepper for the mouth. The head cook didn't like me. He'd always yell at me to hurry up and make more bunny pizzas. I couldn't keep up. I could never keep up. The fish and meat cooks had to take turns helping me make my pizzas. Everyone kind of hated me. The pace was too fast for me and I couldn't do anything right. I remember one night the head cook came over to tell me my bunnies looked sad. I didn't know what to say. *Smooth Criminal* was playing on the radio, and I remember nobody felt like dancing. I worked there for two weeks. One morning, I just decided not to go to work anymore. I didn't answer the head cook's calls. That's how it ended. I'm a depressed bunny.

Someone taps me on the shoulder, and I turn to look. A tiny young woman smiles at me. She's wearing eyeliner with little black dots at either end of her eyelids. She looks like a bird. Her face reminds me of Natalie Portman. She's Queen Amidala in *Star Wars*. "Mireille can't make it, so I'll be showing you the ropes tonight." She smiles again. Any time a woman smiles at me, I fall in love. That's just the way I am. I make up stories, homes, babies. I'm heavy. Amidala introduces herself.

I think her name's either Julie or Sophie, but it doesn't matter, and I've already forgotten anyway: to me, she's Amidala. She explains how to punch in. She types in some numbers on the touchscreen on the wall. She gives me my code. I haven't listened to a word she's said; I'm too absorbed by her eyes. She asks if I've understood and I say, "Of course." "Mireille told me you can't work in the fridges, right?" I feel like an idiot. I'd already forgotten that I told Mireille about my lung disease. A Jedi who can't go in a fridge—not very badass. I don't know what to say. "Don't worry. You're lucky, you know? The meat department is pretty tough. If they ever need a hand, it'll be Akim, the other grocery clerk, who'll go." "What's a grocery clerk?" "Uh, it's the job you applied for..." "Ah, OK." Amidala bursts out laughing. "You're funny!" She smiles at me again. I would have liked to own that smile. I would have liked to build a cabin in that smile and live there a long time and never pay rent again and never have to do any more lung treatments and grow old and die in her smile. Just one little smile is all I'd need.

I'm coughing up a little less blood today. Amidala took me on a tour of all the departments yesterday: Bakery, Meat, Seafood, Fruits & Vegetables. I pictured her wearing a different dress in each department. I have a bit of a thing for the princess's first costume in *The Phantom Menace*, a red dress with golden thread. There's black fur, too, around the double collar and at the cuffs. But what I remember most of all are the big, bright bubbles that run all around the long skirt. I imagined Amidala dressed up just like this as we stood across from the bananas. She introduced me to all the cashiers, but I can't remember a single name. As jobs go, grocery clerk is a lot like me: you have to do anything and everything. That suits me down to the ground. My Jedi days are behind me; now I'm a grocery clerk. As we walked up and down the aisles, I coughed up a huge ball of mucus. I could imagine just how big it was, all covered in blood. My mouth was full. I didn't dare interrupt Amidala. But at the same time, I was gagging at the thought of swallowing the huge gob back down. I just about managed to make a few "OK," "uh-huh," and "sure" sounds, clenching my teeth all the while like an idiot. I had to shake every cashier's hand with my mouth full of mucus, before I spat it out into a trash can in a quiet corner of the lunchroom.

I have McDonald's for breakfast this morning. I try to use the time to write, but I can't. I listen to the soundtrack from *Our Day Will Come* on my headphones and pretend to be thinking. In my head I keep replaying the spa scene where Vincent Cassel jerks off in front of a couple. The lovers are taken hostage by Cassel's crony—I can't remember the actor's name—who's on an exercise bike armed with a crossbow. The couple has no choice but to stay in the spa, and Cassel takes his sweet time getting off. I picture myself jerking off in front of all the people at McDonald's, a crossbow in my other hand. I imagine parents fleeing, their children in their arms. I imagine one of the cashiers crying out in horror. I imagine the assistant manager staring at me with his headset on, mouth hanging open. Anyway. I'm crazy, seriously ill. Only a few hours left to kill before my first real day of work. I don't feel like working. I'd rather someone paid me to eat at McDonald's. I'd like to spend the rest of my life convalescing. I could write poems or stare at the ceiling all day. The only thing that keeps me going is the hope of one day living on Tatouine with Amidala. I spend all day at McDonald's beside a woman in a big fur coat. She looks a bit worse for wear. She seems sad and alone. Like a sad statue staring at a coffee cup someone's put in front of her. I leave the restaurant, get in my car, and play *Fell in Love With a Girl*. It takes less than five minutes to get to the Super C. Akim is pushing a line of carts across the parking lot. Akim is a dead ringer for Lando Calrissian, only without the moustache. He's the one I'm closest to. Amidala introduced us yesterday, and right away he said, "Hi, my friend." Still, he's a fair bit across the parking lot. I wave once, then again. I keep waving, but he doesn't see me. I go inside to punch in. I walk by all the cashiers, but they don't recognize me. I enter my code on the little touch screen, and it tells me I've got the wrong password. "Of course." I try a few variations. "Beep... 2-6-6-2, beep... 2-6-2-2, beep... 6-6-2-2." It doesn't work. Fuck you, you stupid code! I drop it, go for a walk up and down the aisles. I don't know what to do. I feel like

Daniel Day-Lewis in *There Will Be Blood*, only wearing a Super C t-shirt. I walk down the aisles like a prospector looking for oil. I look right to the back of the shelves to see if I can find some. I hear a voice behind me. "What're you doin'?" It's Alan, one of the butchers. He introduced himself yesterday as if he couldn't care less. He probably thinks I'm just another number, with his white apron and hairnet that's too big for him. Alan is a little shorter than I am, mid- to late-thirties. He's very curt. He stares daggers at me. "Oh, I was just rearranging the cans of tomatoes. They weren't straight," I say. "Yeah, that's not exactly top priority right now." His blue eyes are almost white. "I couldn't find Mireille," I say. "No one's really told me what I should be doing." "Chicken's on special today. I'm gonna need a helper. Come with me." He's already at the end of Aisle 7 before I can reply. I hurry after him. I don't have much of a choice. I follow him; I don't want to put people's backs up. Alan gives me a stained old fleece sweater and an apron. He hands me a net and a pair of gloves. "Chicken drumsticks and thighs are on special. Take this knife and cut here, like this, then here, like this. And watch yer fingers. This thing's frickin' sharp." My heart beats faster. I can't remember where I'm supposed to slice, and I don't want to make him go through it again. "OK," I say. All around me, three butchers are busy slicing meat. I try to work out which parts, but I can't tell. The noise in the meat department is deafening; there are hulking bandsaws everywhere you look. I feel like I'm in a carpenter's workshop. Carcasses are piling up with every cut, and everyone knows how to make best use of their time. They move quickly, precisely, and completely ignore me. I could be dancing the cha-cha and no one would notice. I realize that all the butchers are wearing white hats, everyone except me. They look like stormtroopers. I look at the ceiling, expecting to see stalactites or something fall on my head. There's nothing. I realize that the Super C is a bit like the Death Star, and that I have absolutely no clue what I'm doing here. I've been left to my own devices, a giant butcher's knife in my hand. I pick up a whole chicken. Water trickles off it, or it could be chicken fat, I don't know. I try to chop off the first foot, but I don't know what I'm doing. I don't know if I'm going about it the right way. I finally manage to hack the first foot off, and already my gloves are sticky and covered in chicken fat. I cut into the breast. "Shit." I'm supposed to be doing the thighs, but I can't find them. I freak out, stare at my table as the seconds tick by, stare at my stupid one-footed chicken. I start to panic. I walk out of the meat department refrigerator, still holding my knife, my too-big-for-me hairnet still on my head. I wander from aisle to aisle, hoping to bump into Alan, but I don't see him anywhere. The customers are staring at me. They must think I'm a dangerous lunatic. I go back to the refrigerator to drop off my knife, but just before I reach the door, I hear someone calling after me. It's Mireille, waving at me in the distance. I go over to her and see the question marks dancing around her face. She looks at my face, then at the butcher's knife in my hand, then back again. "What are you doing in Meat? That's not your department... I need you over in Soft Drinks." "Oh, sorry." "Go take your knife back and come meet me in Aisle 12." "OK." I scuttle back to the meat department. I'm taking off my hairnet when I see that Alan is at my workstation looking for me. I walk in through the two big doors with my knife and can see the daggers in the look he gives me. "Where the fuck were you?" "Mireille wants me to stack the soft drinks." Alan is a good ways away from me, but two strides later and he's snatched the knife from my hands. He starts hacking away at the chicken drumsticks. I think he would have made a good Darth Maul in *The Phantom Menace*. I can picture him running around like a madman, cutting the feet off every chicken that crosses his path. I quickly hang up my fleece before he busts my ass with his double-bladed lightsaber. By the time I make it over to Aisle 12, there's no sign of Mireille. I decide to wait for her in front of the 7UP. I think about drinking Chemineaud. I'd like to get drunk on Chemineaud, go blind, and die in Aisle 12 of the Super C in Repentigny. An old lady walks past me, her cart filled with cat food. She asks me where the cream soda is. I have no idea, but I don't tell her that. I pretend to know where the cream soda is. I walk slowly down the aisle with her, but I don't see it. There's every drink in the world, just no cream fucking soda. "Ah, it doesn't matter," she says. "It really doesn't matter." But in my head this is terrible,

this is drama of the highest order. "I'm sure we have it."
To make her laugh, I say, "What's your cat going to do
without its cream soda?" The lady bursts out laughing.
When Mireille comes down the aisle, the old dear has
me by the arm and is still laughing. Mireille smiles, too,
and asks me what's going on. "This charming lady is
looking for the cream soda." Mireille points to the tons
and tons of bottles that I hadn't seen. I say to the lady,
"Ah, you see? Your cat's saved now." She thanks me with
a wink. Mireille explains where to find the soft-drink
pallets to bring to Aisle 12. I have to use a pallet loader
and slide the forks underneath the pallet. I manage
to get it all done just in time for the end of my shift.
When I see Alan in the lunchroom, he grins at me like
a maniac, a burned-out cigarette between his teeth. His
teeth are yellow, almost black. Alan is the Dark Lord of
the Super C.

I'm at the café. I'm writing about snow and the planet
Naboo. I have no idea where I'm going with it. My coffee's cold. It took less than two minutes to get cold. What
the fuck? I don't get it. I don't get why the snowflakes
are so huge. I don't get why there's a cute girl sitting
all alone by the window. She's got short blond hair. She
looks like she's waiting for someone. She's not reading
the paper and she's not on her phone. She's just staring
out the window. I think that's nice. It looks like she's
just come from the hairdresser's. Her ash-blond hair
is strangely straight. She looks a little sad on her own.

I'd like to tell her she's beautiful, I'd like to tell her she has beautiful hair, I'd like to tell her her haircut suits her. But I don't; I'm not a nutcase. Outside, the snowflakes are as big as old Mazdas. I've forgotten how to write. I got an email from my publisher. He wants me to tweak some of my poems before they come out in the spring. I don't feel like it; I feel useless. A poet who doesn't want to write poems isn't a poet, he's a chair. I shaved off my moustache before coming to the café. I'm no longer Daniel Day-Lewis. I'm no longer looking for oil. I'm no longer spitting up blood. It's super. It's Super C. I really have forgotten how to write. The girl looking out the window has green eyes. Very pale green eyes. She blends into the row of reeds alongside the windows. Suddenly, someone walks up to her. It must be her mother. The girl in the reeds smiles, and I know I'll never get to know that smile intimately. It's a minor tragedy, and all the chairs in the café know it only too well. The girl in the reeds looks at her mother tenderly. She takes the time to look at her, to talk to her. I never did that with my father. I don't think I made the most of him being there. What could I have done differently? Would he have listened if I'd told him about the girl in the reeds? Would he have let me tell him about my spiritual vision of snow? I'd have told him I think they're the same snowflakes all the time. Snowflakes that are recycled, snowflakes that are reborn, snowflakes that span centuries. When I leave the café, it's still snowing. The snowflakes have shrunk, as if in exhaustion. I am exactly this kind of snow. I'm that little snowflake that gets in your eye and makes you go, "Jesus Christ!" Unless I'm mistaken, life is beautiful. It's just a matter of aim. And if I'm really lucky, I could even end my days in the mouth of a cute girl who's just come back from the hairdresser's.

Today I'm stocking the cereal shelves as I listen to A Soft Murmur on my earbuds. I decide to mix different sounds for each brand of cereal: Froot Loops are a crackling fire. Cheerios are rain. When I turn around, I see Amidala trying to say something to me. It's raining in her mouth. I stop the rain sound. "You look sad. What're you listening to?" "No, I'm not sad. I'm listening to the rain." She doesn't understand. I hand her one of my earbuds. She listens intently to the rain as we stand next to the Cheerios. I smell her perfume, and my heart beats faster. I could spend the whole day here listening to the rain fall with her in the cereal aisle. My blood pressure fluctuates depending on how close Amidala is. I watch her bottom lip and her chin. It's as if her chin is ballet dancing. I imagine us standing next to a field of wheat, with real rain falling. I imagine making love to her in a field of wet wheat like in Woody Allen's *Match Point*. Only at the end of our story, I wouldn't shoot her. I wouldn't kill her at all. She smiles and says, "You're cute." I don't know what to say. I see Akim appear in the aisle and head towards us. He looks in a panic. "Can you come help me in Fruits and Vegetables?" "Sure." Amidala is already gone, disappearing like a ghost. As we walk towards the fruit department, Akim points out to me that it's the first of the month. "The banana rack has to always be full." "The banana rack?" "Yeah, it's the first of the month, welfare day. The banana rack always empties super fast on the first of the month." When I get to the fruit section, there are only two bananas left. I say, "How come people on welfare like bananas so much?" "Shh, not so loud!" Akim moves closer and whispers in my ear, as serious as can be, "Cause bananas are cheap, and they're good for you." "Oh, I get it." "Go get a case of bananas from the storeroom. I'm gonna clean up that crap on the floor. What a mess!" A few feet away there's a huge watermelon splattered on the floor. I can't find the bananas in the storeroom. I see apples and oranges and strawberries and blueberries but not a single fuck-ing banana. The warehouse is huge. I walk up and down two aisles before I come face to face with Darth Maul. I really don't have time for this, but an image pops into my head of me powering up my lightsaber. I picture myself in a lightsaber battle with Alan in the Super C warehouse. I'd be Obi-Wan Kenobi and I'd slice him in two with my Jedi weapon. Alan would keel over into a huge box of cauliflowers. I may be seriously ill, but he turns and runs as soon as he spots me. I find the bananas in two enormous plastic bins. I try to pick up a bin, but it's too heavy. I'm not sure what to do. I start picking up bunches one at a time. By the time I get to nine, my arms are full. I bump into one of the cashiers who's on her break. She's an older woman, and she asks why I'm stealing bananas. "I'm not stealing them. I'm taking them out front." She laughs. She says she's just teasing. I laugh too. When I go back out through the warehouse door, I notice how busy the store is. There are people and grocery carts everywhere. People are clustered in front of the fridges and shelves. I say politely, "Excuse me, excuse me!" with my arms full of bananas. Nobody pays me any attention. In uncomfortable moments like these, my thoughts often turn to the president of the United States. I can't stand politics, but I still like to compare my social standing to that of important people. For example, I imagine I change bodies for five seconds with the president. I'd take his place and he'd take mine. I'd be the only person who knew that our roles had been reversed. I imagine the U.S. president walking around in my body with an armful of bananas. I imagine him with the bananas shouting, "What the fuck?" It makes me laugh. When I set all my bananas down on the display counter, Akim tells me, "That won't be enough. I'll deal with it... They just told me there's a busted pickle jar in Aisle Five. Think you could go clean it up, my friend?" "Sure." I grab the mop, broom, and garbage can, and slink my way like a cat between the grocery carts and crying babies. I take my time lobbing the pickles one by one into the bin as I listen to the rain on my earbuds. Once I've swept up all the bits of glass and mopped up the pickle brine, I head back to take a look at my cereal boxes. They're all mixed up. The Cheerios over with the Frosted Flakes and so on. "Man, what a mess!" The rain is still coming down in my ears. There's thunder and lightning at the Super C. I realize I'm not much good at anything. Aside from writing poems or being the president of the United States for five seconds.

I spend my days at the café before going to work. I force myself to write. Today I brought *The Deserts and Mountains of Cystic Fibrosis* with me. The book is open at a double-page photo of a white water lily. I flip through the pages, stopping at a picture of a flower I've never seen before. I read, "*Pulsatilla kostyczewii*, rare plant that flowers only two or three times. In July, sometimes even blooms near the permanent snow line." One day, Super C supermarkets will be as rare as this flower. After three cups of coffee, I finally manage to finish writing a short poem: "How do you cook rice in water?/It's too much weight on my shoulders/It's too many nights in my hands/It's/I don't know/All I know is that the snow isn't falling/It's rising from the basement to take a walk along my street." I'm tired of writing, I'm tired of thinking. It's exhausting. I wish I had another hobby, like cars or something. I'd like to soup up cars. That's not true; I couldn't care less about cars. I reread the only sentence of my novel: "The days are long." I'm not sure. Maybe that could be the ending, maybe there's nothing more to add, maybe that says it all. Days should last an average of three hours. Give me three hours and I'm sure I'd manage not to get depressed. The server brings me a fourth cup of coffee, and I think my heart's about to explode. I don't tell her I don't want any more. I drink every cupful she pours me. I'm killing myself with every drop of percolated coffee. I emailed my publisher to tell him I'm writing a novel. I made it sound like it was coming along nicely and that I'd be able to send him the manuscript in a few months. He replied a couple of minutes later: "Wow! That's fantastic!" He doesn't know I've only written one sentence so far. And he doesn't know that I'm working at Super C and that I live in a tiny room that I call Dagobah. Which reminds me, I haven't seen Norm in days. We don't see each other anymore, not since I started work. When I spot Amidala from the other side of the grocery store, I wish I could hold her in my arms for four seconds. Just four seconds. I'd like to invite her for breakfast at Chez Rémi. I'd like to listen to the White Stripes with her and to sing along really loudly. I'd be Jack White and she'd be Megan White and we'd be a great duo. We'd do a gig on the roof of the Super C in the pouring rain. It'd be just her and me, and the fans' faces would be all blurry. It'd rain on our hair and on our bodies, and we'd be soaking wet. We'd be so beautiful.

Someone's stealing from the grocery store. The security cameras have caught a guy with a beard and a hoodie swiping beer and shrimp rings more than once this week. The Super C has turned into a police station, complete with investigators, the works. All the employees have become detectives, apart from Alan, that is, who wants to "chop his balls off." I feel a little like Bruce Willis in *Die Hard*. I'm the only one who stops to think how sad the thief must be. I can imagine him in his tiny apartment, defrosting his shrimp. I can just picture his tears. But I say nothing to no one; I'm one of the tough guys. Just call me John McClane. I imagine doing stunts in front of racks of frozen meals. I imagine a freezer exploding and me saving a woman from the flames in the nick of time. My name is John McClane and I'm stacking boxes of chicken nuggets. I see Akim materialize in the aisle. Now whenever I see Akim, I ask him if the bananas are OK. "Hello, my friend!" "How are the bananas?" He laughs. I like making Akim laugh. He laughs like the actor who dubs the voice of Lando Calrissian. Today he seems more serious than usual. I ask if everything's OK, as I do my best to line up the boxes of chicken wings. "I didn't know you were sick," he says. "Oh, no worries," I say. "I'm fine." He steps a little closer. "Multiple sclerosis is no fun. My cousin had it." I'm not too sure what he's getting at. "Ah, I have cystic fibrosis. It's not the same thing," I say. "Oh, OK. Ah, OK. It's your lungs, is that it?" "Yep." "Does it really feel like you're breathing through a straw?" I feel like saying to Akim, "I couldn't tell you. I've never really been able to breathe. I'm pretending to breathe, just like I'm pretending to stack bags of chicken wings in the freezer. I'm not breathing through a straw; I am a straw. It's the things around me that do the breathing for me: my clothes, my car, the bedside tables I bought at Structube. Do you get it, Akim? I'm a straw that wants to go live on Tatouine. An awkward straw, a straw that's never been able to repair anything: when something breaks, it stays broken. Akim, I can't sleep without a ventilator otherwise I hear the mucus gurgling in my throat and it keeps me up all night. I live to the constant hum of ventilators. I'm John McClane climbing through the ventilation shafts. John McClane realizing that his life is constant silence. John McClane trying to start up the ventilators every ten metres so that he no longer has to listen to himself." I don't say any of that. I smile, I pull my John McClane face, and keep stacking chicken wings. I just say, "Yeah, pretty much." "Do you mind me asking you about it?" "Nah, not at all." He puts a hand on my shoulder. His hand is warm. He says, "I'd better be going. Those carts aren't gonna collect themselves." "Good luck. And remember: Any trouble from the bananas and I'm on it, OK?" He laughs as he walks away. I keep on stacking my boxes in the freezer. I kneel and straighten the stacks. I'd happily spend all day inside the freezer. I'd like to be carbon frozen like Han Solo. I'd stay frozen like that in the chicken nuggets section. Tourists would flock to see me. They'd peer at my sick lungs, frozen in carbonite. The thought of it makes me smile. I look around and don't see anyone. I cry inside the freezer. I'm not sad. The tears are as big as my old Mazda. I'd have enough tears to build a small bedroom, with a bed, two bedside tables, and a bookshelf. Thing is, I'm not so good with my hands. I think to myself what a terrible waste all these tears are. I wipe my face and pull myself together. My name is John McClane, hi there. I stand back up and see Amidala on the other side of the glass door. I didn't hear her coming. She asks if I'm OK. She puts her hand on my forearm. "Oh yeah, fine. Thanks. My eyes are watering from the cold." She still looks serious. "If ever you want to talk, I'm here, OK?" "Great, thanks. You, too, eh? I'm good at solving problems. I have a gift." "Really?" "I shouldn't be talking about it. It's a secret. But, well, if you insist... I am one with the Force." She doesn't get it. "I am one with the Force and the Force is with me," I say again. "It's... Jedi powers. Anyways..." She laughs; her laughter is sincere. I don't know why I said that. It could have gone down like a lead balloon. She plays along. "Ah, that's why you're so cute." I'm surprised. I try to keep my cool. "Yep. It's all down to the Force." I roll my eyes and do my best to look blasé. She laughs hard, and I think I'm in love. She looks me right in the eye. I feel a little dizzy. Amidala is defrosting me. I imagine every person on Earth trapped in some kind of bronze mattress. I imagine all the mattresses shuffling along with their frozen faces, on their way to work, going out for a meal, heading to a rock concert. I wish I could freeze the sun and my car and Amidala's laugh. I wish I could freeze Amidala's face and hang it from my bedroom ceiling. I'd stare at Amidala's eyes on the ceiling all day.

One of my testicles hurts. I jump up and down on the spot in my room. The pain hangs on; it won't let go. "Jesus, there's always something." Tonight, I think I heard a mouse in the suspended ceiling. It was scrambling around above my bed and sounded like it was gnawing on something. It kept me up most of the night. I won't say anything to Norm in case he puts down traps. I'd like to tame it, like in *The Green Mile*: call it Mr. Jingles and make it a little bed in a cigar box. The mouse would live longer than me. I'd have to write it into my will. I'd leave it the bedroom set I bought at Structube. I go online to see how long different animals live. My time's going to be up before lots of other critters. Most parrots and whales will still be partying it up long after I'm gone. Bastards.

I'm wearing my best shirt. I got it from Wal-Mart. I'm going for breakfast with Amidala at eleven o'clock. At Chez Rémi. My treat. "No one's ever asked me out to breakfast before," she said. The sun is enormous outside. It hides the sky, like it's lying on its back. I'm nervous. When I get worked up, I want to turn into a ghost, and then I drink Chemineaud. I wonder if Amidala can see ghosts. I just take nine swigs, to make sure I don't disappear. My neck is gone; so is my left hand. My head's floated off somewhere. I can swipe my hand right through my throat and it doesn't even hurt. I try to swipe my hand through my testicle to get rid of the pain, but it doesn't help at all. I brush my teeth twelve times. I hate myself. Norm is reading his newspaper in the kitchen, hunched over the table. He's wearing the reading glasses he always has perched on the end of his nose when he's doing the crossword. He looks like an old moose. He doesn't look up. He says, "Broom made of twigs tied around a stick... five letters." I'm standing by the front door, putting on my boots. "Broom made of twigs tied around a stick... five letters," he says again. I look at him. "You want me to answer?" "I'm stuck," he says. "I'm about to throw the damned paper in the garbage." "Dunno. Sorry. Gotta go." I open the door; the wind whistles through my coat and chills me to the bone. "Tell me," he says, "and I'll knock $50 off this month's rent." I look over at him and say, "Besom." As I close the door, I hear him say, "Fuck me." My testicle is a broom made of twigs tied around a stick.

It snowed again last night. The sun's melted the snow in the streets, but not on my car. The snow on my car is a lot like my face. Poke around a little on my skin and you'd probably find an old purple Mazda. The days drag by. They do it on purpose. They're all the same. They drag on, don't know what to do with themselves. Sometimes snow is what they do. Sometimes they stay as calm as you like. Maybe they're taking pottery classes. I don't know. I'm a lot like the days. I don't get up to much. Sometimes I go to work at Super C. Sometimes I write poems and cry and think I'm pathetic. I'm more than capable of burrowing down into my bed and not coming up for days at a time. My back is a digger that likes going down deeper and deeper. I start my car and put on *Fell in Love With a Girl*, but I don't move. I'm hyperventilating. I want to go hide in my digger. I want to go dig inside me and hide in the semi-basement of my blood. I inch down further in my seat. I'm stuck here. I'd like to go off with Mr. Jingles in my bedroom's suspended ceiling. I could have breakfast in the ceiling, stay there, and end my days without worrying about hyperventilating ever again. Living in the ceiling might also help my testicle hurt less. I open the car window. The cold air goes straight up my nose. I don't feel the air go into my lungs, but I know it's going in through my nostrils. It feels like I'm breathing in light. I look in the rearview mirror. I manage to calm down, buckle my seatbelt, back out onto the road. "I'm going to order breakfast, talk to Amidala, try to make her laugh," I tell myself again. I say it out loud. I drive slowly, but I still manage to miss a stop sign. My hands are clammy. I've forgotten how to chat women up. It's been too long. I should have tried chatting up Mr. Jingles, for practice. When I get to Chez Rémi, I see Amidala sitting at a table at the back of the restaurant. "Sorry I'm late. My car wouldn't start." Amidala pretends to be angry. "Is that so? Car trouble, eh?" "Honest to God. My landlord had to give me a hand. I don't know a thing about cars." A first lie for Amidala. I know it won't be the last. I pile up lies stone by stone, then, at the end of every relationship, I stand back and take a good look at my handiwork. I think that's how they built the pyramids. "No worries, I just got here!" She reminds me of a little wild bird. She's wearing a white blouse with a black sweater. She's put on mascara. The server brings us two coffees. Amidala orders the "Builder's Special": sausage, ham, bacon, pancakes, eggs, and beans. My mouth drops open in mock astonishment. She laughs. "Hungry, are we?" She blushes. "What?!" I order the usual: two eggs over easy–bacon–white bread. "Bor-ring." She grins as she says it. "I've changed my mind," I tell the waitress. "I'll have the Builder's Special, extra sausage." Amidala grins even more; I've never seen her grin so wide. She has big teeth. I like her front teeth. One of them sticks out in front of the other. I am a broom made of twigs tied around a stick in Amidala's mouth. A sweet silence settles in between us. "I love silences," she says. "Me too." "If you were a Beatle," she asks, "which one would you be?" I have a think. "I can't make up my mind. Ringo Starr or Paul McCartney." "How come?" I look thoughtful. "I don't know who's gonna die first. I'd like to be the last Beatle alive." "Ringo Starr's definitely gonna die last," she says. "You'd be better taking Ringo." "Yeah, that's what I think, too. And who would you be?" She flashes me the "peace" sign: "John." "Of course." "Wanna be my Yoko Ono?" I laugh. The server arrives with our order, and I take out my pills. She asks what I'm talking pills for, and I decide to tell her the whole story: my lung disease and the whole shebang. "Yeah, I know about your disease. Mireille told me before

I showed you the ropes the other day... I didn't know you had to take pills, too." "Yep, I'm a little old man." I take a mouthful of pancake. She changes the subject. "What do you like to do in your spare time?" I say, "I like to google questions that people ask." She doesn't get it. I take out my phone and show her. "For instance, I write, 'Can the wind...' and I see what questions come up. You see here, people have asked, 'Can the wind make you crazy?' 'Can the wind knock over a motorbike?'" She laughs. I wish I could be the wind. I feel like asking a few new questions: Can the wind ask for sick leave at Super C? Can the wind go off and live on Tatouine forever? Can Amidala fall in love with a gust of wind that's got cystic fibrosis? "What about you, what do you like to do?" She says, "I like to dance. Anywhere... I'm crazy about dancing... Aside from googling stuff, you must have something you love doing, too, no?" I think for a moment. "I write poems." "Really? I've never read a poem." I find that sad, and I tell her I'm going to fix that. We finish breakfast. I feel like I'm about to explode. My belly is hard as a rock. Amidala looks as fresh as a daisy. Out on the sidewalk, she says, "Can I come to your place, just to read a poem?" "Got a craving for a poem?" It's so cold out. Amidala doesn't answer; she's got her face buried in her scarf. I say, "OK, follow me in your car to my place." I didn't think things would move so fast. Amidala doesn't mess around! When we get to my place, Norm isn't home, and I'm kind of relieved. I feel like a teenager bringing a girl back to his parents' place.

87

I ask if she's thirsty or would like a bite to eat. "Another piece of ham?" She claps her hand over her mouth and pretends to gag. We go down into the basement on Dagobah. Amidala pulls out her phone, puts on *Don't Let Me Down* by the Beatles, and starts to dance and sing in my bedroom. She's a good dancer. I never imagined a cute girl would be dancing on Dagobah one day. Amidala comes over and sits on my lap. She leans in towards me and tells me I smell like French fries. We kiss, I've got a hard-on, I've had one ever since we came down into the basement, but there's no hiding it now. I nuzzle her neck and cheek. She says, "You're drooling all over me." I think of the dog in my lungs. Amidala wants to go down on me, but I forgot to shave my pubes. I say no. She doesn't mind. We get undressed. We take our time. When she's about to come, she grabs my hand and tells me to squeeze her throat. She likes that, and I do, too, actually. We come at the same time, and I think that's a first for me. We lie naked on my bed for a long time. There's a rustling in the ceiling. Amidala asks what the strange noise is. "It's Mr. Jingles, a mouse that lives in the ceiling." "Wow, you've even given it a name?" "Yeah, of course." My testicle doesn't hurt anymore. The room is getting darker. Amidala says she has to go. She gets dressed, gives me a hug, and leaves. I feel a little ball of anxiety warming my tongue. In the kitchen, I tell myself out loud that it'll pass, that it always passes in the end. I realize I didn't read Amidala a poem. I realize it's pitch black in the house. I realize that, even when I'm happy,

88

I'm still sad. I don't know what to do, don't know where to go. I stay in the kitchen until Norm gets back from work. He gets home late. When he turns on the light in the hall, he sees me sitting in the kitchen. "What're you doing all alone in the dark?" I don't know what to say. I feel like telling him I'm not alone, that Mr. Jingles is somewhere in the house, but he'd probably think I was really crazy then. "I just wanted to see your tree all lit up." He laughs. His gap-toothed smile makes me feel better. The ball of anxiety on my tongue has disappeared. I go back to Dagobah. My whole bedroom smells of Amidala's skin. I fall asleep with my shirt still on. I fall asleep with my nicest shirt on, the one I bought at Wal-Mart, and I dream of Ringo Starr dying.

I've been listening to *Don't Let Me Down* nonstop for the past two hours. I feel like standing on a table in the café and tearing my shirt and shouting "Don't Let Me Down!" But I don't. I don't want any trouble with the police. The server appears and refills my coffee cup. I like La Brûlerie cause the coffee is better than at Café Morgane, and refills are free. I give a dollar every time they refill my cup. The servers know a good thing when they see it, and they wait perched at the counter like owls, a pot of coffee in hand. I go to La Brûlerie every other day. The staff knows my routine. When I sit down at a table, I don't even have to order. They bring me over a small, regular coffee and a glass of water. I always get the same thing. When I finally get up and leave, they call out "See ya tomorrow!" and just to be stubborn, I only come back the day after that. Just so I feel like I'm in control of my own destiny. The server is talking to me, but I can't hear her. She says, "What are you taking at school?" I feel like replying, "Oh, I'm not in school," but I bite my tongue. "I'm studying Mandarin." "Oh, wow, OK." I don't think she'd have said "Oh, wow, OK" if I'd told her I wrote poetry. I don't think she'd have said "Oh, wow, OK" if I'd told her I live with an undomesticated mouse by the name of Mr. Jingles. Outside, miniscule snowflakes are falling. They're so tiny they could fit under my fingernails. At the table next to me, two women are talking about their horses. By the sounds of it, it costs $300 to $500 a month to keep a horse. I could never have a horse. Unless I don't pay for its keep and live with it on the street. I'd be the homeless guy in Repentigny with a horse. I'd be like the homeless people who sleep spooning with their dogs. I'd spoon with my horse in a sleeping bag. I google "Can a horse..." and there are some surprising questions: "Can a horse gallop backwards?", "Can a horse live on its own?", "Can a horse vomit?", "Can a horse cry?". I learn that horses sleep standing up so they can gallop off if a predator approaches. It's not snowing anymore. I read an article about sharks. Sharks have to swim while they sleep. They swim constantly, to filter water through their gills. I am a shark. A shark that walks on the sidewalk and doesn't scare anyone. A shark with cystic fibrosis that works at Super C. It's started to snow again. Snow is bipolar. It doesn't look real. It gets pushed about by the wind, as though it's running away from something. I'd like to run away with it. I'd run away with the snow to the next block, then I'd choke and come back to the café and sit back down at my laptop to write nothing. The snow would be raging; it would hate me. I get a text from Amidala. She writes, "The breakfast idea was really original :-)" I'd love to stroke Amidala's back. I ask her if she feels like watching *The Phantom Menace* tonight. She asks me what that is. "The first of the *Star Wars* prequels." "On one condition: I want to go skating afterwards." "Deal." I pack up my stuff, pay, and leave the café. The server calls out "See ya tomorrow," and I think to myself, "Not a chance." I walk slowly, I enjoy the snow, I make up with the snow. When I get home, I clean up on Dagobah. I put on another of my Wal-Mart shirts. I hang around for most of the day. I'm not working today; they cut my hours this week. Amidala arrives at my place looking smart. She takes off her coat and scarf. She's wearing jeans and a black tank top with spaghetti straps. We kiss each other on the cheek, but not on the mouth. She says hi to Norm and, as she's going down to Dagobah, he gives me a wink. I put on the *Phantom Menace* DVD. We sit down on the leatherette couch in the basement, and I'm careful to keep the Ninja Turtles blanket out of sight. As the credits start rolling, Amidala laughs. "You OK?" "Yeah, yeah. I just can't believe you're making me watch *Star Wars*." "Well, I'm an original kind of guy, remember?" "Yep."

"I'm gonna make you watch every last one of them." She asks how many there are. "Eight, but they're not done yet. They're going to be bringing out lots more." Amidala looks dismayed. I laugh. During the movie, she says she thinks Jar Jar Binks and the Gungans are really annoying, and I'm pleased. "I hate them, too." When she sees the real princess Amidala, played by Natalie Portman, I smile but don't say a word. I'm an idiot! She thinks Qui-Gon Jinn's a hunk. "I agree." She manages to sit through the entire movie. I congratulate her in my mind: Congratulations, Princess Amidala. She gives me an exasperated look. "Pfff, whatever... Let's go skating!" At the park where I worked last summer, the city built an ice oval about a kilometre around. There's even a hut where you can change into your skates. My skates are old and rusty. Amidala laughs when she sees them. I'm a bit wobbly on the ice, but after a couple of laps I start to get the hang of it. I overtake a man and his young daughter. Amidala is showing off, doing pirouettes like she's at the Olympics. I pick up speed and glide off, so far off that I'm all alone. The wind blows against my face. The wind blows only on my face. I think about the Google questions about sharks: "Can sharks jump?", "Can sharks drown?". With a little practice, I'd be able to jump on this ice rink. With a little practice, I'd be able to drown on this ice rink.

The snow's coming down like Niagara Falls in the Super C parking lot. I've only ever seen photos of Niagara Falls. Do they really exist? I don't know much. I don't even know the names of most of the world's cities. I have to resort to Google to find out if things really exist. I found out that my favourite planet really does exist. There's a town in Tunisia called Tataouine. It's where they filmed the desert scenes in the first *Star Wars* trilogy. I also found out there's an expression: to go to Tataouine. It means to lose yourself at the end of the world. There's even a variation on it in Quebec: *tataouiner,* to lack speed, to dither. This planet really is my soul mate. It could be my totem. My star sign. I don't want to be a Taurus any longer; I want to be a Tatouine. In an ideal world, the weather would follow my mood. It would rain a lot, but I'd no longer worry about catching cold in the rain. There'd be no more Super C; I'd plant different types of Sidekicks all over the place. On Tatouine my lung disease would be gone; I'd no longer have to work. I wouldn't need to be talented. I'd be able to play *Super Mario Bros 3* all day long. I'd have room for both my tables from Structube beside my bed. I'd be the wisest of Jedi who sleeps in the cleanest of bedrooms. I'd be old Ben Kenobi, only I wouldn't be stuck sleeping in a cave. A horn blares. A car passes right by me; I can feel the wind from the car on my coat. The snow is heavy. I can hardly see in front of me. All I can make out is car headlights crossing in the parking lot. Akim hasn't come in to work today. For once, I have to round up the carts in the parking lot, one by one. I feel a bit sorry for them, trapped in the snowstorm like that. I cough and hack. I wish I could go home and straight to bed. I'd leave a note in the snow in the parking lot, written with a branch. "Sorry, gone home. So, so tired." I don't, though. I need the money: for rent, for food, for meds, for my stupid little Sidekicks that don't grow on trees. The snow is sticky. The snow reminds me of my mucus. It sticks to my coat and my little fluorescent safety vest. I cough up yellow mucus every ten metres. They'll never lose track of me, I tell myself. I'm Hansel and Gretel, both at once. Walking through the snow in ski-doo boots is an art I've mastered, but it's tiring. I can no longer feel my heart. My heart has been wearing pyjamas ever since I turned twelve. I come across a bunch of carts at the end of the parking lot. It takes me twenty minutes to fit four of them together. Nice work, genius! When I breathe in, I can feel every obstacle in my throat. I've never been good with obstacles. I've always backed away from obstacles, always run away from them. I decide to lie down in an empty parking space. I make a half-assed attempt at a snow angel. I think of my dad. He signed me up for ski lessons when I was a kid. I was maybe eight or nine. The instructor showed me how to snowplow to go down the hill. I couldn't stay on my feet. I tried a few times, then, I don't know how, I found myself all alone. Lying there on my back, looking up at the sky for the rest of the ski lesson, while the other children practiced going downhill with the instructor. I remember my father being discouraged. I remember the other parents saying, "Who is that kid?"

Out of the corner of my eye, I can see that my four carts are starting to come apart in the wind. Stupid bloody carts. I run after them. One of them bumps into the door of a parked car. It doesn't leave a mark. I'm glad. I look in through the window. There's a little boy inside, all alone, holding a Game Boy. He looks out at me. I say hi; he doesn't reply. Not wanting to look like a pedophile, I beat a hasty retreat with my four carts. I make my way through the storm, looking for shopping carts, a ghost in a fluorescent vest. There are carts everywhere. They're breeding like rabbits, giving me the runaround. I'll never track them all down. Every time I think I'm done, I see a bunch more waiting for me, just standing there. I hear a voice calling for me in the little walkie-talkie I'm wearing on my shoulder. I am John McClane, making angels in the snow. The sound of the walkie-talkie makes me think of *The Deserts and Mountains of Cystic Fibrosis*: you can hear the Caspian Sea in there, with its one hundred and sixty kilometres of shell beaches. Every sound made by a walkie-talkie must contain at least one hundred and sixty kilometres of shells. It's Mireille; she wants to see me. When I get to her office, she tells me someone filed a complaint about me: they saw me making a snow angel in the parking lot. "Is it true?" "Not really. I slipped on the ice... ended up on my back... and, uh, yeah, I may have flailed around a little." I do the

95

snow-angel thing with my arms. Mireille looks me right in the eye, deadly serious, then bursts out laughing. She laughs for a solid two minutes. Two minutes is a long time to be laughing. I make myself laugh along with her: I don't want to be in trouble over a snow angel. "You're a real number. Did anyone ever tell you that?" I don't know what to say. "I've heard all sorts since I started here, but a snow angel is a first." I scratch my head. "I'm sorry." "It's fine. Just... no more snow angels in the parking lot." "Sure thing." I leave the office and pretend to be hard at work. I bring back one cart every half hour. On Tatouine, there'd be no more customers filing complaints, and making angels in the sand would be right up there as a way to tackle anxiety. Sand angels would replace light therapy. Picturing the battered and broken making angels in the sand makes me laugh. I'm sure I'd fit right in. I could be the sand-angel guru. My sect and I would go from one grocery store parking lot to another to make sand angels. One day the rules would change and I'd get arrested. Life imprisonment for inciting the members of my group to spread their wings under parked cars; crushed to death, the lot of them. As I bring back my one hundredth cart, I pass by an old lady in a purple coat standing by the trunk of her car. She looks like a ship's sail straining in the wind. She's a sorry sight. She's trying to put her bags in the trunk, but her cart has a mind of its own. I grab it with one hand, and put her bags in the car with the other. "Thank you so much," she says, practically shouting. "I didn't see you come up there. Thanks a lot." I give her a thumbs up. I'm a ninja, a powerful warrior who helps the poor and the down-trodden. I'm a ninja in ski-doo boots. I feel a headache coming on, gouging at my temples and eyes. I feel like locking myself away in the staff washroom and taking a nap. One of the employees would try to open the door, but he wouldn't be able to. After a while, people would knock and unlock it from the outside, but I'd jam my foot up against the door to stop them coming in. I'd be like Will Smith in *The Pursuit of Happyness*, only without the kid. My legs are starting to feel like jello. The snow is piling up in the parking lot. I walk in the tracks left behind by the car tires. I'm a ninja and I'm so, so fed up. I look at all the carts I have to round up: they're all out there, by the look of things. I try to count them, but there are too many. Four hours' work for nothing. I go back for another look at my snow angel, but I can't find it. It's been buried alive.

Is it possible to die of darkness? I haven't seen the sun for ages. It snows all the time in Repentigny. The sky is always pale grey. My fingernails are too long. I know I should trim them, but I don't have the energy. It's all so challenging. It's all so complicated. Cutting your fingernails, walking in the snow: same battle. On Tatouine, I wouldn't have to trim my nails: they wouldn't grow. I wouldn't have to wash or get my hair cut, either. My hair would always be just the right length, always clean, always tidy. I go to La Brûlerie, sit down at my usual table. It's pretty quiet. My nose starts to bleed and I go to the washroom. It bleeds for twenty minutes. Electric heating makes my nose bleed. I stay there until the bleeding stops. When I finally come out of the washroom, nobody applauds. I don't write a single sentence of my novel. I watch a couple eating in silence. I watch the server going from table to table, filling up the little wicker baskets with creamers. I watch the snowplows go barrelling past the windows at breakneck speed. Everyone's busy; everyone's got something to do. All I do is bleed on and off from my nose. I hide my fingers. I'm ashamed of my long nails, I'm ashamed of my greasy hair. I flick my hair to the side, but it always falls back over my eyes. I have a little bald spot near my forehead. It's chic, oh-so chic. I'm a very chic ghost in very chic ski-doo boots. I watch people eating while I listen to A Soft Murmur. They're chewing on the rain. I text Amidala. I ask if she wants to come watch *Star Wars Episode II: Attack of the Clones*. She writes back, "Sure, but I'm gonna have to get drunk first, otherwise I'll never make it to the end." I reply, "OK." I leave the café, and go buy two bottles of wine at the corner store. When I get home, I see Norm in the living room, dressed up as Santa Claus. He's the scrawniest Santa I've ever seen. His costume looks pretty sharp, all sparkly. He says, "Whatcha doin' here?" "Oh, sorry, I'm not working today." He takes off his fake white beard and says, "OK." There's a long silence. If I don't ask, it's going to be even weirder, so I say, "It's none of my business, but why are you dressed up as Santa?" He clears his throat, and the pompom on the end of his hat drops down over his forehead. He's serious. "A buddy of mine gets me lots of Santa gigs over the holidays. The pay's good." "Oh, that's cool," I say. "Two hundred and fifty bucks for a seven-hour day. It's nothin' to sneeze at." "Wow, OK, no, for sure." He's the first gap-toothed Santa I've ever met. "They're looking for an elf at the mall. I can ask my buddy for you, if you're interested." "Oh, no, really, I'm fine thanks, Norm." He takes off his suspenders. "Oh yeah? You sure? I mean, I still haven't got your rent cheque for this month." "Oh, you haven't?" He takes off his pants. He's wearing white briefs. His legs are hairy, and there's a long scar on his left knee. "No, I haven't." He's not angry; he just seems a little impatient. I say, "Hang on a minute." I check my bank balance on my phone while he's pulling on his workpants. I eye the two bottles of wine at my feet. My mouth feels a bit dry. There's only a hundred and four dollars left in my account. My next pay's not until next week. I'm not working enough hours at the supermarket. At minimum wage, I hardly make enough to cover the rent. "OK. I'll be an elf." Norm keeps a straight face. "OK. I'll call my pal... You're gonna have to do an interview." "An interview to be an elf?" "Yep." Norm pulls out his phone and dials a number. He stares out the living-room window. The Santa costume is lying in a heap on the sofa. "Hey, Mike! Listen, I think I've found you an elf... Yeah... Hang on, I'll pass you over." Norm hands me the phone.

I realize I'm about to do an over-the-phone interview for a job as an elf. "Hello?" "So you wanna be an elf?" "Yes." Mike asks me if I've ever been an elf before. I say I haven't. He asks me if I've got good people skills, if I like kids. I lie, "Oh yeah, I love kids." It strikes me that, taken out of context, that's a strange thing to say. Mike asks how much I weigh. "You big or small?" I think for a moment. "I'm average." He asks me how I feel about wearing tights. My first thought is, "No fucking way." Norm is busy folding the sleeves of his Santa suit, and he glances up at me every now and then. "No problem. I don't mind wearing tights." Norm smiles at me. "OK, good. Can you come in Saturday with Norm?" "Sure." I wonder what I've gotten myself into. I haven't even taken my coat off yet. Mike says, "Great then. See ya." He hangs up. I pass the phone back to Norm and tell him I've got the job. "Alrighty!" If I was on Tatouine, I wouldn't have to dress up as an elf. I could drink wine all day long and put the hate on every kid in the world. There's a distance that sets me apart from things. A gap that I probably create subconsciously. Little piles of mental snow that I sprinkle wherever my gaze settles. I have nothing to shovel it with. I wait for the snow to melt. Sometimes it doesn't melt at all. Sometimes, it's me who has to melt instead. I grab the two bottles of wine and head for Dagobah. I stretch out on my bed and wait for Amidala. I feel like writing a poem, but I can't summon the energy. I haven't heard Mr. Jingles for a while. I hope nothing bad's happened to him. Without meaning to, I fall asleep on my back. I hear Amidala knocking on my bedroom door. The sound wakes me, and I see her there, smiling like a flower. She's not wearing makeup, and it suits her. She's got on a loose-fitting sweater with a moose on the front. "Nice sweater!" "Hey, don't make fun of me!" "I'm not. I like your sweater." She lies down on my bed and kisses me on the cheek. I open a bottle of wine and we pass it back and forth. Amidala says, "No need for glasses." I say, "Fuck glasses." I tell her about my novel that's not going anywhere. I tell her about my budding career as an elf, and she bursts out laughing. I elaborate: "I'm going to have to wear skintight tights. The kids are all going to be checking out my crotch." Amidala laughs at my borderline pedophile joke and says I'm an idiot. Amidala's laugh makes me forget all about my snowbanks. I feel light. We finish off the first bottle in no time. She opens the second, takes a long swig, and sets the bottle down on the bedside table. She undoes my pants. I realize I still haven't shaved my pubes. We spoon and make love. Amidala's hair is warm, and it tickles my nose. I feel good. I'd happily die buried in her hair. I nuzzle the back of her neck and her ear, and tell her she's beautiful. She orgasms quickly. I don't have time to come, but I don't care. We get dressed and go into the basement living room. I put on the Episode II DVD, and when the soundtrack starts to play, Amidala pretends to hang herself, her tongue sticking out to one side. "It's way better than the first. I can't wait for you to see Kamino." "What's Kamino?" "It's a planet where it

rains all the time and where they produce a clone army."
"OK." I wish I could clone Amidala thousands of times
over, just so I could bump into her on every street corner. I wish I could clone her laugh. That way, there'd no
longer be a gap between me and stuff. All my snowbanks
would melt. I'm a bit tipsy. I feel like a smoke. Amidala
has her head in my lap and falls asleep in thirty seconds
flat. I reckon she's doing it to get out of watching the
movie, but I let her get away with it. I stroke her hair.
I brush it gently with the tips of my fingers. I'm waiting
for the scene where Samuel L. Jackson says, "This
party's over." I try to carry Amidala over to the bed, but
I'm not strong enough. She's as light as a feather, and I'm
as weak as a kitten. I stroke her forehead and tell her she
should go sleep in my bed. She stands up like a robot,
works out the distance to the bedroom, and goes off to
collapse on the mattress. I tuck her in, go to the bathroom, take a hot shower. I try to open the little bathroom
window, but it's stuck shut with the cold. I'm completely
naked, standing on the edge of the bath, straining at the
window to let the steam out. Nothing doing. Every window in the basement will be steamed up. Too fucking
bad. I'm a kitten. I dry myself and put on my ripped, old
pyjamas. I look in the mirror, but I can't see myself.
There's too much steam: all I can see is my outline.
I wipe away the condensation so that I can see myself,
but it doesn't work. The window's frozen shut, and
I don't know when I'll be able to open it again. Amidala
wakes me up during the night because I'm breathing

loudly; she can hear the bubbles in my lungs. I tell her that's nothing unusual. She rubs my back. Her hand's cold. She warms her hands on my back. "Your back's like a furnace." "Yep, and I don't know how to turn it off." I roll over and try to find her lips in the dark. My thumbs find her collarbones, neck, chin, lips. Her face is tiny in the dark. I kiss her. "I can't see you," she says. "I can see you," I say. She asks how. "Jedi powers." "You never miss a beat, do you?" She laughs. Can you really die from too much darkness?

I feel weak. It starts in my thighs and runs all the way up to my forearms. I think I've caught a cold. I'm a little short of breath. I don't want to tell Norm I can't do the elf thing. He's been waiting for me in the car for the past five minutes. I haven't had time to do my treatments. When I go outside, he's got *Satisfaction* by the Rolling Stones playing full blast on the radio. Norm is in great form. "C'mon, Santa's Little Helper. Time to go!" His car smells like a mix of steak and modelling clay. Norm is already wearing part of his Santa suit. He drives fast. I notice he still wears his wedding band. I feel like I know him well enough to ask. "You still wear your ring?" Norm gives me a funny look. I get the feeling my question is going to remain unanswered, and I kick myself for bringing it up. After a pause, he turns down the radio. "I can't take it off." "Have you tried soap?" He smiles. "No, not like that. I can take it off, only I can't. I tried for a while, and it feels like part of me's missing when I don't wear it." Norm turns left, takes a street I've never been down before. He says, "I was really depressed after my wife left me. The Santa Claus thing came later. It's one of the things that helped me through it." "Sure, I get that." The parking lot is full when we get to the mall. "All these people coming to see Santa. I don't believe it," I say. Norm smiles, but his good mood soon disappears when he can't find a parking spot. I feel like drinking Chemineaud. I imagine an elf drunk on Chemineaud acting up in front of the kids. The elf who tries to toss them up into the air and catch them. I might be able to throw them, but I wouldn't be able to catch them. I can picture the scene: a whole pile of dead kids, skulls cracked, lying on the floor in the mall. I'm a real idiot. Norm opens his trunk and takes out a huge hockey bag that contains the rest of his costume. A big, fat man is waiting for us at Door 5 by the pharmacy. He's wearing a winter coat that's too small for his belly. His coat is unbuttoned and flapping in the wind. His gut is impressive. He and Norm shake hands like a couple of old truckers, wrists straight and elbows bent as though they're arm-wrestling. Mike has eyes like a toad, an enormous double chin, and not a hair on his head. He's also missing a tooth. The gap-toothed stick together, by the look of things. I'm not a member of that particular club yet. "So, you're the elf, huh?" "Yeah." He hands me a garbage bag. I open it and see a pair of tights and a hat and little bells and shoes and I think to myself, Oh my God. I stay cool. "Great," I say, and I think how ugly I am.

"The place is fuckin' packed," Mike tells Norm. "Bob's here already. Hurry up and get changed, the pair of you." By way of explanation, Norm just says, "There were no friggin' parking spots." Mike doesn't say another word. I follow Norm to the washroom inside the pharmacy. Norm asks the cashier if he can use the staff washroom. She gives him a funny look. "I'm Santa," Norm says. Her expression changes, like she's just realized she's talking to Bono. She points over towards the washroom. Norm turns to me. "Last year," he explains, "I was stuck in the mall washrooms for half an hour, signing autographs for the kids." I get changed first. I start with the stockings. They're too small. I should've told Mike I was on the beefy side, so he'd get me a bigger costume. I try to yank the tights up over my hips, but they get stuck halfway around my butt. I put the elf shorts on over them and it doesn't show. I put on the hat, the shoes, the green shirt, a gold-coloured jacket cut just like Aladdin's. I take a look in the mirror. Ouch. I don't look like an elf at all. I just look like a fucking weirdo. I come out of the washroom, and Joe Pesci bends over double. I've never seen him like this. Tears are streaming down his face. He can't stop laughing. "Oh my God, I don't believe it. Oh my God," he gasps. "Fuck you, you shitty Santa," I think to myself. Norm goes off to get changed. I can still hear him laughing on the other side of the door. When he comes back out, he gives me a little twirl, arms in the air, proud as you like. His costume is so big, it's hanging off him. His fake beard is so big, I can't see his face. It's

105

like a Santa parody. We make quite the team. We walk over to the throne. I have to admit, they've made a good job of it: oversize plastic candy canes, reindeer, brightly lit trees, artificial snow, the lot. A long red carpet winds its way up to a huge armchair. At least fifty people are waiting in line. When the kids catch sight of Norm, some of them start shouting; others burst into tears. Norm takes a bow. Some of the parents applaud. Norm tells me to stick close to make sure the crowd keeps it together. "OK." I'm introduced to Bob, the photographer. He's dressed up in *Nutcracker* gear: a red overcoat with gold buttons and a black top hat. "You took your sweet time," he whispers. "Sorry." Norm sits down on his throne and some of the parents spill over as far as Bob. "Go on, get to it!" Nutcracker Guy tells me. I say, "We're going to need a nice, straight line for Santa or there'll be no gifts for anyone." I feel like killing myself. No one listens. It's Bob who raises his voice and gets them all back in line. I've gone weak at the knees; my head is pounding. A little girl wants to know my name. I hesitate. "Qui-Gon Jinn," I say. She doesn't understand. "Elfis, my name is Elfis." Her mother is satisfied. I start clowning around, walking like I've got a sore back. I pretend I'm slipping on ice. A little boy laughs. I'm thirsty, I keep coughing, my mouth's full of mucus, but I can't spit. I swallow each gob down until I feel sick. I wish I was on Tatouine. I think about my cold, my wobbly knees. I've no choice but to spit out a huge yellow gob into the artificial snow. I do it as discreetly as I can. I don't think anyone saw me. I have to go work at the store tomorrow and I don't know how I'm going to manage. I'm pathetic. Real elves don't have cystic fibrosis. The day drags by. I don't eat anything; I don't have time. Dozens and dozens of young children file past. They cry, they shout, they whine. I'd like to go sit on Norm's lap and ask if he'd pay my rent for a year. I'd like to curl up and sleep in the mall's artificial snow. I'd like it if someone would wake me up next year. I'd like to lose weight every time I blink. I'd be able to fit in my elf costume; I'd be able to disappear in my elf costume. I'd be Elfis, the ghost at the mall.

The children keep on filing past and they all have the same face. I'm starting to get used to them. I like the ones I feel sorriest for. A little boy introduces himself. His name is Adam; he has a bowl cut. He stares at me with big, brown eyes. He tells me what he wants most of all is a little dog, but not a real one. "Dad says a real one is too much work," he says. I laugh. I tell him he needs to ask Santa, not me. He asks what I want for Christmas. I don't know what to say. He's caught me off guard, the little rascal. "I'd like to see my sister who lives in New York." He asks me how come she doesn't live at the North Pole. I'm an idiot. I'd forgotten I was in character. "My sister's an elf, too. She does scouting for Santa Claus in New York." "Oh," he says, and then it's his turn to see Norm. Sheesh. A mother of four tells me my nose is bleeding. I hadn't realized. "Oops." I pinch my nose, but it's too late. My gold jacket is ruined. I motion to Bob that I need to go to the washroom. He motions back that I should be quick about it, probably so as not to traumatize the kids. I take my time making my way to the washroom, pinching my nose all the way. On the cubicle door I stare at a badly drawn heart with the initials "B.M. + S.D." The bleeding is starting to slow. Every piece of toilet paper I stuff up my nose comes out paler than the one before, until the last little paper cone comes out perfectly white. I stare at the cone for the longest time, blinking hard. It doesn't want to disappear. For once, I wish the paper were still red. I wish I could spend all day in the washroom. I go over to the mirror and try my best to mop up the bloodstains from my Aladdin shirt with wet hand towels. I manage to remove some of the blood, but I think I split the crotch of my tights. When I get back to my elf duties, I feel like I'm in everyone's way. The whole vibe has changed. Bob is managing the queue and taking photos at the same time. I feel like I'm always in the wrong place. It's the same at Super C. The only difference is that at the Super C, I can slip away. I can sneak off to another aisle, find something else to do, or even just pretend to be hard at work. Here, in my elf costume, there's nowhere to run. I wish I could just turn off the shopping-mall lights so no one can see me. I stand beside a giant plastic candy cane and stare straight ahead. An old woman taps me on the shoulder. She really needs to go to the washroom, but she doesn't want to lose her place in line. She asks if I can keep an eye on her granddaughter. I say, "Sure." As I go over to the queue, I see Norm watching me out of the corner of his eye. The parents are wondering what I'm doing there. The little girl looks like she's afraid of me. "Hi, I'm an elf. My name's Elfis." She stares at the bloodstains on my shirt. I ask her what her name is, but she doesn't answer. She's shy. I have to admit, if I were her, I wouldn't have replied to a blood-spattered guy named Elfis either. She looks like she's about to burst into tears. Please, anything but that! I ask her what she wants for Christmas. She stares straight at me and shrugs. "A puppy?" I start barking and stick out my tongue. Her face is a blank. I ask her how old she is. She doesn't know. "I'm a thousand years old." She couldn't give a damn. I wonder where the hell her grandmother has gotten to. "Well, Santa Claus has told me a lot about you. He can't wait to see you." She still doesn't say a word. A boy standing in front of us turns and asks excitedly, "What about me?" I think to myself, "Not you, you little shit," but I say, "Of course, you too!" He looks too old to visit Santa. He tells me he wants a game for his PlayStation. I couldn't care less. The grandmother finally gets back from the washroom. She's happy I didn't kidnap her granddaughter. "Thank you so much." I leave them and see Norm gesturing to me. I lean in towards him and he mutters, "I'm thirsty as all hell. Go buy me a bottle of water, will ya? I'm roasting in this thing." I'm relieved to escape to the food court at the far end of the mall. I buy a bottle of water and a slice of pizza. I eat my pizza standing next to a garbage can. All the tables are taken. I watch the giant screens hanging above the people sitting there. One of them is showing the weather in different countries. It's hot everywhere, especially in Puerto Rico. My head hurts. I feel shaky. I feel trapped in my costume. I finish eating and realize they haven't shown the weather forecast for Tatouine. I don't feel like going back to Santa's Village, I just want to get the fuck out of here. I feel like going to bed and taking a long nap. I feel like just pressing "pause." I imagine myself heading out into the snow in my blood-stained elf costume. I'd probably get pneumonia. Norm would probably kick me out for leaving in the middle of my elf shift. I decide to go back to my job and phone it in. Norm has two kids sitting on his lap. I hand him the bottle of water and go back to my place near the queue. A parent asks me if Santa's elves are paid to do their job. "I dunno." I hadn't even asked about the pay beforehand. Either way, every dollar will go into Norm's pocket to pay the rent. My legs hurt; I feel ashamed. I overhear a woman talking to her son about his swimming lesson. It reminds me of the smell of the municipal swimming pool and of my dad in his swimsuit. I remember I didn't want to jump off the high diving board. All the other kids had jumped except me. I can still see my toes curling over the end of the diving board and the people in the water urging me to jump. I never did. I've always been a chicken and a bit different from other kids. My dad had to climb up the ladder to bring me down. It was the first time I felt shame, I think. If I'd known then that I'd be working at the age of thirty-one as an elf in a shopping mall, I think I would have jumped head first onto the deck of the pool. I cough. I'm short of breath again. I hork up enormous gobs of mucus into the artificial snow every time the coast is clear. This day is going to have to end eventually. I'll catch my breath at some point. I've been living on a diving board for thirty-one years. I live on a floor-level diving board and there's no water.

I dreamed that I tried to kill myself by jumping off a bridge. I succeeded, only to wake up in a luxury hotel room. A woman who reminded me of Meryl Streep asked me if I still wanted to die. I didn't really know what to say. She told me to think it over, said she had the power to fix my stupid mistake. I stayed for a long time in that in-between world. I was happy; I could order fries and drink beer. In the lobby, I bumped into some people I knew from way back who asked what I did for a living. I told them I'd committed suicide, and they all said, "Oh no, oh no!" I asked Meryl Streep if it would be OK if I stayed there. She didn't understand. I wished I could stay at that hotel for the rest of my days, eating French fries. I kept telling her everything was "less complicated here." She didn't want me to stay. It wasn't easy, but I decided to die a second time. I remember it was super emotional. Whatever. I've been in bed for the past two days. I'm not spitting up blood, but I feel weak. My mucus looks like newborn kittens. Maybe I've got an infection; I'm in denial. Maybe I'm just short on motivation. I've started on Cipro, an antibiotic I have to take twice a day for two weeks. I'm not supposed to eat dairy with it. I need the doctor's permission to take Cipro, but fuck it, I still had a whole bottle of it left. It's kinda my last chance to avoid having to get a PICC line put in. The Super C called seven times. I finally told them I was sick, that I was sorry I hadn't picked up earlier. I know I should go to Montreal to get a doctor's note. I stay in the dark on Dagobah. I eat peanut butter on toast and go back to bed. I do my treatments, too. I'm a robot. I fill up my vials using a syringe. I'm a medication mixologist. I'd be a good barman for sick people. In my bar, there wouldn't be any fights: people would be too frail. They'd just ignore each other. There'd be super-comfy seats and fancy spittoons. Outside, there'd always be a lineup of sick people looking to have a little fun. Yeah, whatever. With the money from my elf gig and the supermarket this week, I was able to pay Norm for December. But two bags of sandwich bread and a jar of peanut butter later, my bank account's nearly empty. I drink water and eat toast and feel depressed. I consider going on welfare. I still can't open the bathroom window. I haven't heard Mr. Jingles in the ceiling for days. He must be dead. I'm sad for him. I lie alone in my bed and cry for a mouse that I've never seen and that may not even exist. I haven't heard from Amidala, and I try to convince myself that that's OK. I don't want her to see me like this. I feel the little ball of anxiety in my throat. It's smack in the middle of my throat. I don't know what to do. I call my sister. She doesn't answer. I go up to the kitchen and freak out even more. I have to do something. Maybe this will be my last Christmas. I watch a horror movie to take my mind off things. The same questions run through my mind as when I was in elementary school, standing there on the big pile of snow in the schoolyard. I was useless at school, but I used to dream of studying for years at university. In class, I'd come up with the wildest scenarios. I'd imagine myself as a rock star, an airline pilot, or an ambulance technician, out saving lives. My dreams were realistic: I never wanted to be an astronaut because I knew I was always short of breath. I just stared at the girls in class while the teacher was explaining stuff. Every day, I would fall in love with a different girl. I'd picture myself snowboarding with a girl in my arms. High school was even worse. I was hopeless at geography, history, math, physics, pretty much everything. I was often depressed. I had lots of friends, at least; I was lucky like that. I've never had a good memory. I could never remember what I learned in class. The number of things I studied and memorized, and that I don't remember at all now, is just crazy, man. It's ridiculous, man. If I had to redo my exams, even my elementary school exams, I'd fail them all. I can never remember the number of provinces in Canada. Nine? Ten? Is Nova Scotia a province of Canada? What the fuck? I've never been to the rest of Canada anyway. I'm sitting on a chair in the kitchen. I listen to my breathing. One of my nostrils is blocked. My breathing's loud, louder than me. It's drowning me out. The screen on my phone lights up. It's my sister. "Hello?" "What's wrong?" "Oh, nothing. I was just wondering how you were. I'm sorry. I didn't mean to bother you." "You're not bothering me. *I* phoned *you*." "OK." "Elliott Smith's sick. We changed his food, and now he's doing a bit better. I'm working crazy hours at the minute." I say, "Oh, OK. And you're hanging in alright?" "Yeah. How are things with you?" I can't answer that. There's a sob in my throat. I take too long to reply. She says, "Okaaaay... So, what's up?" "I'm not really sure. I'm kinda confused." I start crying. I can't keep it together. The tears tumble down my cheeks, tickling me on the way. I can't see a thing. I don't have the strength to wipe my eyes. "Come on, talk to me... Are you gonna kill yourself or what?" There's no malice in her voice. Her tone is light. She's managed to defuse my sadness a little. It feels as though she's asked if I'm really planning to go apple picking stark naked in a busy orchard. "No, no, of course not... It's just, I don't know, with work and everything, I'm having a hard time making rent and, I dunno, I feel kind of alone." "Did you pay this month's rent?" "Yeah." "Well then, come spend the holidays with us." "With you? In New York?" She seems to have her mind made up. "Sure. I'll pay your bus fare. I'll send you the reference numbers, and all you'll have to do is pick up your ticket at the bus station. I'll put it in your name." "OK, but I've never been to New York. I don't know. And I'm supposed to be having turkey with Norm for Christmas." "With Norm? Jesus. Just tell Norm you'll be having turkey with your sister this year, will you?" "Yeah, OK." It all happens very quickly; everything always happens quickly with Cammy. I have a bus ticket from Montreal to New York City for the very next day. When Norm comes home from work, I tell him I won't be able to have Christmas dinner with him after all. The words gush out of my mouth. I don't want to leave Norm in the lurch, poor guy. "No worries, kid." "You can come with me to New York, if you like. We could go to SantaCon." "No way, Jose. Quebec is the place for Santa and nowhere else." I laugh. We examine the Santa question from every angle. I go downstairs to sweep my room. I gather at least a kilo of dust. If dust was worth something, I'd be a billionaire. I'd go to the bank every day and cash in my kilos of dust for hundreds of twenty-dollar bills. I'd be able to buy myself an indoor pool, which I'd install in my room on Dagobah. It would be a heated, silo-shaped pool in the floor. There'd be underwater lights to light up the little waves. It would be at the foot of my bed, and I'd be able to go for a swim without leaving my room. Yeah, right. I'm lying on my bed, thinking about New York. I've always wanted a t-shirt with "I ♥ New York" on it. I think about all the different variations of "I ♥" you could put on a funny t-shirt: "I ♥ Repentigny, I ♥ cystic fibrosis, I ♥ Super C, I ♥ Norm dressed up as Santa, I ♥ the bathroom window that won't open." I miss Amidala. I write her a very long message that ends with, "I'm leaving for New York tomorrow to visit my sister. I know you can't wait to see

115

Star Wars Episode III, but you'll have to hang on a little longer. I miss you." The rest of the night drags by. The minutes are black and trudge down to my heart. I try counting sheep, but I don't see any. All the sheep are off bounding over tall buildings in New York. All the sheep have come to die in the snowbanks of Repentigny.

I wake up with a sore throat. There's also a pain in my left foot. I don't get it; I didn't bump it on anything. There's no swelling, no bruise. The pain's concentrated beneath my big toe. It hurts when I flex my toes. I go online and click on a link, *Eight Pains You Don't Want to Ignore*. I can't find exactly what I have. It must be something really rare. Maybe it's stage-two foot cancer. It says black spots tend to appear on the skin when you've got foot cancer. Maybe my spots are still in the process of appearing, or maybe they're just invisible. I might have ghost spots. I'm starting to feel stressed. I can walk, but the pain creeps up on me. I get dressed, make my bed, eat two slices of toast. I notice a box of clementines on the kitchen counter. It's not often that Norm buys fruit. I steal ten of them. I leave my car in the driveway and walk to the bus stop. It's not far. I feel disoriented. I listen to *Here Comes the Sun* as I wait for the bus. Here comes the sun, here comes the bus, here comes my foot. I think about my foot. All I have in my backpack is two sweaters, a pair of underpants, a whole cocktail of meds, and my passport. Plus, I remembered to bring *The Deserts and Mountains of Cystic Fibrosis*. It's nice out, but it's freezing. Minus twenty-eight, according to my phone. My hand takes less than a minute to freeze every time I take it out of my coat pocket. The sun is a white marble, a soundless drum. I can't put too much weight on my foot or else it hurts even more. I start to worry. I go back home, take the car, and drive to the pharmacy. The place is empty. A woman is stacking perfume bottles and says hello as I limp inside. I go to the back of the pharmacy, and a young woman in a white lab coat comes over. "D'lk to see da pharm'cis." My voice is weak and throaty. I hadn't noticed I'd lost my voice as well. My sentence comes out all wrong; they must think I'm from the country. The pharmacist is a very poised Vietnamese woman. She looks like she's around my age. I never trust people my age, especially when it comes to medicine. I don't trust people who grew up playing *Super Mario Bros 3* at the same time as I did. "How can I help you, sir?" I mumble, "Sor'foot. D'nno why. No swelln, no boose. No bmps." She looks at me, more than a little perplexed. She says, "How long have you had the problem for?" I don't want her to think I'm crazy, so I say it's been for two days, at least. "It's probably just a sprained ligament... Take Tylenol or Advil if there's any swelling." I joke, although it's also partly to reassure myself, "'k, s'not canc'r?" The pharmacist doesn't get it. "Cancer?" she asks. She's impassive, but I can see her judging me as she looks at me. "No, I really think it's muscle related." There's a long silence; she steps back. "Take Tylenol every day, and if the pain lasts more than five days, go see a doctor about an X-ray." "Tanks." I walk back to my car and I'm ashamed. I turn up *Fell in Love With a Girl* as high as it will go. I drive back a little faster than I should. I only half glance over my shoulder. I flip my middle finger at the sun. I leave the car in Norm's driveway, take my backpack, and go hunting for Tylenol in Norm's medicine cabinet. I take ten of them. Maybe there's a black market for Tylenol and clementines. I go back to the bus stop. I wait for ages. I could have waited on a chair in the kitchen, but it's too late now. The bus is here. I drop my fare into the slot, listen to *Here Comes the Sun* again. Everyone on the bus looks like they want to throw themselves off a bridge. I take the metro and get off at Sherbrooke. I limp my way over to the Montreal bus station. My bus doesn't leave for another five hours; I'm way too early. I don't want to miss the bus in case my sister kills me in my sleep, so I sit down and open *The Deserts and Mountains of Cystic Fibrosis*. I come across a lovely picture of sand dunes, just like the ones you see in the movies. "These elegant variations in the sand are shaped by the shifting winds," I read. "While the dunes themselves are fashioned by the fluctuating flow of the wind, their rippled effect stems from its swirling action." The wind is fashioning my foot. I google "sand" and read: "coral sand, glass sand, immature sand, gypsum sand." I'm trying to make a model of my heart, but it always ends up too small. My lungs are kinetic; they ooze and move around, melting inside my ribcage. I manage to nap for a bit. The hours are warm and smell of the metro. I pick up my ticket from the Greyhound counter. I didn't think my sister's trick would work. I'm so naïve; I don't get out much. The sun's already on its last legs, and it's not even four o'clock. The bus is packed. I flop down in the front seat, completely exhausted. The seats are blue and have little printed greyhounds racing across them. I'm sitting on a bunch of little blue dogs. A guy my age sits down next to me. He's wearing a heavy gold chain, diamond-stud earrings, and a big black coat. He catches me looking at his chain. He tells me straight up that it's worth $7,000. I give him the thumbs up. I could live for at least a year and a half and not have to work if I had a chain like that. I picture myself at the grocery store, trading two links of the gold chain for a whole shelf of Sidekicks. He shows me his fingers and tells me how much each ring cost. Then he moves on to the earrings. I couldn't care less, but I don't want him to beat me up, so I pretend to be impressed. He says his name's Yannick. I tell him my name's Jacques. He doesn't seem convinced, and I curse myself for not coming up with a name that goes with my age. "Call me Jack," I croak. "Never did like the name my parents gave me." He laughs. He laughs hard. I wish I'd never noticed his chain. It's the first time a gangster has ever spoken to me. Maybe Yannick will teach me how to be streetwise. I might end up a rapper. I'd be the first rapper with an Ewok name: Wicket Warrick the rapper. Yannick won't stop talking. He talks about the girls he's seeing, his work at the garage, the house he wants to build in five years' time. I nod, not really listening. I move my foot. It hurts when I stretch it a certain way. The bus starts up, and I breathe a little easier. I peel a clementine while Yannick goes on and on about plywood. I've lost my voice, I've lost my strength. I look outside as I chew. The streetlamps light up the bits of peel in my hand. Yannick is really going into detail as he describes the boobs on his ex. I make a sign that I need to go to the washroom. I stay in there for a long time. I stare at the peel that I still haven't thrown away. Someone tries to open the door. After five minutes, there's a loud knock. "Dammit!" I say, but it sounds more like "Duh." I don't want to go sit back next to Yannick. When I come out of the toilet, a girl glares at me. "S'rry." As I make my way back up the aisle I check to see if there are any other empty seats, but it looks like they're all taken. When I get back to the front, the gangster has his eyes closed and his headphones on. I quickly do the same. It smells like eucalyptus in the bus, and it makes me feel queasy. I look over my shoulder and see the girl with the glare. She must be the one who smells like eucalyptus; it must be her glaring eyes that smell like eucalyptus. I manage to nod off for a bit every fifteen minutes or so. I dream that I'm in space. I dream that I'm as light as a feather. I dream that my voice is clear and suave, and that I'm making a moving speech to some unknown nation. I ride on the back of a greyhound, a greyhound from space. My greyhound trip lasts for a good while. I realize I'm still clutching my clementine peel. I stuff it in my coat pocket. The bus comes to a stop and the driver turns off the engine. People start to get up from their seats. I'm a bit lost. It's probably obvious from my expression. Yannick tells me we have to go through Customs, and shows me his passport. I hadn't thought about this part of the trip. I hadn't realized I'd have to talk to an agent with my disgusting voice. I'm in the middle of the queue, and I see the Customs officers get on the bus to check the luggage. After a few minutes, I spot a Customs guy who looks like Charles Grodin get off the bus carrying my backpack. "Sh't." He looks around asking whose bag it is. He's Charles Grodin only paler and closer to sixty, not the one in *Beethoven*. I raise my hand. "Mine." He gives me a serious look and motions for me to come forward. I'm a bit stressed, I picture a Saint Bernard leaping out of my backpack. He asks for my passport. A second officer approaches. My bag is open. Charles Grodin pulls out *The Deserts and Mountains of Cystic Fibrosis* and passes it to the other guy. He tells me to follow him into an office. "OK." The office is tiny; it's a tight squeeze. I sit down on the only chair. The Customs agents start to pull out my pill bottles one by one, then my compressor and syringes. When I see my syringes, I break out in a sweat. Charles picks up my compressor and asks me what it's for. "It's for my lungs," but it comes out as "S'four m'long." The two agents don't understand and I try to mime it instead. I point to my lungs, I pretend to cough, only it makes me cough for real. The other guy asks why I have syringes in my bag.

Meanwhile, Charles tosses my clementines one by one into the garbage and tells me I'm not allowed to bring citrus fruits into the United States. I tell him I didn't know. I apologize: "Oh, sorr', sorr'." I pull the peels out of my coat pocket and throw them away, too. I feel like Kevin Spacey in *K-Pax*. The agent asks me if I have a doctor's note for my disease and all these meds. I say I don't, and that I didn't know I needed a note. Charles asks me what's the purpose of my visit to New York, how long I'll be staying in New York, where I'll be staying in New York. I tell him I'm going to my sister's place, that she lives in New York with her boyfriend Aaron, and that it's just for Christmas. Charles asks me where I live and what I do for a living. I say, "I liv' 'n R'p'nt'gny 'n w'rk at S'p'r C." Charles says, "Super what?" I say, "S'p'r C, S'p'r C." The two Customs agents look a little dismayed, and I probably do, too. I wish I could do a Kevin Spacey and just disappear in a beam of light. "'sa sup'rmark't." The two men leave the office, and I try to calm my breathing. I'm a candle that's gone out before it's even burned. I start to suspect my visit to the U.S. of A. isn't going to happen. And I wonder how I'm going to get back to Repentigny. I don't feel like spending the rest of my money on a cab ride home. Maybe I could pitch a tent near the border and live here. I'd have a view of the booth and I could watch people get searched all day long. The Customs people could feed me with citrus fruit. I wonder if you're allowed to take Sidekicks into the States. I'd be the luckiest guy in the world if I could

122

collect all the packets of Sidekicks that are confiscated at the border. I look around. The fluorescent lights in the office are blinding. I'm pathetic. I try to say, "I'm pathetic, I'm pathetic," but it won't come out right. I'm losing my voice more and more. Soon, I'll have to communicate by blinking. One blink for "Yes," two blinks for "No," three blinks for "I'm hungry," four blinks for "I could sleep on the floor of the Customs office for seven years," five blinks for "I love Amidala," six blinks for "I'm gonna get my life together, I'm gonna become a lawyer, I'm gonna make lots of money, I'm gonna travel the world, I'm gonna get married and have kids, three kids—two boys and a girl—a girl I'll call Charlotte or Juliet," seven blinks for "I don't wanna live anymore, I can't stand myself anymore, I wanna go to Tatouine, all I wanna do is cook Sidekicks on Tatouine," and eight blinks for "I don't have a bomb on me, I swear." The Customs agents come back and tell me I can put my stuff back in my backpack. When I'm done, Charles tells me I can go to New York, but he warns me that next time I'll need something in writing to explain my meds. I smile and say to Charles, "Oh, tank you ver' m'ch, sir." I walk out of the office, my heart still beating a mile a minute. I get back on the bus. Everyone is sitting there, ready to go. Judging by the look on Yannick's face, they've been waiting a long time. The girl who smells like eucalyptus likes me even less now. The gangster doesn't seem so fond of me now either. I avoid catching his eye; I don't want to set him off. He elbows me on the arm. Yannick is staring at me, his mouth wide open. He's got a gold tooth I hadn't noticed before. He laughs, lifts his arm, and holds his hand out. I reach out my hand, and he gives me a manhug. "Man, you're a fuckin' badass, Jack! Jack here's been held up at Customs for a fuckin' hour!" He says, "Ever heard of Mos Def?" "Uh." Yannick jams his headphones over my ears. I listen to the words: "It's a brand new day." I nod, look serious. This makes Yannick laugh. I feel exactly like an Ewok rapper. The driver starts the bus, and we cross the border. I feel like I'm floating. It's a brand new day for the guy with cystic fibrosis who's sitting up front on the bus. It's a brand new day for all the world's clementine pickers. I close my eyes and keep the headphones on until the end of the song. I like the tune. I wonder what I'd look like with a gold tooth. I picture myself stocking the shelves with Pepsi at the Super C with my gold tooth. I am the greyhound from space, I am the syringe smuggler, I am the Ewok rapper, I am the gangster from Tatouine.

Elliott Smith's barking like mad. I'm sitting in the back seat of Aaron's car, and the dog's licking my cheek and mouth. "Wuh. Easy d're, d'ggie." Cammy asks, "What's up with your voice?" I shrug. Aaron has perfect hair. He's wearing a long beige coat, the kind you only ever see in the movies. I'm wearing a snowboarding jacket that's a bit too small and a bit too worn. I wish I could wear a long coat like his, but it doesn't look very warm. I'd catch cold, for sure. Anyway, I don't have the money to buy a coat like that. Elliott Smith's still barking. He runs back and forth from one window to the other, jumping over me each time. My sister shouts at him, "STOP IT, ELLIOTT, STOP IT!" Aaron turns left and mutters, "Fucking idiot." Another guy just cut him off. Aaron's cologne is discreet and distinguished. I smell like clementines. There's classical music playing in the car. I say, "What're you l'stening to?" He looks at me in the rearview mirror; he didn't understand my question. My sister repeats it for him. "Oh, ahem, Chopin." "'K." My sister turns to me and asks how my trip was. I don't know where to start. I'm about to explain, but she cuts me off, "How'd it go in Albany?" "'lb'ny?" "Yeah, Albany? It's like the ugliest and trashiest bus station ever!" I remember the bus stopping at one point at a station, but I didn't know it was Albany. "OK." I'm exhausted. I don't want to talk for another ten thousand years. My sister can tell from my face and turns to me. "We'll be there soon. We live in the Upper East Side." Needless to say, that means nothing to me. I look out at the cars and the passersby. The people don't have necks; in New York, people don't have necks. That's how they protect themselves against the cold. It's just as freezing here as it is in Repentigny. It's all perfectly normal, nothing exceptional about it. People are breathing, people are talking, people are walking. A fat guy waits for the light to turn green before crossing the street. He's carrying a bunch of plastic bags, and I can see his lips moving. It looks like he's talking to himself. It looks like he's saying an ancient prayer. We turn the corner and I silently bid him good-bye. I like saying goodbye to people in my head. I often do that when I'm in the car or on the bus. Sometimes I'll say, "Small world" out loud. It's funny cause most of the people I see in the street I'll never see again. Elliott Smith is lying on the back seat with his head on my leg. I think about the novel I'm not able to write, I think about the poems I haven't written for ages. I think I'm all out of things to say. I think I've said all I have to say. Maybe I need to come up with a new dream. It's hard to come up with new dreams. I could get paid to walk my sister's dog through the streets of New York. I stroke Elliott Smith's head, I rub his left ear. My sister tells me the pancakes are really good here. I say, "Oh, cool." I don't like pancakes. It strikes me it's been a century since I last had breakfast at Chez Rémi. I start to nod off. The heat inside the car is soothing. My nose is runny; my left nostril's blocked. I've got nothing to blow my nose on. I wonder if Chopin ever had to stop in the middle of a concert to blow his nose. We turn a few more cor-ners, and my sister says, "We're taking a little detour. I just want to show you something." I watch Aaron's eyes in the rearview mirror. He looks fed up. I try to put myself in his shoes, and I get how he must feel: having to go pick up your girlfriend's retarded, depressed older brother two days before Christmas is hardly the most exciting thing in the world. We eventually drive past a gigantic Christmas tree. My sister shouts, "Look! Look! It's *Home Alone 2*!" She looks over her shoulder at me and smiles. I laugh. When we were young, we'd watch *Home Alone* all the time over the holidays. Elliott Smith starts barking again. Aaron honks at a car that's stopped right in the middle of the road. Cammy looks at me and seems happy to have made me laugh. I say, "Thanks," but it comes out as "Tanks." I pat Elliott Smith, and he calms down. I feel like crying. I spend the rest of the ride home looking out the window. Eventually, we arrive at 95th Street. All the buildings look super luxurious. When I get out of the car, I realize there's no snow here. It's not going to be easy getting around in my ski-doo boots. As we walk up to the apartment, my sister says we're right beside Central Park. There are tons of stairs; they go on forever. I'm out of breath, and stop to take a rest. When we get to the top, I see that Cammy lives in a tiny one-bedroom apartment. It's stylishly and simply decorated. The apartment smells of Aaron. I'm in Aaron's microcosm. It reminds me a bit of where the crazy guy lives in *American Psycho*. Cammy says I'll be sleeping in Aaron's office. There's an inflatable mattress on the floor, and a bedspread with flowers on it. She asks if I'm hungry. "No tanks." I'm having trouble breathing. I take a shower. The bathroom is spotless and tiny. I stare at the blue tiles for a while. I use Aaron's shampoo. I'm going to smell of Chopin-meets-raving-lunatic. I picture Aaron fucking in front of a mirror, flexing his pecs. I picture my sister naked for a split second, which makes me more than a little uncomfortable. I give myself a slap. I'm such a moron. My foot hurts a bit less now. The pharmacist must've been right: it's not cancer. When I come out of the bathroom, the only light still on is in the kitchen. Cammy is standing there with a big glass of water. She asks if I'm OK. I nod. "J'st turd." "OK, help yourself to anything in the fridge." I nod and watch her disappear as she closes the bedroom door. I turn out the light and go into the office. I snoop through Aaron's papers for a bit. It's all numbers and tables, that kind of thing. It all just makes me feel incompetent. I open the closet just in case there's an axe hiding somewhere. Negative. I turn off the light and lie on my back. The mattress is only half inflated. My back's almost touching the floor, but I don't have the energy to blow it up. I picture Aaron running about butt naked, wielding a chainsaw. I picture him chasing me around butt naked, wearing nothing but his very white running shoes. I'd be dead in no time: he'd have no bother catching me in my ski-doo boots. I can hear nothing but my breathing in the dark. I'm not breathing very well; I can hear the mucus gurgling in my throat. I cough and cough, but nothing comes out. I'm disappointed: I'm breathing just like I'm still in Repentigny. I switch on my phone. No messages from Amidala. My screen lights up part of the ceiling. I can't see anything beyond the light. I'm the light's New York shadow.

I get up super early. Everyone's still asleep; even Elliott Smith ignores me from his little bed in the living room. I sit on the sofa. I should have brought more than two sweaters with me. Tomorrow I'll be wearing the same clothes I wore yesterday. I'm going to look like a bum. I take all my morning meds. I make myself two slices of toast with American peanut butter. It doesn't taste the same; I don't feel at home at all here. I cough and hork up more mucus than ever into the sink. My mucus doesn't feel at home at all here. I walk around the apartment twelve times. My foot's barely hurting at all now. It's nine o'clock, and nobody's up yet. Maybe Aaron's killed my sister and gone out. He's killed my sister while flexing his pecs and listening to Chopin, and I didn't hear a thing because I was fast asleep. I hear a sound, and it's my sister who comes out of the room first, her hair all tousled. "Up already?" "You bet." My voice is better than it was yesterday. I have to speak softly, but my words are coming out right at least. I'm glad. My sister asks if I've eaten yet, and I nod. Aaron is still in bed. I say, "New Yorkers get up late." Cammy doesn't bat an eyelid and says, "It's the holidays." "OK." She makes some coffee, then tells me she has to walk Elliott Smith. "I can go, if you like. It's not like I've got anything else to do." "Uh, sure. OK." She hands me the leash and tells me how to get to Central Park. I say, "Do you have any shoes I could borrow? I only have my ski-doo boots. I'll look stupid with them on." My sister lends me Aaron's running shoes. They're not white, much to my disappointment. As luck would have it, we're about the same size. "Brothers in feet," I joke in my gravelly voice. Cammy rolls her eyes and goes back to the coffee maker. Outside, the humidity grabs me by the retinas. Elliott Smith seems to know the way; he yanks on his leash, and I follow. He sniffs at some of the trees along the sidewalk, picking them out with care. We walk past a basketball court. There's a kids' playground beside it. Elliott Smith wants to go in, but I won't let him. I want him to take me to Central Park. He seems to understand, and keeps going along 95th Street. After a moment or two, just as I'm starting to feel uncomfortable, we finally hit 5th Avenue. I can see that Central Park is just opposite, but I can't figure out how to get inside: there's a wall in the way, and it's about twice as tall as I am. Central Park is on lockdown. I don't feel much like scrambling up a wall with a dog in my arms. I turn left and follow the wall, but there's no end in sight. Central Park is a nightmare. I'm coughing and coughing, already tired, and my foot is starting to hurt again. I realize that Aaron's shoes are way too small for me, after all. Brothers in feet, my ass! Eventually, I wind up on the corner of 90th Street and 5th Avenue. I'm exhausted. Elliott Smith feels like a million bucks. I want to scoop him up and warm his little feet, but he's having none of it. He gives me a look: What the fuck? "OK, OK," I tell him. "I just wanted to warm you up, for fuck's sake." At last I find an opening to the right and I'm in the park. On the other side of the wall, there's a never-ending roadway for runners, bikes, and cars. I end up on another road a little further on. This one seems reserved for people who went for a walk and got lost. Central Park is a deathly boring labyrinth with a couple of roads cutting across it. I see two sets of stone steps opposite me and, in the centre, a memorial to John Purroy Mitchel. I walk over and learn that he was mayor of New York City for four years. He died before the end of his term. They've reconstructed John's head, neck, and shoulders. His bust is made of gold and smiling a little. I wonder if I'll ever have my own memorial in Repentigny. I can just picture the plaque: "Super C grocery clerk for several weeks; died on the job." I think I'd look the part in gold from the shoulders up. I hope the sculptor makes me look super sad, shouting at the top of my lungs. Elliott Smith goes for a pee just below John. When he's done, we walk up the stairs and come out right in front of the big lake. There's a shooting pain in my foot, my heels are on fire. I don't think I'll be able to go much further. Central Park has been a bit of a let-down. "Central Park is shit," I tell Elliott Smith. I head back to 5th Avenue. I follow the stone wall again. I walk slowly, limping a little. I wish I could just drink Chemineaud and sleep here against the wall. I'd try to put Elliott Smith inside my coat like homeless people do, but he wouldn't want to. He'd end up dying of cold and, lying there on the sidewalk on 5th Avenue, I'd tell him how stupid he was. I make it back to my sister's in time for lunch. It took me all this time, and I haven't even done anything. I walk up to the first floor, ring the bell, and my sister buzzes me in. I walk up the never-ending steps. There are twenty-seven of them. Cammy opens the door, dressed in her nice clothes. My sister is always dressed nice. Everything mixing and matching perfectly. I don't know anything about fashion, but to me she looks like one of those models who wear sunglasses on magazine covers. She works for a swimsuit company. I don't remember the name. But anyway. In the summer, she wears big floppy hats that really suit her. If I wore a big hat, I'd just look like a dolt. I take off Aaron's shoes and my socks. My heels are bleeding. Cammy says, "Oh, his shoes are way too small for you." I feel like saying, "No shit, Sherlock," but I don't. I'm just visiting, and visitors don't go about pissing off their hosts. "Yeah... I thought they fit OK." I sit down on the sofa, my pants hitched up, in my bare feet. It feels good to be on the sofa. My legs are like jello. If I'd had to choose between going for a walk in Central Park or sitting here on the sofa, I'd have chosen the sofa. My sister comes back with a bottle of peroxide, cotton pads, and some little plasters. While I'm getting cleaned up, she asks if I want a sandwich. "Oh, yes please." Aaron is sitting in the kitchen reading a book. I walk over and sit down at the table. "What are you reading?" He's not listening. Either he's too caught up in his book or he's an asshole. My sister says, "Aaron! My brother's talking to you!" Aaron looks up. "Oh, sorry man. I didn't hear you." "It's OK, I just wanted to know what you were reading." "Oh, it's *Catcher in the Rye*... A Christmas classic." He smiles and gives me the thumbs up. As she takes the cold cuts out of the fridge, Cammy tells me he always reads it over the holidays. I say, "Oh, nice, it's a great book." There's a bit of a silence. I rack my brains for something else to say. Don't find anything. Aaron goes back to his book. My sister brings me over a baloney sandwich. She bought some just for me. She and Aaron don't eat baloney. "Thanks." I can see the trouble my little sister's going to just to be nice to me. I know she's a good sister. I know I'm not always there for her, not like she is for me. I'd like to tell her that I love her, but I can't. Talk about clichéd. Which reminds me that I never told my dad I loved him before he died. Another cliché. If I'd known when he was going to die, I'd have prepared myself and told him the night before. I'm sure it would've come out all wrong. I'd probably have spluttered and stammered my way through it, but at least I'd have said it. It's too late now; that's life. That's what I always say when I want to explain myself: "That's life." My sister's sandwich is good. Cammy is eating a chickpea salad and asks if I liked Central Park. I say, "Oh yeah. I really liked it." "I saw the big lake," I add. "It's nice." Cammy stabs a chickpea with her fork and corrects me: "It's a reservoir, not a lake." "Oh, OK." "Um, I forgot to tell you we're going to Aaron's parents' place for Christmas this year." "Oh yeah? Do they live near here?" "About an hour away, in Bedford." "OK." Aaron glances up at Cammy then looks down again at his book. Cammy asks what I plan to do today. It's two minutes past noon. As far as I'm concerned, my day's already over. I'd be happy to go lie down on my deflated mattress and sleep until tomorrow morning. "My feet are a bit sore. I don't think I'll do much walking today." "C'mon, you're only here for three days... Christmas is the day after tomorrow! Make the most of it! You like art. I looked it up and there's an Edvard Monk exhibit not far from here. We could go." I'm guessing she means Edvard Munch, but I don't correct her. She just made me a baloney sandwich, after all. I say, "OK, good idea." I put on my coat and big ski-doo boots. I feel like an astronaut. My sister's boots are dainty, and they match her coat perfectly. My boots match the ugliest buildings in New York. When we leave, Aaron is still buried in his book. I thought we'd take the car, but my sister wants to walk. My feet don't hurt as much in my boots, but I walk really slowly. Cammy says, "Seriously, you call that walking?" "I'm not Elliott Smith, y'know." We laugh. She strides ahead and eventually looks back over her shoulder at me, "My God, it's gonna be closed by the time we get there!" I ask her where the exhibit is. "At the Met Breuer." I guffaw. I'm getting my second wind now. I try to walk just like Cammy, even though I'm wearing huge boots. I swing my hips, toss back my imaginary long hair. I imitate her voice, adding a little French accent: "We urr walkeeng in ze city of New York and we urr go-ink to ze Mette-Brue-Heure." She laughs so hard she has to stop and lean on a tree to catch her breath. Cammy can make fun of herself with the best of them; that's something we have in common. "Asshole." We keep walking along Park Avenue. All the buildings are beige, brown, or grey. We don't see a single café, restaurant, or store. The wind is howling. With all the tall buildings, it's like being in a

134

wind tunnel. My legs are exhausted, I drag my feet on the sidewalk. I know it'll destroy the rubber soles of my boots, but I don't care. "Is it much further?" My sister says we'll be there in five minutes. I'm like a kid asking what time it is. I'm relieved every time we get to a street corner and we have to wait for the light to turn green before we can cross. I close my eyes and rest my feet. The light goes green. I see all kinds of faces I'll never see again. Every time I look into a face, I mumble, "Farewell, farewell, farewell." A man coming the other way bumps into me. "Wow," I say. "What?" "I think Robert Downey Jr. just ran into me!" "Huh?" I'm all excited, "Seriously, the guy really looked like Robert Downey Jr." My sister stares at me, unmoved; she couldn't care less. "Yeah, could be." "Whaddya mean, could be?" "This is New York. I once saw Tom Hanks out for a jog." "No shit," I say. "Life is like a box of chocolates. You never know what..." I can't remember the rest. "Ah, fuck it." She laughs. My sister has really white teeth. I love making her laugh. When we turn onto 75th Street, we come to a building with two red banners announcing The Met Breuer. "Ah, OK, *Met Breuer*, that's how you spell it," I think. We go in, and Cammy pays for me. We leave our coats in the cloakroom. Cammy whizzes past the paintings. I stand there for ages looking at each one. She has time to visit the whole exhibit several times over, stopping each time to see me standing in front of the same painting. In the foreground there's a man with a moustache wearing a little hat. His skin looks grey. Behind

135

him, there's a big red house with a white picket fence. The house looks like it's on fire or possessed or something. The red doesn't go all the way round the upstairs windows. There are no leaves on the trees; it looks cold. The man looks ill. I wonder if he's wearing ski-doo boots, I wonder if his feet hurt. I turn to my sister. "Want to go get a coffee?" "Yeah, good idea." We go to a café over on Madison Avenue. Cammy orders a cappuccino, and I get a latte. For the rest of the afternoon, she tells me about trips she's been on, all the places she wants to travel to. She says she's thinking about getting a new job even though she makes good money. She seems happy. I'm happy. When she gets up to go to the washroom, I check my phone. No messages. I scroll through the news. I come across an article: "Mystery surrounding accelerating expansion of the universe." I look around the café, I see a cute girl working on a laptop. I look at her lips, her chin, her neck, the way her hair is done up. She's wearing a slim black watch around her wrist, and I feel a hard-on coming on. I picture her naked in a bedroom. I picture myself alone with her on an uninhabited planet. When my sister gets back from the washroom, I shrink back down in a matter of seconds. I shrink so much that I disappear into one of my ski-doo boots. I am the mystery surrounding the accelerating expansion of the universe.

I open my eyes and I'm in Aaron's office, still in New York. The mattress has deflated again. It's Groundhog

Day. I check the time on my phone; it's late. Elliott Smith is asleep in his doggy bed. My feet hurt. My sister has left a note on the kitchen counter: "Hi, gone out to run some errands. Left some money if you want to go sightseeing." There's a twenty-dollar bill next to the note. I get dressed. My sweater stinks. I go into my sister's bedroom, rifle through the drawers, and snitch a white t-shirt that belongs to Aaron. It's a bit small; it makes my belly look bigger than it really is. Too bad. At breakfast, I spill orange juice down the front of Aaron's t-shirt. "Fuck me." I go into the bathroom and try to rub the orange stain away with soap and water, without taking off the sweater. I feel like I'm in a sexy carwash. My chest is soaked and my nipples are sticking out. I'm sure I'd get great tips at the carwash. I prance around in front of the mirror. I laugh out loud, I'm a moron. When I look in the mirror, I notice I need a shave. It's not something that usually bothers me, but this morning, I'm feeling on top of my game. I rummage through the cupboards until I find an electric razor. I shave; it feels good. I look fatter without my stubble. I've got a double chin, another bulge near my neck. And I shaved too high: now one sideburn is shorter than the other. I try to even them up, but one side is still higher than the other. "Fuckin' retard!" Now I look like a total idiot. I break out in a sweat. It's Christmas tomorrow, and I can't go out looking like this. I decide to shave the whole lot off. I start by shaving a line straight up from my forehead. "Jesus, what am I doing!" I run the razor through my hair. It takes ages, but I finally manage to shave the right side clean. I try to be careful, but clumps of hair still drop in the sink and onto the counter. I'm tired. I wonder what the hell got into me. All I feel like doing now is putting away the razor and going to lie down with half my head shaved. Just when I think I'm done, I notice a few little tufts I missed. I have a tiny skull with a bulging neck. I'm the world's worst barber. I've got grooves all over my head. I go back over with the razor ten, twenty, thirty times. There always seems to be more to shave. In the end, I get fed up and go get the garbage can from the kitchen. It's tiny. I manage to stuff all of my hair clippings in it, and wipe the bathroom counter fifty times. I'm suddenly dying for a hot dog. I put on my coat and boots. My hat feels twice as big as it did before. Elliott Smith runs around my feet. He wants to come, too. "Sorry, not today, pooch." Out in the street, the air is as humid and vicious as ever. The wind pushes against my eyes. I feel more fragile without my hair. I check the map of New York on my phone. I see there's a McDonald's not far, at the corner of 95th Street and 2nd Avenue. Fuck the hot dog. My feet hurt. I wish I had a jetpack to get around like Boba Fett. My cough is phlegmy; when I turn the corner, I spit up an enormous gob. I lean in to examine the slimy mass and see flecks of blood. I feel a bit dejected, but the McDonald's is only a few steps away from my spit. Everyone eating there looks like they're homeless. I order a Big Mac Meal, and the girl at the cash brings me my order in record time. I don't see any Monopoly coupons. I say, "Nomoremonopolycoupons?" The girl doesn't understand a word I've said. "Wha'?" "It's OK." I sit down next to a homeless guy who's really dark-skinned. He looks as tired as I am. He's got a tiny cup in front of him. He's wearing a purple sweatshirt. I take a bite of my hamburger and eat two fries. I feel cheap. I give my fries to the homeless guy. He's missing a few teeth. "Thanks, man," he says. I think he's drunk. I seem to hit it off with people who don't have all their teeth. I walk towards the nearest subway station and spit up seven gobs of blood along the way. I look for the station that'll take me the furthest away. I change lines. It smells of garlic the whole way. I try to doze a bit, but the smell is making me feel sick. I get off the subway and go up thousands of steps. By the time I get outside, the sun has nearly set. I check my phone; I'm in Brighton Beach. I walk along the Coney Island boardwalk. There's hardly anyone around. The few people I do see seem to be speaking Russian. I pass by the New York Aquarium, but I can't see in through the beige concrete wall with seashells on it. New York is nothing but walls and roads. As I get closer, I can hear moans. I stand there, back against the wall, for at least half an hour, listening to the strange noise. An old guy walks up to me and stops, staring at me all the while. His hair is white, he's wearing a little black hat. A large dog, a Labrador I think, follows him. The man says, "This is the cry of sea lions." "Oh, OK, thanks." I watch him walk off, while the dog stops to sniff my knees. I don't dare pet it in case it bites me. I hear the old man call, "Come on, boy, come on!" and the dog ambles off after its owner. Are those really sea lions crying on the other side of the wall? The old guy was probably pulling my leg, but I guess I'll never know for sure. I go down onto the beach. It's cold and windy. The sand is white and speckled with tiny little shells. I'm all alone. It's calm. You can hear the waves lapping in the background, despite the wind. I see a pile of big rocks jutting out of the sand. I climb onto one of them, careful not to fall. The rocks are frozen, slippery. I'd like to see Amidala on one of the rocks on Brighton Beach. I'd hold her hands. It wouldn't stop her falling, but she wouldn't hurt herself. She'd lie there on her back, laughing, eyes closed. She'd pick herself back up and I'd brush the sand from her cotton coat. I'd pick the grains of sand off one by one. It would take forever. That way, I'd get to live forever. The phone rings; it's my sister. She wants to know why there's hair all over the toilet. "I don't know," I say. "I cleaned it all up before I left." She can only half make me out because of the wind on the beach. She asks where I am, and I say, "Brighton Beach." "Why did you go all the way out there?" "I wanted to hear the sea lions crying." She doesn't understand. "I'm on my way back," I say. The daylight has fallen away quickly, as though the call from my sister has sped up time. I walk back, following the ski-doo bootprints in the sand. I feel weak, I don't feel like doing anything anymore, apart from maybe eating a hot dog. Are the sea lions crying because they're not allowed to eat hot dogs? I manage to get lost on my way back, even with the light from my phone. It takes me forever to get to a subway station. I head back to Manhattan; it takes forever. Manhattan is a haircut that never ends. It's late by the time I get back to my sister's apartment. Cammy looks pissed. I haven't even taken my boots off yet and she's asking why I shaved my head. I explain the whole razor thing. She says, "Omigod!" and rolls her eyes. It reminds me of Dad, and that makes me sad. She can tell from my face, and that calms her down a little. I eventually get to take off my boats, my coat, my hat. She says, "You haven't shaved the back of your head properly. It looks like a vagina, for God's sake." She doesn't laugh. Aaron smiles from the sofa, where he's watching TV. He gives me a little wave. I go into the bathroom; I can't see the back of my head. Cammy takes out the razor, covers the vanity with a long towel, and shaves my head properly. Little clumps of hair fall onto the towel. When all the hair's been thrown away and the bathroom is clean again, I take a long shower. I watch the little hairs slide down off my shoulders. I want to die. I get out of the shower and see that my three sweaters are clean and folded on the dryer. I hide Aaron's white t-shirt at the bottom of the laundry basket. Cammy asks if I'm hungry. I say I've only eaten a Big Mac. She looks a bit discouraged. She warms up the supper I missed earlier: shrimp stir-fry with rice and a citrus salad. I help myself to seconds and thirds of the shrimp stir-fry with rice. Elliott Smith stares at me the whole time. Aaron laughs at a joke a talk-show host just made. I get up and go over to the sink. I hear my sister call out from the living room that there's no need to do the washing-up. I ignore her. I sit down in the armchair for fifteen minutes. Cammy is curled up against Aaron on the sofa. I feel a little ball of anxiety warm my throat. I focus on something else, tell Cammy supper was lovely, and she gives me a little smile. "Sorry to be such a bore, but I'm gonna hit the hay. I walked a ton today." "OK, goodnight." Aaron is watching his program. My sister gives him a little jab in the ribs. He turns to me. "Oh, goodnight, my friend." "Thanks, you too." I close the office door; it's roasting in here. I turn down the thermostat, open the window a crack, turn on the little lamp on the desk, take out *The Deserts and Mountains of Cystic Fibrosis*. In the Close-up on Deserts section, there's a double-page photo of a huge lizard sticking out its tongue: "Bitterly opposed to any and all intrusions into its territory, this hissing grey monitor puts on a most unsettling performance." I'm already starting to get cold. I close the window and turn the heat up a bit. I've got grains of sand from Brighton Beach stuck on my heart. I've got a close-up of a desert on my heart. A really cold desert. I've got a lizard head, too. I warm myself under the desk lamp. If my sister opened the door now, she'd see a two-hundred-pound lizard sticking out its tongue. I turn off the light and lie down on the bed. I don't know what I'm doing here. It's Christmas tomorrow, and I haven't bought a thing. I am a lizardman who lives beneath the frozen rocks on Brighton Beach.

I spat up blood on the floor next to my bed. I cleaned it up, then spat out another cup of blood into the bathroom sink. Some people swallow swords or eat fire: I spit up blood. I'm sitting at the kitchen table with a glass of orange juice. I'm cold; my head feels a bit fuzzy. My arms are weak, and my thighs feel like they're about to fly off someplace. The others are still in bed. I imagine my sister coming out of her room and seeing me levitating. I'd be upside down, and my thighs would be touching the ceiling. It would look a bit strange at first. I get an email from my publisher: he wants to see me to talk about the poetry collection that's coming out in the spring. I don't feel like publishing it anymore; it feels like old news now. The poems should all be about the blood-spitting lizardman who lives on Brighton Beach. The bedroom door opens, and Aaron comes out in his boxers. He gives me a wave on his way into the bathroom. Cammy comes out a little later and asks if I slept well. "Yeah, great. Thanks." I don't tell her about the blood. The whole hair thing wasn't great, and I want my sister to be happy for Christmas. My breathing comes in bubbles. I can feel them in my throat, I make an effort not to cough. Cammy makes bacon, eggs, and hash browns. I say, "It's really good." She's sitting with her legs crossed and sticks up a thumb, her mouth full. When we've finished eating, I say, "I'm sorry. I forgot about the gifts... I'm hopeless." "Don't worry about it. It's just nice that you're here." As she says it, she opens her eyes super wide to show she thinks that I'm cheap. I laugh. She smiles. Aaron doesn't pick up on it. "We're gonna leave pretty early," she says. "We help Aaron's parents with the cooking every year." "OK, no problem." She takes a last forkful of egg and gives me a look. "Are you OK? You look pale." I take a sip of water. "Yeah. Just a little tired, that's all. The mattress keeps deflating. I'm too heavy for it." I pat my belly with both hands. Aaron laughs behind his newspaper. My breathing is shallow. I cough. "Treatment time. I'll go into the office." My sister nods and watches Elliott Smith chase his tail around the kitchen. I close the door behind me, start preparing the colimycin, suck up three millilitres of sodium chloride with my syringe, mix the chloride with the colimycin powder. I know the drill. I put the mix into the nebulizer and start the compressor. It makes a hell of a racket. My compressor's just like me: take it out the country and its personality changes completely. My compressor has a New York accent now. I breathe in and out into the mouthpiece, watch the white smoke escaping from the little plastic nebulizer in my mouth. I cough, and my heart stops beating every time I cough. I die a lot. I spit up red mucus into the little office trash can. I hide it with layers of Kleenex. I'm making a blood lasagna. My sister opens the door. "What's with all the smoke? Leave the door open. We don't mind... I used to see you with your pump all the time when we both lived at home." "OK," I say, my mouthpiece still in. I notice that my sister's already wearing her dress. I take the nebulizer out from between my teeth, let the smoke blow out into the room. "Dammit, I forgot to bring some-

144

thing nice to wear. I didn't think we'd be going to Aaron's parents'." Cammy says not to worry, we'll find a solution. Finding solutions has never been my forte. I'm one of those people who never looks on the bright side. I can't help it. I try to put things into perspective, I try not to be dramatic, but there's always a wave of darkness that catches up with me. Stupid wave of darkness. I finish my treatment, turn off the compressor, make sure you can't see the blood in the trash can. Aaron motions for me to follow him. He's wearing a swanky grey jacket and white shirt. I'm a bit jealous. He leads me into his room, stands in front of the closet. My sister is doing her makeup in front of a mirror. She's putting on mascara and says I should pick out whatever I want from Aaron's stuff. I'm glad, happy that I'm going to look a bit like Christian Bale. I imagine myself all dressed up and running around with a chainsaw. I choose a dark blue jacket and see a change in Aaron's eyes. My sister laughs behind me. "That's his favourite jacket." Cammy tells Aaron it's his own fault: he should have put his jacket away if he didn't want me to pick it out. "It's OK, I can take another one, no problem." "No, no, it's fine, man, I'll give you the shirt that goes with that." He hands me a shirt and khaki pants. "Oh, and the sneakers," he says. He digs around at the back of the closet and emerges with a pair of cream-coloured shoes. I go into the bathroom, try on the pants. They're a little tight. I can't close the button, but I can do up the zipper. I put on the shirt; it's a bit tight around my belly. It's not easy doing up the buttons. "What a surprise," I say to myself. It feels like I'm back dressing up as an elf, only this time at least I'm going to be the chicest of elves. I come out of the bathroom, and my sister says I look nice. I can't bend my knees, I can barely spread my legs, but I don't tell her that. I'll spread my legs tomorrow. Aaron says, "Looks great." "Thanks." Cammy tells me to put the shoes on and I think, "Shit, I should've put the shoes on before the shirt." The buttons are going to come flying off, right down onto Elliott Smith's little head. I sit down on one of the kitchen chairs and slowly work the shoes on. The buttons survive. My throat goes on making bubbles. I get up, take a look at myself in the mirror. My cheeks are red; my cheeks are always red. Cammy looks at me looking at myself. I pretend to be super comfortable. "Look at me. I'm a supermodel." She rolls her eyes and goes back to her makeup. I go make my bed, watch my belly stretch the buttons as far as they'll go. Elliott Smith sniffs at my feet and looks up at me, his tongue hanging out. "Yeah, I know. I'm fat," I say. But he keeps sniffing me anyway.

I look out the little office window. The sky is an off-white colour. The sky has a big belly and a jacket that doesn't fit. It looks cold out. I feel a headache coming on. For some reason, I think about Norm. I wonder what he's up to today. I wonder how he's doing. Cammy comes into the office and asks if I'm ready to go. I'm losing all notion of time. I don't know. Everything goes so fast.

People get on with their lives and I watch them doing it, and I find it comforting. I like watching people whose lives seem to be working out. I picture myself in their shoes, I picture myself spending their money on *Star Wars* figurines or comic books. I put on my snowboard jacket. There goes my look! Aaron smells of his discreet and distinguished cologne again. He's loaded down with gift-wrapped parcels and bags. Cammy asks if I can take the dog. I scoop up Elliott Smith in my arms. I sit in the back of Aaron's Volkswagen. All the gifts are piled on the seat beside me, so Elliott Smith has no choice but to sit on my lap. He squirms and puts his front paws up on the window so he can see outside. In there among all the presents, I feel bad, like I don't belong. Aaron puts on his classical music again and drives along the Henry Hudson Parkway, which runs alongside the river. I'm feeling a bit carsick. Elliott Smith eventually calms down and curls up on my lap. I try to relax, too. I close my eyes and focus on the music. I hear Cammy whispering something to Aaron. I think about Amidala and her big soft sweater with the moose on the front. I finally nod off. When I open my eyes, I realize I forgot to brush my teeth this morning. I'm going to be the weird French Canadian with bad breath and clothes that are too tight. There are trees on both sides of the road. It reminds be a bit of the boulevard near my home. My sister eyes me in the rearview mirror and tells me we're already in Bedford. "When there's no traffic, it's a piece of cake!" Aaron turns left onto Henkers Farm Lane, and I notice that all the properties are gigantic. There are majestic trees and enormous white houses. I've never seen such big white houses. They're all huge, set far back from the road. Long driveways wind their way through massive grounds to multiple garages. I feel a bit like Tom Cruise in *Eyes Wide Shut*. It's like I'm being driven to a masked ball. The only problem is, I don't have a mask. Just my red cheeks. Maybe Christmas Eve will wrap up with a big orgy. So long as I don't see my sister naked. I'm nuts. Aaron finally gets to the end of the road and turns just before the dead end onto a road that leads to his parents' property. We're still a ways from the house, but it looks huge. It's a friggin' mansion. "Oh, nice little place..." My sister turns to me with a grin. "Yeah... Aaron's dad is a surgeon." "Oh." The place has four garages, and I can't even begin to count all the windows. I notice the huge windows over the main entrance. "Is he George Lucas's surgeon?" She gives me a look. I notice there are already a few cars parked in front of the garages. I start to feel a bit nervous. I don't know these people. I have no idea what I'm going to talk to them about. I bet not a single person has heard of the planet Coruscant. Aaron parks behind a luxury car. I've never seen so many shiny cars. I get out of the car holding Elliott Smith, trying all the while not to split Aaron's khakis. I think of Norm, all alone for Christmas, and it makes me sad. I wish he could have cooked his turkey or made his rigatoni cake at our Bedford mansion. I cough, careful not to spit up a big bloody gob in front of Cammy and Aaron. I wait until they walk past me, their arms full of gifts, before horking into one of the countless bushes lining the driveway. Elliott Smith trembles in my arms. I tell him that everything's going to be OK, that I'm here. Aaron opens the door. "Hello, everyone!" I go into the front hall and see people approaching us from every which way. They call out, "AARON! AARON AND CAMMY!!!" and I stand there like a big idiot. I don't see any naked people in masks. I don't know what I'm doing here. I take off my snowboard jacket and a maid whisks it away. I'm stunned; I've never met a maid before. Lots of people shake my hand. A tall guy who looks like Tom Brady grabs the back of my neck. It's all a bit intense, I think. He's with another smaller, muscular guy. Tom Brady says to me, "Dude, can you just speak Frenchie one second? Like, tell me a sentence with a horse." The two guys crack up, their arms draped over each other's shoulders. I don't get it. Cammy appears next to me. I say, "I don't understand." Tom Brady's mouth is wide open; his teeth are straight and they sparkle like diamonds. He flicks his friend's chest with the back of his hand. "I donunnerstan," he says in my voice. I turn and stare at Cammy. "This is Jimmy, Aaron's brother... He thinks French is hilarious. Don't mind him. He laughs at my accent, too." My sister tells him, "Hey, leave him alone!" Tom Brady gives my sister a big hug. She obviously finds him funny and sweet, and they seem to know each other well. When I was in high school, I wasn't the kind of kid who'd let himself be bullied.

I remember one day in music class, another kid started calling me names. I lost it. I stood up, grabbed his music stand, and threw it at him. He wasn't hurt, but he toppled over backwards off his chair. It was quite spectacular. I was suspended for three days. So, yeah. An old man comes up to me and gives me a hug. He smells like aftershave. He has white hair and perfect teeth. I'm sure you have to tick all kinds of boxes to get to live in a mansion, like having very white, very straight teeth. The man is wearing a yellow sweater. He asks if I'd like something to drink. "Yes, please." "All right, kid, come with me." I say hello to a few ladies we meet on the way, giving them air-kisses. They tell me their names, but I forget them just as quickly. I see a girl on the staircase staring at me. I give her a little wave, and she ignores me. She looks a bit creepy. We go through a living room, then another. Enough already. I wonder how many more living rooms I'll have the energy to walk through. We come out into another room and walk past another staircase. This house is outrageous and ridiculous, I think to myself. I think about Dagobah and one of my bedside tables in my closet. Here, there's room for millions of bedside tables from Structube. The carpet feels thick beneath my thin shoes. My heels are starting to hurt, but I don't let on. A huge bookshelf runs all the way around the room. There are thousands of books; I don't know where to look. I sit down on a big leather sofa. "So, what would you like to drink?" I don't want to be difficult. "Same as you." He smiles, and his smile reminds me of

Bob Barker. My grandma was really into *The Price Is Right.* "Alright, kid." I hear him drop a few ice cubes into our glasses and pour something into them. I stare at my fat thighs, I stare at the seams of the khaki pants that are stretched to the limit. Bob Barker hands me my glass. "Cheers, kid." "Cheers." I take a sip and think, "Oh man, crème de menthe, great." "So, where do you live?" "In Quebec." "Yeah, but where in Quebec?" "Repentigny." "OK, I don't know that city." "It's OK, I didn't know Bedford before I came here." Bob Barker bursts out laughing. There's a bit of a silence, while he stares at his glass. "When I was young, I spent a few days in Montreal... I met a beautiful woman there. Her name was Sandra." "Oh, OK." He continues, "I was so in love with that girl." There's a long silence, he stares at my shoes. I down my drink. "Another?" I give him a thumbs up. He laughs. I realize I don't even know his name. He looks too old to be Aaron's dad. "Are you Aaron's father?" He hands me my glass and bursts out laughing again. "God, no." He sits and takes a sip of crème de menthe. I take long sips to get through the uncomfortable silences. I look up and see Cammy come into the room. "I've been looking everywhere for you... Whatcha drinking?" "Crème de menthe." "Yuck." Bob Barker tips his head back and guffaws. "Come on, I want to introduce you to the rest of the family." I finish off my drink. "Thanks for this." Cammy says, "Sorry, Donald, I want to introduce my brother to everyone." "No problem, beautiful Cammy." He gives me a little wink. As I leave the room,

I already feel a bit woozy. Maybe I have a lower tolerance for crème de menthe. We go back past the staircase and the living rooms. "Who was that?" I ask. "What, you didn't introduce yourselves?" "Not really." "Pfff... he's one of Aaron's dad's brothers." "OK." I'm feeling a bit lost. Cammy introduces me to at least thirty people; I have no idea who's who. People come up, kiss me on the cheek, shake my hand. Then, Cammy sends me to the kitchen to slice carrots on an island counter that's as long as my old two-bedroom apartment. A very nice lady comes up and kisses me on both cheeks. She says her name's Lily, and she asks if I'd like a beer. "Oh, sure, thank you." I'm surrounded by women, and I listen to their lively conversation. I laugh along with them, even though I don't know what they're talking about. Cammy has disappeared. I take the time to really look at the women: they all seem to be in their fifties. I'm in good company; I feel more at home here than with the men. I don't know shit about sports or cars. Lily brings me another beer. "Thank you, beautiful Lily," I say, and immediately kick myself. The women all turn to me and break out into hysterical laughter. There's just one who doesn't appear to like me much. She has short, dyed-red hair, and I'm guessing she's the oldest lady here. I knock back the beers that Lily keeps bringing me. Time flies. I must have sliced every last vegetable in Bedford. It's already dark out. I'm boiling hot in Aaron's jacket. I'm sweating buckets, my back is soaking wet. Cammy finally comes back to the kitchen; I have no idea what she was doing all that time. "Man, you're all red... Your face is all blotchy. You alright?" "Blotchy?" I start feeling even hotter. I'm such a hypochondriac. "I'm gonna go to the bathroom. Where is it?" My sister thinks out loud: "You take that door, keep going, turn right, then right again, then go straight and it should be on your left." "Christ! OK." I'm lost as soon as I go through the door. I go down the hall, turn left, go through a living room. I haven't seen this one before. I turn right and end up in a corridor. I see the creepy little girl from earlier sitting on the floor with her phone. I ask what she's playing, but she doesn't answer. I try to be friendly, to get her to like me. "Do you know I work for Santa?" She looks like she doesn't believe me. I want to tell her that I'm Elfis the Elf, but I change my mind. She keeps staring at her screen and says, "There's no such thing as Santa." I stay quiet. My vision's gone a bit blurry. I ask her where the bathroom is. I'm about ready to burst. She completely ignores me. I decide to keep heading straight. My face is boiling. I open a door, stumble into a bedroom. I open four other doors, and each leads either to a bedroom or a huge closet. It's a nightmare. I'm tempted to take a leak in one of the closets, but I think better of it. I try to go outside, but there's a huge window in the way. I can hear laughing. I go up to the window and see a group of old guys smoking cigars on the lawn. Cammy and Aaron are with them, each holding a glass of white wine. I can't believe how comfortable Cammy is around these people; it's like she grew up in their world. I wonder if she ever thinks about our dad, I wonder if she remembers the suppers he'd make with baloney and peas. Not because we didn't have any money, just because he didn't know how to cook much else. I hear someone walk up behind me. I feel a hand on the back of my neck and give a little jump. It's Tom Brady, asking me what I'm doing. "I'm looking for the bathroom... Can you help me?" He laughs and says I should follow him. He walks super fast. He turns on the ceiling light in an immaculate white bathroom. Everything's so clean, so tidy; everything smells of jasmine. I piss at least a litre of pee. I wash my hands, wipe them on one of countless white towels hanging on a rack. As I look in the mirror, I notice there's a big, red splotch on my left cheek. I take off my jacket; my shirt's soaked through. I splash my face with water, take a few deep breaths, but it makes me cough, and I spit up blood into the sink. I'm getting water everywhere; the bathroom's no longer sparkling clean. I'm such a slob. Tom Brady is staring at me wide-eyed when I go back out. He asks if I'm OK. I say yes. "Come with me," he says. We walk down hallways, climb a set of stairs. I'm lost, but that doesn't surprise me anymore. We go into a large bedroom that has two desks, four computer screens, a huge plasma TV on the wall, and an enormous corner canapé. There are medals and trophies displayed in a glass case, some of them for sports I've never even heard of. There are also framed diplomas on the wall. I should do the same on Dagobah: I'll frame my high-school diploma to make myself look important. "Oh yes," I'll say.

"I finished high-school math. I really am a genius." Brady opens a closet and hands me a New York Rangers t-shirt. "Oh no, it's OK, thanks." He insists. I try to take my shirt off, but the sleeves are stuck to my arms. Tom Brady gives me a hand. That's much better. I really am a lizard. I'm starting to get really hungry now; I'm starving. I ask Tom Brady what time it is. It's nine-thirty. I can't believe it. I've never eaten so late in my life. I've always eaten around five o'clock; I'm an old woman. "What time are we eating?" "Real late," he says. Fuck. He goes over to one of the desks and throws me a bag of sunflower seeds. "Thanks." I stuff twenty seeds into my mouth, shells and all, and swallow them. Tom Brady asks if I'm thirsty. "Yes." He opens the door of a dresser to reveal a huge selection of booze. I'm in hell, and every American in this mansion is a demon. He asks what I'm drinking. "Crème de menthe," I reply, my mouth still full. Tom Brady guffaws, asks if I met Donald. "Yes." He laughs some more. Probably best to stick to that. He rummages around in the bar, but comes up empty-handed. He'll be right back, he says. I go over to the bedroom window. A tall tree is all lit up by a light on the lawn. I'm in the mood for a little defenestration. I always feel like throwing myself out a window when I'm drunk. I take out my phone, put on *Fell in Love With a Girl*, and start dancing. I sing into an imaginary microphone, play air guitar, pretend I'm Jack White again. Tom Brady comes back with a bottle of crème de menthe and pulls a face. "Oh God, I hate this song!" He pours me a glass, and I knock it back. He pours me another right away, and I take small sips. "Jack White is a god," I say. "Nah, man. Bruce Springsteen is a god." "No, um, Ringo Starr is a god." He laughs, says I'm funny. He asks what French music I listen to. "Play a Frenchie song for me." I scroll through my music. I can hardly see straight. I finally settle on *Juste une p'tite nuite* by Les Colocs. The music plays, and I close my eyes. Tom Brady is getting into it. He asks what the song's about. I take a step closer and put my hand on his chest. "A broken heart." I'm so drunk. Tom Brady laughs. He can't stop laughing. I want to punch him in the mouth: no one laughs at Dédé. When the song reaches the chorus, I climb up onto the sofa and sing along with Dédé Fortin. "CÂLISSE RESTE DONC, JUSTE UNE P'TITE NUITE, PIS ON VA S'AIMER, JUSQU'AU MATIN!" Just fucking stay. Just one little night. And we'll love each other till the morning. Tom Brady is sprawled on another sofa, egging me on as he drinks his Jack Daniel's straight from the bottle. He keeps saying, "Caliss rest' don'." We could start a band. We'd call ourselves Crème De Menthe and tour the U.S. of A. doing covers of old Colocs songs. I take a swig from the bottle, too, then climb down from the sofa and lie down on the floor on my back. Tom Brady is still slumped there. "Caliss rest' don'," he says again. My head's spinning; it won't stop spinning. I need to sleep. I need to disappear. I can't take this anymore. I leap to my feet and bound out of the room. Tom Brady shouts at me from the sofa: "Caliss rest' don'!" I walk with my

156

head down, stare at the carpet. I hadn't noticed the carpet before. It reminds me of the one from *The Shining*. I'd have liked a little tricycle to get around this place. That would have made things way easier. I start to retch; I keep going, head down, sticking close to the wall. The music's still playing on the phone in my pocket. I can hear Dédé Fortin singing. "Tassez-vous de d'là y faut que j'voye mon chum. Ça fait longtemps que j'l'ai pas vu y'était parti y'était pas là..." I take a right and come out onto a staircase. I want to go outside, get some fresh air. I start walking down the stairs, can't shake the feeling I'm going to be sick. I start throwing up against the wall. I put my hand to my mouth, but there's too much of it. I'm choking. I vomit my way down the stairs, and it's all green. There's crème de menthe everywhere; it's up my nose. I'm sick on Aaron's shoes and khaki pants. I'm like that little girl in *The Exorcist*. Let Jesus fuck you! I don't go down the stairs with my back arched, but I vomit with the full force of little Regan MacNeil. The long, devastating streams of vomit are a surprise even to me. The carpeted staircase just won't end. I feel like I should curl up into a ball and roll my way down. I focus on the Senegalese guys singing in the song "Balma balma sama wadji. Khadjalama yonwi. Djeguelma djeguelma sama. Wadji khadjalama yonwi..." I catch sight of the woman with the dyed-red hair who doesn't like me. "Shit." She stares at me with wide eyes from the bottom of the stairs and shouts for Aaron. When I reach the bottom, I say to the old woman, "Outside. Where's outside? Outside?"

She doesn't answer. I glance at the staircase out of the corner of my eye: the wall is green, the wall is green all over. Balma balma sama wadji and Merry Christmas, everyone! Cammy appears, flanked by Aaron and a woman I don't remember seeing before. "Jesus," Aaron says. I tell my sister I want to go outside. She leads me to the front door, helps me put on my winter coat, and goes outside with me onto the porch. I sit down on a step by the door. She's angry. She asks why I drank so much. "Dunno." "Come on. Seriously. Get some help." There's a long silence, then I hear the front door open and shut. I'm alone on the porch. The music's still playing on my phone, and I feel like throwing it as far as I can. I take it out of my pocket to turn down the volume and see a text from Amidala. She's sorry. She dropped her phone in the street and had to buy another one. She misses me too and is looking forward to *Star Wars Episode III*. I know that's not true. I know she couldn't care less about Episode III. I know that's why her text has such an effect on me. I'm crying. I'm no use to anyone; I'm pathetic. The door opens again, and I wipe my tears away. I hear Bob Barker's voice asking if I'm OK. "Yes, thank you." He tells me to come inside, that it's cold out. He helps me to my feet, helps me put my coat on a hanger in the hall, helps me make it to a little bedroom. I lie down on the bed. The mattress is so soft that I start grinning like a lunatic. Bob Barker turns out the light and closes the door. My head has almost stopped spinning. I'm going to manage to disappear after all.

Relief. I look at the screen on my phone; the light is blinding. I manage to read Amidala's text again. I didn't make the whole thing up. I'm glad. I hold the phone carefully, scared I might delete the text. I read it another dozen times, then set my phone down on the table and roll onto my side. I think about my planet. We'd be able to teleport on Tatouine. There'd be no phones anymore. I'd be able to reach out and touch Amidala's hand here and now. I'd be able to throw myself off a bridge here and now. I'd be able to change my mind and come to my own rescue. Save me from myself here and now.

I wake up in my clothes, my mouth dry. I missed Christmas altogether. I look down at my khaki pants, I stare for a long time at the dried vomit on them. I don't dare try to stand up, I don't know where I'd go anyway. I cough. My cough has never been so deep. My lungs are a mine, and I'm claustrophobic. I lie there for an hour, staring at the ceiling. I text Amidala: "Hi, still in NYC. Drank too much crème de menthe yesterday. Ugh! Home tomorrow. Will call when I get back." I sign it with a kiss, capital X. One capital X is worth three small ones. I cough. I cough and I cough. I can't stop coughing. I hork up an enormous blob from deep in my chest. It fills my mouth. No garbage can in sight. I go to the window, turn the swivel, and am about to spit it out when I spot the mosquito screen. "F'ck," I mumble. Someone's knocking at the door. Cammy comes in with Elliott Smith. The dog sniffs my feet. My sister asks if

I'm OK. She doesn't look mad anymore, but there's a bitterness in her expression when she sees the state of my pants. "You alright?" "G'tta spit." She tells me to follow her, and she shows me to a bathroom I hadn't seen before. I wonder how many bathrooms there are in this mansion. We don't see anyone on the way, and I'm relieved. I spit and take a leak. I feel dirty. When I come out of the bathroom, I ask my sister if I can take a shower. "Yeah, wait here. I'll get you some clothes." She sounds kind of resigned. As she's walking away, I apologize to her in my head. She comes back with some sweatpants, underwear, socks, and a gift-wrapped package. "What's that?" "It's your Christmas present." "Oh... thanks." Cammy doesn't say anything. She just walks off calling Elliott Smith, who's sniffing the curtains. I close the door and take off my khaki pants. My thighs can breathe again at last; my thighs are my new lungs. I pile all my dirty clothes in one corner of the room. I wish I could burn that pile of clothes, wish I could live in the fire of my burning clothes. The shower is a big glassed-in cube. There are dozens of bottles of shampoo, conditioner, shower gel, you name it. I take the time to read every sentence on every bottle. I wish I could publish my poetry collection on a shampoo bottle. I turn the hot water up higher and higher; I want to melt. I carefully wash every inch of my body. I turn the knob to cold and drink a litre of water. I spit up blood in the shower and make it disappear with my foot. I poke the mucus down the drain with my big toe. I wish I could squeeze myself through the drain hole and never come back. I wish the drain hole would lead me straight to my bed on Dagobah.

I step out of the cube, towel myself off, look in the mirror. I'm pale. I look at my lips, examine their colour. When I had anemia, the doctor told me that pale lips are a sign of low hemoglobin. Since then, I check my lips at least two hundred times a day. My lips look pretty normal today, so I decide to go ahead and unwrap my gift. I'm naked as I tear off the wrapping paper. It's a white "I ♥ New York" t-shirt. I smile as I unfold it; I'm really touched. It's like my sister read my mind. I wanted that shirt so bad. I get dressed, stuff my dirty laundry in the gift box, and go out into the hall. Without meaning to, I pass by the staircase where I threw up, and I see that everything's spic and span and that there's not all that many steps after all. I can hear Elliott Smith barking, and I follow the sound. I end up in the kitchen, where Aaron is standing at the island counter eating pancakes. He sees me coming and gives me a little smile. He opens the fridge and pours me a glass of orange juice. "Enjoy." I smile. "Thank you." Elliott Smith is barking like crazy. He's hungry: he wants to eat pancakes, too. Aaron serves me a plate and invites me to sit at the table next to the counter. I pour syrup over the pancakes, take two bites, feel queasy. I'm exhausted. "Sorry, I'm not very hungry..." He laughs. "It's OK." My sister walks into the kitchen at the same time as the maid. When the maid sees me, she stares daggers at me and walks back out. Cammy and Aaron notice, and they chuckle, but my sister quickly turns serious again. "She's the one who cleaned up your puke last night." I don't say anything; I feel miserable. "Where is everyone?" "They all left last night. Aaron's parents have gone for a hike." "Oh." There's a long silence as my sister wipes the counter with a wet cloth. The mood is tense. I just want to get the hell out of here. "Thanks for the t-shirt." "Eat up. We've already finished." "I tried, but I'm not really hungry." "OK, let's go, then." I get up, pick up my plate, empty it into the garbage, rinse it in the huge sink. Aaron doesn't look like he's in any hurry; he's standing at the counter reading the paper. I follow Cammy to the front door. I put on my coat and Aaron's vomit-specked shoes. My heels are killing me. I never want to wear these shoes again. I never thought I'd be so keen to see my ski-doo boots. I never thought I'd be so glad to leave Bedford and New York and get home to Repentigny and see Amidala and drive my old purple Mazda. Cammy calls Aaron from the front hall. I cough, I'm already roasting in my coat. I go outside, I cough, I gag, I struggle to breathe, I spit up blood. "Jesus, you alright?" "Yeah, I'm fine." "You're not fine at all. You're coughing up blood, for God's sake!" "I'm fine." "We gotta get you to the hospital." "Forget it, I'm not going to the hospital here." "Oh yes you are. Didn't you see what you just spit up!?" She leans over to examine the mucus, looking both amazed and disgusted. "Cammy, I'm OK. I'm used to spitting up blood. I'll go to the hospital when I get back to Montreal. They won't do anything about it here, and anyway, I don't have insurance. It'd cost me a fortune." "Oh, come on! I'll pay. I'm taking you to the hospital!" My emotions are starting to get the better of me. I raise my voice. "Hey! Forget about the hospital, will ya? Do you have any idea how many times a month I spit up blood?" She doesn't answer. Elliott Smith barks in her arms. I feel weak. There's a lump in my throat; my eyes fill with tears. "I think home... you ticket today pay?" I've forgotten how to talk. I can't speak human language anymore. I feel like E.T. I just want to go back to Dagobah and eat Sidekicks. Aaron joins us outside, a big smile on his face. But when he sees our expressions, his cheerfulness evaporates. We climb into his Volkswagen. My sister hands me Elliott Smith. I stroke his head, tell him he's a good doggie. My sister tells Aaron I've been spitting up blood. He looks at me in the rearview mirror. He looks surprised, like he feels sorry for me. He starts the engine and we pull away from the mansion. Cammy searches on her phone for a ticket from New York to Montreal, buys it, and tells me I'm lucky cause there's a bus leaving in three hours. I'm relieved. "Promise me you'll go straight to the hospital when you get to Montreal?" "Yes." The drive back passes in total silence. I try to sleep, but I can't. Whenever I feel like escaping, I try to sleep. When we get on the Henry Hudson Parkway, the road that runs alongside the river, my sister tells me she had a good long talk with Jimmy last night. "He was pretty drunk, too. I've never seen him so hammered. He kept apologizing. He said it was his fault, that he gave you too much to drink." "I'm a big boy. I'm the one who felt like drinking. It wasn't his fault." There's a woman jogging along the sidewalk. She's going nearly as fast as the car. I wish I could run that fast. "Anyway, he really liked you... He told me you played a sad song for him... What was it?" I smile. "*Juste une p'tite nuite* by Les Colocs." She laughs. Aaron doesn't get it. "What?" "Nothing," my sister says. When we get to the apartment, I open the car door, but Aaron says, "No, no, stay in the car." Cammy says he'll go get my stuff for me. Aaron gets out and opens my door; he reaches for the dog. I give Elliott Smith a little peck on the head before handing him over, then I find myself alone in the car with my sister. She stares straight ahead. I don't know what to say, I never know what to say. I can't see her face, just her carefully styled, curly hair. I hear her sniffle. "You crying?" "Course not," she says, as she continues to stare out the front window. Aaron comes back with my backpack. "There you go." He drives me to the bus station. The sun looks like it's about to set even though it's only just past two o'clock. I clutch my backpack tightly, a little nervous. Aaron pulls up in front of the station, stops the car, and reaches over to shake my hand. "Take care of yourself, my friend." "You too." I get out of the car, and so does my sister. She closes the door behind her, we walk a few steps away, then stop. Tears well in her eyes. I give her a hug; my throat is on fire. "Don't worry, I've spit up blood a hundred thousand

times before, and look at me! Look! I'm in top shape!"
I back up a bit and try to dance like Charlie Chaplin. I'm
a terrible dancer. I'm out of breath in no time, I cough a
bit. She smiles through her tears. "I think I'm gonna call
you the Grinch, the Grinch who stole Christmas." She
laughs. It's not a mean laugh. I say, "Well, it wouldn't be
the first Christmas ruined by crème de menthe." I pretend to throw up on her. She rolls her eyes. "I love you,
brother." I take her in my arms and hug her for a long
time. I finally manage to say, "Me too." We say we'll call,
we say we'll see each other soon.

I manage to sleep on the bus. Another passenger shakes
me awake when we get to Customs. As we cross the
border, I get a text message from Cammy: "Aaron forgot
to give you back your book on Russia." I look in my backpack and realize she's right: *The Deserts and Mountains
of Cystic Fibrosis* is gone. I write back, "No worries, you
can keep it. I was done anyway." I close my eyes, start
to dream. I'm at the Super C, in a mine. The only way
I can be happy is by tunnelling down to the centre of
the Earth. It's snowing inside the Super C, but it's not
cold. My sister's dog is next to me. He talks to me, he's
polite and encouraging. He tells me not to give up. I hear
voices behind me. Lots of people are staring at me from
the fruit section. I can't tell if they're ghosts or statues.
I don't have the strength in my arms to lift the pickaxe.
Elliott Smith looks me in the eye and tells me it's OK; at
least I did my best. It's still snowing in the Super C. At

the end of my dream, I realize that I'm the ghost. I realize that I was the only ghost.

I let Google autocomplete sentences beginning with "A hair on..." It comes up with all kinds of stuff: "A hair on Fifth Avenue, a hair on my neck, a hair on an elephant's bottom, a hair on my chin." I'm Ben Kenobi emerging from his cave in *A New Hope*. I'm in a little room, waiting to see the doctor. I stand up and walk around the room. It takes me seven seconds flat. I touch the paper covering the little exam table. I put my hand on the paper and press down onto the table. I crumple the paper, tear it a little. I am this paper: I don't look nice for very long either. The doctor comes into the room. He's young. He must be late thirties tops, and he looks like an X-wing pilot. He says, "So, you've felt better, eh?" I don't answer, just nod. He says they're going to give me a PICC line, and I'm not particularly surprised. "Although, since you had an allergic reaction the last time... the baboon syndrome... we'd like to keep you in for observation for a few days just to make sure everything's OK." "OK." He sees the worry on my face. "Just in case," he says, adding, "They'll call you as soon as a room's free... I'll request the PICC line right away. You might not have it by tomorrow, but we'll be able to give you your antibiotics all the same to speed things up." He leaves, then comes back after a long time and sits in front of me. I stay sitting, don't move. I've forgotten how to move; I no longer know how to move the right way. He looks at his computer screen. "I don't know if they mentioned it," he says, "but you've picked up a bug. There's a new strain of bacteria in your lungs." "I didn't know." "After your last IV treatment, the blood tests showed a new type of germ." I don't say anything. "Just so you know, you have *cepacia*... or, if you want the full name, *Burkholderia cepacia*. Back when the bacteria were first discovered, when a patient had it, it was assumed they would die right away... So a lung transplant was considered top priority. Nowadays, studies have shown that it's not as bad as it looks. We've come to realize that it doesn't really change much. But, in terms of what it means for you, you're going to have to start coming to our Friday afternoon clinics. That's our day for patients with *cepacia*. And you'll no longer be hospitalized on the same floor as cystic fibrosis patients, to avoid contamination." I don't know what to say. I am Ben Kenobi with a bacteria I've never heard of. I don't like the shade of blue on one of the walls. It's too blue; I hate that blue. The doctor asks if I'm OK. "I'm OK," I say. I leave, walk past the long glassed-in waiting room on the twelfth floor. I can see the Jacques Cartier Bridge, all lit up. It reminds me a little of the sea. I take the elevator and head back to the Champ-de-Mars metro station. I think of my sister. When I came back from New York, I didn't go straight to the hospital. I lied to Cammy. I went back to Repentigny to sleep in my own bed. Then I got up early and took the bus back in to Montreal. I didn't want to spend all night at the ER. I am Ben Kenobi, taking the bus back and forth between Montreal and Repentigny. I wait for the next metro. I put on my headphones, open up A Soft Murmur, and listen to the rain. I look at the people waiting for the metro in the rain. A guy sits down near me. I feel like I know him; I think he might be on TV. I close my eyes, pull up my hood, think about my bacteria, and start to cry. I cry in the rainless rain. I'm wasting away. I don't want to suffer. Please, don't make me suffer. I feel out of it. I'm moving, though I'm not aware of it. I'm on the bus, still listening to the rain. I look down at my hands, try to come up with a reason to love them. I miss my stop, get off, walk home. Norm's sitting in the kitchen. He looks up. "Hey, I haven't had a chance to talk to you since you got back. How was New York?" "OK, I think. It was OK." I'm not talking like I usually do. Norm can sense something's wrong. He asks me how I'm doing. He stares at me, legs crossed, his newspaper on his lap. His glasses are perched on the tip of his nose. I think he looks good like that; he looks like a fur trader in New France in his checked shirt. "Not great." I take off my ski-doo boots. He stands up and walks over. I can feel the unease between us. I know Norm is the type of man who never cries. I don't want to break down in front of him, but the tears come all by themselves. My eyes do their own thing. Maybe they're going to take off and make a new life for themselves someplace else. Norm says, "Look, son..." He steps closer, holds me in his arms. I wasn't expecting that. I cry on his shoulder, pour myself out onto Norm. I'm not even embarrassed when

I hear myself sobbing. I never thought I'd find myself crying on my landlord's shoulder one day. Norm asks if I'm hungry. My nose is all snotty. "Yeah." He makes me a ham sandwich; I eat it in seven seconds flat. He asks me what's up. I tell him about the illness, the bacteria, the hospital. "Don't worry about the rent, son. We'll work something out." I don't know what to say. I thank him, tell him I'll dress up as an elf free of charge for Easter. He laughs. I go off to Dagobah, take a long nap. My phone rings. I open my eyes; it's already dark outside. I answer the phone. It's a man from the hospital. "I'm calling to plan your stay at the hospital." "OK." "Are you free tomorrow?" I think of Amidala. The reunion will have to wait. "Yes." "What time can you come?" I don't know what to say. "I can choose the time?" "After supper? Say, six or seven o'clock?" "Sure. Seven o'clock." "Go to the sixteenth floor, Pavilion C." "OK." I hang up; I can't fall back to sleep. I turn on the lamp, play *A Hard Rain's A-Gonna Fall* by Bob Dylan. I've always liked the album cover for *The Freewheelin' Bob Dylan*. I'd like to go for a walk in the slush with a girl hanging from my arm, too. I pack my little suitcase. Most people pack to go on vacation; I pack to go to hospital. I'm depressed. I'm starting to feel a ball of anxiety in my throat. I have to think positive. I think about Amidala dancing in my room. I decide to start dancing, even though I don't feel like it. I twirl around, make circles with my arms. I do the snake; I shimmy my knees really fast. I am Justin Timberlake. It takes me an hour to pack a single pair of socks in my suitcase. I'll get there, I'll get there. I am the ghost of Ben Kenobi. If I have a band one day, I'm going to call it Cepacia. People won't come see me play, in case they catch it. I'll do gigs with a hospital mask over my mouth. I'll choose which mask, depending on my mood. Today, I'd be wearing a mask with Bob Dylan's mouth on it. Tomorrow, a mask with Ben Kenobi's beard. I pack a second pair of socks. I'll get there, I'll get there. One day, I'll manage to get rid of the hair on my heart.

I get to the hospital on a Thursday night. I've forgotten which pavilion I'm supposed to go to. I head to reception, where a lady is sitting behind a gigantic desk. I've only just gotten there, and I'm already lost. "I'm meant to be staying in a room on the sixteenth floor." She tells me to turn right, then keep going straight to the elevators. It's easier getting around the hospital than that big house in Bedford. Sixteen floors is a lot. The elevator stops at every other floor to let more people on. I'd rather have had the elevator to myself. I feel like shouting, "Everybody out! I want the elevator to myself! I repeat: I want the elevator to myself!" I find myself hemmed into one of the corners. An old lady and her husband, who's in a wheelchair, are taking up all the room. I feel like saying to them, "Aren't you ashamed of yourself, ma'am?" I need to calm down. I pull myself together, think about when I'll die. I still don't know how long I'll live for. It's playing havoc with my peace of mind. By the time we reach the sixteenth floor, I have the elevator to myself. My prayers have been answered. I am a voodoo doctor. I step off, walk through some doors, see a cute girl, dressed all in blue, waxing the floor. I stop at a counter. "I'm here for a hospital stay." It sounds like I'm on a package tour. It feels a bit like that time I went to Mexico with my ex. The woman I'm talking to looks like Oprah Winfrey. She hands me a bracelet with my name and date of birth on it. Now it really does feel like I'm at Club Med. I look around for the sea or the pool or the bar. Which way to the bar, Oprah? I feel like dancing again. I want to dance the night away with Oprah Winfrey. "You're in Room 16-09." "OK." She tells me to take a left and keep going to the end of the hallway. I walk past lots of rooms full of sick people. They're all old and bedridden. I'm surrounded by mummies. What am I doing here? I am the pharaoh of the sixteenth floor. I'm impressed by my bed when I get to my room; I've never seen the likes of it. There are green lights on each corner of the mattress, and a huge white nightlight that lights up below the bed. It looks like a spaceship. I'm ready for liftoff. I'm ready to get the hell outta Dodge. I turn on the light; the room's walls are orange. I have huge windows. The blinds are magnetic, trapped between two glass panes. I'm in the Millennium Falcon. I bet the Millennium Falcon has magnetic blinds, too. My room looks out over the Ville-Marie Expressway. Cars are driving under the conference centre. I can see the courtyard behind Montreal's city hall, and the courthouse. The area behind the city hall is huge and completely vacant. I'd like to build myself a house right in the middle of it. I could have a farm there with Amidala; that would be great. I'd have horses, cows, and chickens—lots of chickens. A man in his fifties comes into my room. He says his name's Jean-Luc and he'll be my nurse for the evening. Jean-Luc has a big, round belly and long grey hair that stands up on his head. I can see scabs on his scalp. He seems nice. He gives me a questionnaire to fill out, says he'll put in a peripheral line until the central one can be installed. His voice is unsteady; his voice is gentle. I ask him what the difference is. "For the peripheral line, I put it in a vein in your arm. The central line is inserted surgically in a vein in your chest." "Oh, OK." Jean-Luc tells me he'll be right back. I sit down in a big leatherette armchair at a little round table by the window. I take a look at the questionnaire: "At home, do you need help to wash yourself? Do you need help eating? Do you need help brushing your teeth?" I feel like ticking yes for each question. I imagine the nurse's aide spoon-feeding me even though I can do it myself. I picture having my teeth brushed while I watch a movie on my laptop, or having my ass scrubbed while I stare at the ceiling. It makes me laugh. Under "Psychological Condition," they ask if I suffer from anxiety. I check "Yes." They ask if I've ever considered killing myself, had any suicidal thoughts. I check "No" (I don't want to end my days in a psych ward). Jean-Luc comes back with all the stuff he needs. He hangs three bags of meds from a tall pole on wheels. He punches something into a little machine attached to the stand. "That's a lot of bags," I say. Jean-Luc chuckles. He gently squeezes the biggest bag. "This is just your basic saline solution. Don't worry, I'm not going to inject the whole lot into you." Jean-Luc tells me to put on my hospital gown. I go into the bathroom, get undressed, keep my socks and underwear on. There's a shower in the corner with a little curtain hanging from the ceiling. I put on the gown, but I do the ties up all ass-backwards. I look at myself in the mirror. The pharaoh's gone. With my shaved head, I look more like a young cancer patient. I'm gradually turning into a mummy. When I come out of the bathroom, Jean-Luc is waiting for me with a tourniquet. I lie down on the bed. Jean-Luc slaps my arm and finds a vein in the crook of my left elbow. He puts my line in and flushes it with NaCl; so far, so good. He sticks a transparent patch over the spot where he injected me. "I'm putting an Opsite dressing on, just a little Opsite to hold the line in place and protect you from infections." "That's fine." "I'll be back in two minutes." I stare at the crook of my elbow, I stare at the ceiling, I stare at the little plasma TV screen on the wall facing my bed. I can't afford cable in my room. The LG screen is turned on, but the picture doesn't change. All you can see is the slogan "Life's Good." "Life is good, my ass." I get up to turn off the screen, but I can't find the button. I peer behind the screen and finger all the cables plugged into the wall. I pull out the fattest one. The screen goes black. I walk over to the spaceship, push the buttons on the little touchscreen at the foot of the bed. I turn off the night light and the green lights. My bed looks gloomy now. I press on a little "up" arrow to raise the mattress. Jean-Luc finally comes back. He reprograms the machine attached to the IV pole. He sighs loudly; he seems overworked. The hallway is dead quiet. He tears open an alcohol swab, cleans the tip of my line, flushes it again. This time he's not able to push in the syringe full of liquid. "Oh-kaaaay. What's going on here?" He wrestles with the syringe, applies more pressure, tries to force the liquid out. I'm afraid my vein's going to explode. "I don't think it's working." "Yeah... Well, I'm gonna have to remove your line and find another vein. This one's decided to block." He sighs. I feel like I should apologize, but I don't. Jean-Luc peels off the transparent patch and pulls out the line. With my other hand, I apply pressure to a cotton ball on my arm. He slaps my left arm again, looking for another vein, but he can't find one. I try to lighten the mood: "I've got a big vein on my forehead. Maybe you could stick it in there." He laughs. Jean-Luc is my new best friend. He finally manages to find a vein in my wrist. He goes through it all again and sticks the needle in. "Ouch!" "Sorry." He flushes the line with NaCl, and this time it works. I'm sweating a bit; my mouth's all dry. He sticks on another Opsite and I notice a bit of blood pooling in the sticky patch on my wrist. I don't dare move my hand in case the line blocks again. To distract myself, I think about the taste of crème de menthe, but that just makes me feel queasy. "I feel sick." Jean-Luc hands me a little garbage can, and I throw up into it. "You OK?" I spit twice into the bin. "Yeah." My puke is acidic and orange. It matches the walls in my room. Maybe I should go into interior design. Jean-Luc hooks up my first IV antibiotic. I need one right after the other: ceftazidime and meropenem. Each takes about forty minutes. Jean-Luc tells me to press the buzzer once the first one's done so he can come hook up the other one. He leaves, and I'm left alone with my noises. I wait, I stare at the white dresser at the far end of the room. I notice there's a little black key in one of the keyholes. I pick up the questionnaire where I'd left off. Now I'm at the "Cognitive State, Behaviour, and Communication" section: "Do you have memory problems? Do you have hearing problems? Do you have difficulty speaking? Have you ever experienced an episode of temporary confusion?" I could say "Yes" to all of them. I'm nuts, I'm already a crazy old guy, I'm already a mummy. I check off "No" to all of them. I'm tired, I'm fed up. I skip ahead a few pages. I get to the section called "Understanding of the Situation." They ask how I feel about what I'm going through. I don't know what to answer. Sometimes I'm a Jedi, other times I'm a lizard. But I don't write that. It doesn't feel like it's me going through all this. It feels like I'm watching someone else's life, only it's me who's suffering. But I don't write that. The IV bag is empty, so I press the yellow "Help" button on the wall. A nurse I've never seen before and two nurse's aides appear within seconds. The nurse asks me what's wrong. "My medication's done." The nurse looks furious. He comes over to my bed and presses the green button on the wall twice to turn off the buzzer. "You're not supposed to press that button. You have to take the white clicker here and press the red button, like this." "OK." They all leave without doing anything about my meds. I stay there hooked up to an empty bag. I stare at the huge IV bag next to the empty one, and I notice it starts to drip to keep my line open. I feel like sinking my teeth into that big bag of IV solution. I feel like sucking up all that solution into my mouth, pressing the yellow button, waiting for the nurses to come, and spitting it all in their faces. I'm Tom Hardy in *Bronson*. I'm gonna strip naked in my room and cover myself in black paint from head to toe. I'm gonna press the yellow button and beat the shit out of every nurse and orderly who darkens my door. Jean-Luc comes back half an hour later to inject me with the other antibiotic. He says he's sorry he's late. "No worries, man." I notice he's shaking a bit when he injects me with my second dose. That makes me nervous, but I keep my mouth shut. He leaves again. I'm already getting used to my new routine. I stare at my feet, rub my toes against the scabs on my heels, listen to the sound of the vent above my head. I need to piss. IV antibiotics always do that to me. I cross my legs for a whole hour, until Jean-Luc comes back and unhooks me from the pole. I'm so afraid I'll piss my pants I practically bound like a gazelle straight to the bathroom.

I look at myself in the mirror and turn off the lights in my room. I take off my gown; it's smothering me. Everything's smothering me. I leave the blinds open. The night is as dark as a plum. I lie down on my side. I take off my underwear; I always sleep naked. I watch the cars coming and going along the Ville-Marie Expressway. Where are they going? I think back to the final question on the hospital questionnaire: "If there was just one thing the nurse could do for you today, what would it be?" I'd like a nurse who could see into the future and who'd practice healing rituals. She'd place precious stones on my forehead and neck and chest and arms and legs, then she'd light candles and burn incense and chant spells while banging on a little gong to save me. Goodbye, degenerative disease. I think about reincarnation. I've probably been reincarnated a hundred times over, but only ever as a caterpillar. In my one hundred caterpillar lives, I've had cystic fibrosis one hundred times. A nurse's aide comes into my room. All I can see is a dark silhouette looking at me. She wants to check if I'm still breathing. She wants to know if the spell has worked. She wants to know if I still glow in the dark.

Oh, boy. I get woken up at five in the morning. The first thing I think to myself is, "Oh, boy." An Asian nurse's aide is standing at the foot of my bed. I'm still groggy. She says she needs to weigh me. What the fuck! Why would anyone want to weigh me at five in the morning?

I see her punching numbers into the touchscreen. By the look of things, my bed is so high-tech, it can weigh me. She says, "75.2 kilos." "Oh, boy. I don't think so!" "No?" She punches in some more numbers, doesn't understand. She asks me to stand up so she can reset the scale. I hesitate a moment as I realize I've got a boner. Fuck. I try to control my morning erection, try to think about things that turn me off. I look outside, look at the magnetic window blinds, look at the line in my wrist. I've still got a boner; everything seems to turn me on. She says it again. "Please stand up, sir." "Yep, hang on a second." I grab the flannel blanket, ball it up, and hold it in front of my crotch. I put one foot down on the floor; it's freezing. I set the other foot down and stand up. I'm naked, hunched over, shivering. I feel like I'm about to fall apart. It takes ages. She can't figure out how the machine works. She finally tells me to lie back down again. I still have a hard-on; I'd be good in a hospital porn flick. "90.8 kilos," she announces. "That's more like it," I say, and give her a thumbs up. She doesn't crack a smile. She walks out of the room, and I'm alone again at last. Now I'm wide awake, and it's ten past five in the morning. I try to go back to sleep, and I'm almost there when someone calls out, "Good morning." It's a new nurse. He introduces himself. His name's Willy. He calls me "sir." He's very polite. Willy is tall and black and muscular. He looks like he's been carved out of marble. He reminds me of a Greek statue. I feel all vulnerable next to him. I'm naked, with a beer gut and what's left of my hard-on. Willy hangs two bags of antibiotics on my pole, while a nurse takes a blood sample from me. The tourniquet is so tight I can't feel my forearm. She fills up dozens of little vials. It's never-ending, and the pain from the tourniquet is unbearable. "Do you think you could loosen it a bit? "Oh, sure, sorry." I hear the snap of the rubber tourniquet. "Phew." Willy flushes my line. "I'll be back in forty minutes to give you the other antibiotic, sir." "OK." I check the time and realize that it's too early for them to inject me with antibiotics; I have a schedule to follow. I start to stress out. I don't want to die because they gave me my meds too soon. I press the buzzer and wait... five, ten, fifteen minutes. Nobody comes to see me. I could be dying here. I press the yellow button on the wall, and a nurse's aide shows up in four seconds flat. "You're not supposed to touch that button. It's for the care team." "I want to see the nurse. I think he hooked me up too early." She doesn't get it. "I want to see the nurse!" She looks unimpressed. Willy arrives and asks what the emergency is. I tell him he hooked me up too soon. He comes over to the bed; he looks angry. He raises his voice, "Sir, I have twelve other patients waiting for me, so I have no choice but to start you early." "I'm sure you have your hands full. I'm just wondering if it's dangerous." "No, sir, it's not danger-ous." "OK," I answer, and he disappears back down the corridor. I sit on the edge of my bed and watch the drops fall one by one into the little plastic cylinder. There's a bunch of tubes hanging from the pole. They all lead into my vein. I manage to doze a little. When I wake up, Willy is beside me, programming the machine to give me the other antibiotic. He avoids catching my eye, then leaves. My stomach spasms. "Typical." I've never needed to shit so badly in all my life. It's absurd. I stand up, I'm shaking, I unhook the two wires connected to the wall. "You're not gonna shit yourself, you're not gonna shit yourself," I keep telling myself. The machine on the pole starts beeping like a microwave. I'm naked in my room, clinging to my coatrack on wheels. I roll the pole over to the toilet, sit down, empty my bowels, arm in the air. The machine beeps every five seconds. I wipe myself. Beep. I wipe myself again. Beep. I wipe myself some more. No end in sight. Beep. The paper's so thin. Beep. "Shut it!" I tell my pole. I stand up, go back over to the bed, plug my wires back in to the wall. The beeping stops. I put my boxers back on, my hospital gown, too, and lie down on the bed. I clasp my belly with both hands. Daylight is slowly beginning to make its way across one of the walls of my room. I hear someone shout out in pain in the hallway. I'll have to start sleeping different hours or else I'll go crazy. I heard a guy repeating "Code blue, code blue, code blue" over the speaker in my room in the middle of the night. I'll never get any rest here. I take another look at the antibiotic bag hanging from the pole; it's starting to become an obsession. I can't see the drops falling anymore, and the bag is still half full. "Fuck." I press the red button and wait. The Asian nurse's aide who weighed me earlier

180

appears in the doorway, and I say to myself, "Shit, not her." She comes over, pushes twice on the green button on the wall, and stares at me. I tell her my antibiotic has stopped flowing. "No, no. It's still going, sir." She points at the big bag of solution, and I tell her that's not the antibiotics. "Yes, it is, sir." I repeat what Jean-Luc told me. "No, that's just my saline solution to keep my line open." She doesn't know what to say to that. She stares at me, looks completely stumped. Oh, boy. I ask to see the nurse. Willy reappears at my side, pokes at a few buttons, sighs loudly. He's really going to hate me now. I feel a pounding headache coming on, right in the middle of my forehead. I try to think of something else. I take out my phone and see that Cammy has sent me ten messages. I take a selfie lying on the bed, my hospital gown clearly in view. "All good," I write. Then I read the earlier message from Amidala again. I write to tell her I'm in the hospital. She writes back seconds later, asking which hospital. "The CHUM," I write. "What floor?" I don't want her to see me like this. She'll never want to speak to me again. I don't reply. She writes, "???" I say I'm on the sixteenth floor; she asks for the room number. I say I'm not at my best. "No one's going to mistake me for Brad Pitt," I write. "I knew that already!" she replies. I laugh. "16-09," I write. She's coming to see me tomorrow night. I lie down on my side and look out the window. I can't feel my headache anymore. I know it's still there somewhere, but I don't feel it. Daylight is everywhere in my room now. Maybe I'm cured. It's a miracle. I feel like pressing the yellow button to share the good news. Willy comes to unhook me. I get up and spend the day in the leatherette armchair by the window. I don't eat much; I've lost my appetite. I didn't have any breakfast or lunch to speak of. I drank a little juice and ate some jello. The doctor comes to see me late in the day. "You'll be spending the weekend in hospital. They don't put in PICC lines over the weekend." That's depressing. "You're on the waiting list." I ask how long it might take to get one; he says he doesn't know. I just want to get out of here. I want to do my treatments at home, sleep all day on Dagobah. I tell him about my bowel problems and the headaches. "That's normal. It's just the antibiotics." "Wonderful." He smiles, a wry smile to show he feels for me. Then he walks out of the room, and I'm alone again. I force myself to eat some dinner. I swallow the pills they brought me with the food. Each pill is sealed in an individual pack. A mountain of empty packs piles up at my feet. I'd like to set fire to the lot of them. I'd like to be hermetically sealed in an individual pack. I wouldn't need to pay rent anymore. I'd just live in a pack. It'd be cool. I could just walk around naked with a hard-on in my hermetically sealed pack. I stick my fork into my asparagus quiche, raise the food to my mouth, chew on it, swallow. It tastes of nothing. I can't taste anything anymore. I try to read one of the books I brought with me, I try watching a movie on my laptop, I try writing a poem. I can't concentrate. Everything's a mountain. My mood is getting worse, along with my condition, it seems. I'm going stir-crazy. I feel like a bit of a vegetable; maybe they'll send me to an asylum. I'm going to end up cuckoo like Jack Nicholson. I'll end up strangling an orderly. That said, I'd still like to be friends with a really tall Indian guy. I think of the most useless little things. I wonder what the person who put up the magnetic blinds was called. Are they happy right now? Are they living in a hermetically sealed pack? I can see images being projected onto the grey courthouse outside. It's impressive. I can see waterfalls, then soccer players, then a woman walking in front of playing cards. I don't quite see how the pictures all fit together, which makes it even nicer. At one point, the images seem to be some kind of tribute to Canada. I spot a moose, then a Mountie in a ridiculous hat. I wish I could swap my hospital gown for a red RCMP outfit. I want a ridiculous hat of my own. Every time a nurse came into my room, I'd leap to attention, arms by my side. I wouldn't wear the pants, but I'd have the big hat and the red jacket. I'd salute solemnly to the hospital staff, with a hard-on, of course. I wonder who on earth is watching the projection apart from me. I'd like to be part of it. They could come film me in my hospital gown, sitting in my leatherette armchair. I'd spread my legs and everyone would see my dick on the courthouse wall, and the closing scene would be me flashing a peace sign at the camera.

I wake up to Willy's masked face. For a moment, I don't remember I'm in a hospital. It feels more like I'm staring at a madman who's doing crazy experiments on my body. He won't learn much. He'll just see that my body is half Sidekicks, half Chemineaud. Willy is wearing gloves and a yellow gown that covers his arms and the rest of his body. I really feel like a guinea pig now. "Good morning, sir," he says, as he flushes my IV line. "Hi, Willy." There's a pause, then I ask him what the mask's for. He says I've been put in isolation. I don't get it. He sees the worried look on my face and says that, as a precaution, everyone who comes into my room will have to put on a mask, gloves, and a protective gown because of my *cepacia*. My spirits sink even lower. I wonder why they didn't wear masks and gowns the first day I was hospitalized, but I don't want to bug Willy with my questions. His mask glows in the dark, and his shaved head is blue and shiny in the half-light. He has gigantic forearms, but he handles the alcohol swabs and syringes with an unbelievably gentle touch. He really is a fine-looking specimen of a man, I think to myself. Willy leaves my room, and I watch him take off his gear in the hall. I feel like an old mummy. An orderly appears in the doorway with my breakfast. She sets the tray down on a little cart outside my room and starts suiting up. She looks well and truly fed up with her job. I feel like telling her, "Go home. Don't worry about it. If anyone asks, I'll tell them you're around here somewhere." Eventually she comes inside and puts the tray on a little table that she wheels over to me. "Thanks." She doesn't answer and walks out. I feel like some kind of rare specimen. The hospital trays are beige. The toast is soggy; the crusts, hard and dry. "Stupid toast." I drink my juice, eat my cereal. All the cereal could fit in the palm of my hand. I miss the breakfasts at Chez Rémi. The nurse on duty this morning comes to unhook me. She doesn't smile either. She leaves like a ghost. I get up, walk around the room twelve times. I'm glad to be free: I have a busy schedule—I have to take a shit then look out the window all day. I'm not human, I'm a cat. All the people in hospital are cats. The Ville-Marie Expressway is quiet today. I realize it's Saturday. People take things easy over the weekend; people are lazy. I never take it easy: I'm still sick on weekends. I won't be seeing the doctor either. He's taking a break from the mummies. He's eating caviar, jerking off with a harem back at his place. I wish I could take a little break too, just two days off. I don't want a harem, just some time to put my feet up. I want to go back to Repentigny and sleep on Dagobah. I stare out at the horizon. I think if I craned my neck, I might just be able to see the Old Port from here. My nose starts bleeding, both nostrils at once. It's never happened to me before. I'm dying, clearly. I pinch my nose and run out to the desk. An orderly spots me making my way down the hall and tells me I'm not allowed out. "Sir! You're in isolation, sir!" "Yo, my nose is bleeding!" I've never said "yo" in my life. It sounds completely absurd; it must be the stress. I keep heading for the desk. I hear

185

the woman shout, "You have to go back to your room, sir!" I'm still pressing down hard on my nostrils, but the blood keeps coming. It's getting everywhere. I'm leaving a trail behind me. I want to die. Where are the sharks? When I reach the desk, I see the nurse sitting there, writing. She looks up at me in shock. She leaps to her feet, races around the counter, and asks me what's going on. Still pinching my nose, I mumble, "Nosebleed." "Your face is covered in blood!" She brings me Kleenex, I let go, and my nose runs like a tap all over my gown. She tells me to pinch hard. She brings me back to my room. The bleeding slows to a stop after a few minutes. The nurse tells me not to worry, that these things happen. "So, I'm not dying, then?" "No." She hands me a new gown and leaves me alone in the room. My nostrils are bone dry; I can feel little clots of blood forming in my nose. I go to the bathroom and change into the clean gown. As I'm coming out, a woman who looks to be in her fifties walks into the room. I see she's not wearing an isolation suit, and that cheers me up. I sit down on the leatherette armchair. She tells me she's a nutritionist, and asks what meals I'd like this week: "Chicken thigh or tuna steak? Beef with mushroom sauce or roast turkey? Hawaiian pork with rice and mixed vegetables or Pennine primavera?" It takes me a while to answer each question. I hesitate, afraid to make the wrong choice. "There's no right or wrong answer. Just whatever you prefer." "OK," I say, but I still have trouble deciding. I think it over. I take my time, as if my life hangs in the balance. I feel lonely. I wish the nutritionist would stay with me. We could discuss Hawaiian pork all night long; it'd be so much fun. The nutritionist's eyebrows are pencilled in. They're so high they're practically halfway up her forehead. I find it original, and vaguely arousing. I feel myself getting hard beneath my gown and I want to punch myself in the face. I'm a friggin' psychopath, a lunatic. I cross my legs. She asks what I'd like for breakfast. Would I like a muffin? I tell myself, "OK, cool it, there's nothing exciting about a muffin, down boy, down. Think about the muffin, think about the muffin, think about the fucking muffin." She's staring at me with her pencil poised, waiting for me to say something. "Yeah, a muffin, great idea." "One muffin? Two muffins?" "Errr, OK, two muffins. Yeah, two muffins." "Yogurt, fresh fruit, a banana?" "Uh-huh, OK, yogurt, fruit, a banana." She laughs. "Do you still want toast?" "No, no more toast, please." "OK, fine. I'll come back next week so we can go over your menu again together." I give her a thumbs up. "Great, thanks." She gives me a smile and is on her way out the door when she suddenly stops and turns around. "Ah, I almost forgot your card. Because you have cystic fibrosis, you're entitled to a thirty-dollar meal card for the cafeteria that you can renew every day." "Thirty dollars a day? What for?" She doesn't understand my question. "Uhh, to eat." "But, isn't it the same food as I get here in my room?" "Well, yes and no. They serve other meals at the cafeteria too. Different desserts, soups, salads, cheeses, and stuff. It's worth checking it out." "OK, great. But why do people with cystic fibrosis get the card?" "Because patients with cystic fibrosis generally need more fats. They're usually thinner and smaller than most people." She pauses and looks me up and down. "In your case, you're lucky: you have a good build." She's probably the only person I've ever met to confuse being overweight with being well built. I take it as a compliment. All the other CF patients are little hobbits, and I am Sam Gamgee. Before she leaves, the nutritionist tells me I can call the cafeteria on my room phone to make changes to my menu or cancel a meal. "OK." How cool is that! It's like being at a hotel. I'll have lobster, I'll have caviar, just like the doctors on their weekends off. I pick up the phone and dial extension 31890. A voice answers. I say I'd like to cancel my dinner meal, and I give my room number. The voice says "Fine, no problem. Have a nice day." It's like magic. I laugh alone in my room. I have a new goal in life: to become a regular at the hospital cafeteria.

I feel exhausted, so I decide to lie down and take a nap. I fall asleep in no time; I dream I'm killing people. All of a sudden, I feel something touch the hair on my leg, and I wake with a jump. It's Amidala in her isolation gear. I'd forgotten Amidala was coming today. I check the time; I slept for four hours. It's already dark out. Amidala's eyes are teasing. She's wearing a mask, but I can tell she's smiling by the way her eyes are screwed up. "Are you laughing at me?" I ask. "No, no. I'm just glad to see you." I smile and give her a hug. "Hey, we're not supposed to touch. You're contaminated," she says. "Hah, I contaminated you a long time ago." She laughs. "How did you know I was in isolation?" "A lady told me I had to wear this thing if I wanted to see you." "OK." She asks me how things are going. "Meh." "You've got a nice room, anyway." "Yep, and a nice view, too." She looks out the window. I point out the magnetic blinds. "Wow." I've impressed her. "What's that building over there?" she asks. "That's City Hall." "Oh." I ask if she's hungry, but she's already eaten. "Too bad. I could've treated you." I flash my VIP card and give her a wink. "Oh, well, in that case, OK." I grab my pants and my "I ♥ New York" t-shirt, and I go to the bathroom to get changed. I can't go to the cafeteria in my hospital gown; I'll scare everyone. When I come out of the bathroom in my street clothes, Amidala says "Hey, you running away?" "Yep," I reply with an exaggerated grin. We leave the room, Amidala takes off her gear in the corridor, and we walk past the reception desk. We bump into Jean-Luc, who's just starting his night shift. I've been caught red-handed. I ask him if I can go to the cafeteria. He says that, since I'm in isolation, it would be best if I stayed in my room. I look at Amidala, then back at him. "You see, I have a very important visitor." He looks at Amidala, doesn't say anything. I promise him I'll wear a mask and be on my best behaviour. He laughs. I feel like a kid asking his dad if he can go play outside. "Alright, then." "Thanks, Jean-Luc!" I feel excited as we leave my ward. In the elevator, I pretend to be afraid when we start going down. It makes Amidala laugh. I don't want to go back to my room; I just want to get the hell out of here with Amidala. I'd go to a bar, drink beer, and dance all night long. The cafeteria is huge. We go through the turnstiles and end up right in front of the desserts. I check the prices. Everything's so cheap it makes me laugh. I put three slices of pie on my tray. Then two small shrimp pizzas, a cheeseburger, three bottles of Perrier: being sick is great. Amidala serves herself a big salad with pollock and vegetables, cream of spinach soup, and raspberry cheesecake. The cashier adds it all up and tells me I still have ten dollars left. It's ridiculous! "OK, hang on." I rush over to the fridge and grab a box of sushi and three bottles of orange juice. This VIP card could be the start of a promising black-market career. I could sell my food for a tidy profit. I could move into my hospital room. I could live out the rest of my life here. It'd be way easier: I'd move in the bedroom set I bought at Structube. My two bedside tables would fit on either side of my bed with plenty of room to spare. I wouldn't have to pay rent anymore, it'd be fantastic. I manage to find us a little round table. The place is pretty full. Amidala thinks it looks like a university cafeteria. "Yeah, you're right." I eat until I'm nauseous. I hold my belly with both hands. I open my mouth and pretend to scream. I pretend to explode in the cafeteria. Amidala can hardly breathe. She laughs and laughs, but no sound comes out of her mouth.

We talk a lot; we've never talked so much. She tells me she's going to quit her job at Super C. She says that Akim misses me. "I miss him too," I say. "I like Akim." I look at the clock on the wall at the end of the cafeteria. I try to make the moment last for as long as I can. I don't want to go back to isolation. I talk about every subject that comes to mind. I go on and on about *Star Wars*. I keep coming back to Han Solo's biceps. Amidala rolls her eyes every time. We end up walking back slowly to my room. I'm exhausted, but I don't let on to Amidala. I don't want her to leave. Jean-Luc is sitting in the same place he was earlier. I give him the thumbs up on my way past, and he smiles. Amidala puts on a new yellow gown, a new mask, and new gloves. She makes a show of putting on the latex gloves, like she's a porn star. "Ready for your rectal, sir?" She stretches the latex glove as far as it will go and gives me a look. I laugh and look away. I notice there's another projection outside on the wall tonight. I point to the courthouse and she says, "Wow." She asks why they're doing that. "Because they've got nothing else to do." She thinks it's pretty. We both stare out the window for a while. I see the Mountie appear in his hat and I smile. She says, "I'd better go." "Oh, come on. We should watch a movie on my laptop. The night is young." "I'm opening the store tomorrow." "You're quitting soon anyway." "Yeah, but not right away. I want to be feeling OK tomorrow." I give emotional blackmail a try. "Sure, I get it. You only came for my VIP card." She laughs. She says she didn't even know about the card until she got here. "Whatever." She gives me a little shove and tells me to stop. "Hey, you can't push a sick man." I can just about make out a smile behind her mask. She looks at me all serious and says, "OK, then. So, what did you want to watch?" "*Revenge of the Sith*." "Oh no! Anything but that." I lie back, eyes closed. "It's my dying wish." "Don't say that, you idiot." "I'm just kiddin'. I'm sorry." I take her hand. I wish I could feel the skin on her fingers, but all I can feel is latex. My head's covered in latex, my ideas are covered in latex, my heart is covered in latex. "OK then. Just an hour, though, OK?" "Deal." I turn off the lights in my room, plonk my laptop down on the little wheely table beside my bed, and tell Amidala to come lie beside me. She asks if that's allowed. "Absolutely." "Oh, boy." She lies down and snuggles up against me. For once, she doesn't fall asleep. She follows the plot, and that makes me happy. She forgets all about the time; I think she might actually make it through the whole movie. I'm more focused on watching her out of the corner of my eye than following the plot. The last scene ends with a shot of the legendary desert planet. "It's nice," she says. She likes the two suns. "Yeah, it is nice. It was shot in Tunisia." "I didn't know Tunisia had two suns." "Ba dum tish." She giggles a little behind her mask. She seems to have forgotten she's wearing a mask. I think for a while as I watch the credits. "I'm thinking about going on a long trip. Would you come with me?" She doesn't answer, doesn't look away from the credits. "I can't really," she eventually says. "I don't have any money to travel." I pretend I didn't hear. "We could live in a tent in Tunisia like the Sand Men." She stays serious, but she plays along. "OK, as long as we can be Sand Women." "That's fine with me. I don't mind being a Sand Woman. They're cool, too." I hear the door open. A nurse's aide comes into the room and sees me in bed with Amidala. She looks irritated. Amidala gets up and goes over to the window. I say, "Yes?" "Just wanted to see if everything's OK in here." "It's more than OK." She leaves without saying a word. Amidala looks out the window. "The projection's stopped." I stand up, begin to worry a little, look outside. "Yeah, it's gone." Amidala holds me in her arms. I say, "I'm gonna miss you." "You'll be out of here soon. I'm sure of it." "Yeah." She adds, "We can talk on the phone tomorrow, if you like." "OK, sure." She picks up her purse and walks out of my room; I follow her as far as the door. She takes off her mask, her gloves, her gown. She's lovely. I tell her to come closer; she says she can't and laughs a little. I insist and she moves in and I kiss her and stroke her ear. She says, "You're stroking my ear. I'm not a cat!" "Now you're *really* contaminated." She smiles. "See you soon." I say, "See you soon, my little Sand Woman." I watch her go, I watch her back; the hallway is long. Amidala grows smaller and smaller. Her back takes a right, her back disappears. Her back doesn't turn around.

I wake up in the middle of the night, scratching my ass. "Ah no. For fuck's sake." I get up, I'm trembling with adrenaline. I go over to look at myself in the bathroom mirror and see the big red splotches. They're under my armpits, too, and on my sides. Baboon syndrome, again. I go back to bed, ring the buzzer. Willy comes into my room. "I think I'm having a reaction to the meds." "Can I have a look, sir?" I pull down my boxers a bit, show him the red rash near my hips. "Hmm, it is very red... OK... I'll call the respirologist. I'll be back soon, sir." I don't answer. I just stare at the ceiling and freak out: I don't really even see the ceiling. Willy is back in a flash, and he injects me with Benadryl. "We're going to stop giving you the intravenous antibiotics. The allergist will come see you Monday." "Monday?" I repeat. "Yes, sir. Today's Sunday. There are no allergists on Sundays." "Fucking allergists," I say to myself. Willy leaves. I can't get back to sleep. I watch the light change in my room; it barely gets brighter. It's a grey day, a pale day. It's six o'clock in the morning, and I already have the blues. The line in my arm is starting to annoy me. I feel like ripping it out and hurling it down the hallway. My wrist is a little sensitive; my wrist is all sensitive light. I am Sam Gamgee with baboon syndrome. I go to the bathroom, take off all my clothes, pull the little curtain closed, take a shower, taking care not to wet the line in my wrist. The water goes everywhere; the drain is too small. I wash quickly and dry myself with five little white towels. I sponge up the water on the floor, kick the little puddles towards the drain. I'm tired already. I have the head of a cat. I go over and sit on the leatherette armchair and stare outside. Two people are walking along Rue Saint-Antoine. They're far away, so far away they're just black specks. They look like tiny shadows. I wish I was walking along Rue Saint-Antoine. I want to be a tiny shadow, too. I can't find a way to stay positive. There's a black cat in my throat. I spot my VIP card on the little round table, and I decide to go to the cafeteria, to take my mind off things. I put on my pants, a mask, and my ski-doo boots, cause my feet are cold. I keep my gown on. I'm breaking out of here. I am Sam Gamgee who doesn't give a shit about the Ring, and who'd rather eat pie on the sly. I walk down the hallway without spotting a single orderly. I'm relieved. I don't think I have the strength to explain my plan. I suddenly feel dizzy and exhausted in the elevator. I rub my eyes, pull myself together. My legs are so heavy. My ski-doo boots have never felt heavier. I don't get it. The elevator goes down, stopping at every floor. Everyone seems taller than me. We're in Middle-earth. I am a hobbit, after all. People look at me out of the corner of their eyes; it feels like they're judging me. I feel like scaring them. I feel like taking off my mask, shoving two fingers down my throat, and throwing up in the elevator. I feel like making myself invisible, but I don't have the Ring. I'm waiting for the Nazgûl to come kill me in the hospital elevator. I get off at the second floor and walk quickly, imagining the Dark Riders are on my tail. I'm such an idiot. On my way to the cafeteria,

195

I have a brainwave: earlier this morning, Willy injected me with Benadryl, so that would explain why I'm so tired. I'd totally forgotten about it. I'm such a genius. I'm the very first hobbit with cystic fibrosis to win the Nobel Prize for Imbecility. I go through the cafeteria turnstile. My mouth's dry. That must be the Benadryl, too. It feels like I don't have any lips, just teeth. Not a pretty picture. I grab a tray and pile on six slices of pie: three lemon and three chocolate. I take three big bottles of water, while I'm at it. I've never been that crazy about desserts; I don't know what's come over me. I'm feeling a little woozy, and I'm still dizzy. I wish I could put on the Ring and become invisible, and stop being dizzy, and steal all the desserts in the cafeteria, and escape from this place, and start my life over. I hand my VIP card to the woman at the cash and sit down at a long table. Alone. I eat my pie methodically, taking my time. I alternate: one lemon, one chocolate, and so on. I drink two bottles of water, but my mouth's still dry. I manage to eat all six slices of pie. My belly is swollen under my hospital gown. I feel like I'm pregnant. My shoulders are heavy, and I move slowly. I could go for a nap right here on the long cafeteria table. Someone would call security. They'd check my hospital bracelet and take me back to my room. If I had the Ring, nobody would see me. I could just stretch out and take a nap. I won't let it go. I think about Willy's forearms. I get up and leave my tray on the table, along with what's left of my revolt. I shuffle back to the elevator. Everything seems so far. My feet

196

are hot. I'm sweating; my socks are soaking wet. When I get back to my room on the sixteenth floor, I hear an orderly call out, "There he is!" I take off my boots, my mask, and my pants. I lie down on the bed. I'm happy to be back in my hospital bed. The day nurse, whose name I can never remember, barrels into the room. She stares at me, wide-eyed. "Where were you?!" "The cafeteria." "You're not supposed to leave your room! They gave you a big dose of Benadryl." "Yeah, I'm feeling a bit woozy." She doesn't answer, just takes my blood pressure. The machine flashes; my pressure is high. She pricks my finger, takes my blood sugar reading: it's through the roof. "You're hyperglycemic. Do you have diabetes?" "I dunno. Don't think so." "It's really not normal." "I ate six slices of pie." She stares at me in dismay. "Three lemon and three chocolate," I add. My day nurse is a Nazgûl. If she could, she'd probably run me through with a sword. I'd lie there in agony, my mouth hanging open, staring into the void. She leaves the room. I fall asleep right away, and dream about my slow death. When I wake up, I see the janitor. He's sweeping the floor, four feet from my bed. I wave at him. He nods, smiles. I watch him sweep, I stare at the floor. He sweeps over the ray of light that's projected onto the floor. I bet he thinks it's paper. That's what I thought, too. We're two nutbars trying to gather up scraps of light from the floor.

In the evening, Jean-Luc comes into my room. No mask, no gloves. He couldn't give a damn about isolation rules. He hasn't bothered tying up his yellow gown, and it's wide open in the back, the shoulders sagging down around his biceps. He's short of breath as he asks if I'm OK. "Yep." He takes my blood sugar; it's normal. We're both happy about that. He tells me they've prescribed me a cortisone cream for my rash. He shows me the tube. "I'll put it on for you." I don't get it. "You're going to put it on for me?" "Yes." "You're gonna put it on my butt?" "Yes." I'm not feeling super comfortable here. "Oh no, that's fine. I can do it myself." "You sure? I don't mind." "No, really, I'm good." He looks disappointed. "OK then, I'll leave the cream here on the table." "Thanks." I watch as Jean-Luc leaves the room, gown flapping in his wake. Jean-Luc, the butterfly. I go into the bathroom and smear cream on my ass in front of the mirror. I fan it with my hand, so it dries faster. I wash my hands four times, just to be sure I don't go blind if I rub my eyes. I go back to bed and lie down on my side. I'm still digesting the pie. I think about Jean-Luc wanting to put cream on my ass for me, and I laugh out loud. Jean-Luc is no Dark Rider; he's an Elf. I fall asleep and dream about Elves versus Nazgûl. I come to the conclusion that I'd rather have an Elf rub cream on my ass than have to talk to a Nazgûl.

I'm lying on the operating table. A bald and very nice orderly came to get me early this morning with a wheelchair. Whenever I have to sit in a wheelchair, I always get the feeling that life has caught up with me. I examine my hands: I'm pale. I've been in hospital before, but now I realize that I'm slowly dying. Dying a little bit at a time really takes it out of you. The radiologist says hello. I can just about see him out of the corner of my eye. He looks really young, and I secretly hope he's never played *Super Mario Bros 3*. His assistant preps my right arm. It's red. The radiologist numbs the part of my bicep where he'll put in the line, and says, "It's going to prick, it's going to feel hot, it's going to burn." I can't see a thing, but I know all the steps by heart anyway. He inserts a thin needle into my vein to make a little tunnel. Then he sticks the line into my vein and pushes until the tip reaches a bigger vein. It takes a while. I can feel him pushing on my arm, but it doesn't hurt. Has the radiologist numbed my will to live, too? I could use a mini radiologist of my own. I'd keep him in my shirt pocket. I'd take good care of him; I'd feed him breadcrumbs and give him orange juice to drink. Any time I felt depressed, I'd ask him to make my heart go numb. I'd be happy all the time, I'd be numb all the time. I stare at the ceiling. I can't feel a thing; I'm a machine. I am Anakin Skywalker who turns into Darth Vader. The radiologist stops pushing on my arm. I see him leaning over me. He secures my PICC line with a couple of stitches and says, "There you go. Have a good day!" I'm left alone with my arm covered in dried blood. The assistant comes back, gives my arm a quick wipe, then sticks a see-through patch over the line. "You're not allergic to Tegaderm, are you?" "What's Tegaderm?" "It's what I'm using to cover your PICC line." "Oh, OK. No... I don't think so." He helps me get up, tells me to wait in the wheelchair until someone comes to take me back to my room. I am Darth Vader in a wheelchair. I try to mentally strangle every person who walks past. Nothing doing. The bald, very nice orderly from earlier comes in smiling. "Me again!" I smile back at him and attempt to strangle him mentally using the Force, but it doesn't work. He wheels me back to my room. For a good part of the day I sit in the armchair and stare at my hands. I try reading a book, but I keep getting caught up in the blank margins. I avoid reading the words. If I read a word, I'll burst into flames. A woman arrives with my lunch. It's the first time I've seen her. She's wearing gloves, a gown, and a mask, and she carefully carries my tray over to me. I feel like one of the X-Men. Today's lunch is macaroni stir-fry with cauliflower. I eat slowly. I'm not very hungry. I think about which X-Men character I'd like to be. I think about Mystique, the blue girl. I'd like to be the blue girl and change into whoever I want. I'd be George Clooney, and I'd stroll the hospital corridors wearing my George Clooney smile. Two masked girls come into my room. They're with a very thin, elderly man. I realize I'm no longer attractive; I've lost all my powers of seduction. The doctor introduces himself. He wants to look at my butt: he's the allergist. I don't care if he's a denturist, I'd still show him my bum. I am Mystique. I take off my gown and transform myself into Leonardo DiCaprio. I have an audience, and they have come just to see my ass. I don't want to let them down. I do it right, play it by the book. I pull down my underwear and bare my bum. I am Ryan Gosling. I display my rash-covered ass to two masked women and an old man I don't even know. I am Ryan Gosling, I am Ryan Gosling, I am not embarrassed, I have no inhibitions, I am so relaxed. I'm willing to show my ass to the whole world if it means I can get the hell out of here. The allergist has very pale green eyes. He's balding. He mutters to himself, "Uh-huhh. Fascinating. Absolutely fascinating." I feel like I'm in a freak show. I feel like jumping out the window; I feel like jumping into the body of Ben Affleck. "We're going to stop giving you ceftazidime and continue with just the meropenem." He adds, "We're fairly certain that your allergy is linked to the ceftazidime." "OK, great, OK." The allergist tells me he'll be back tomorrow to see how my rash is doing. He leaves the room along with the two mute, masked women. I am a grumpy George Clooney, baring my ass like a baboon.

I have a nap. I wake up. It's already time for supper. Jean-Luc is starting his shift. He says, "So we're sticking with the meropenem and stopping the ceftazidime?" "Yep." He laughs. I'm a comedian. "I'll come back and hook you up around 9:30, OK?" I am Will Smith. "OK, great. OK, thanks." I ask Jean-Luc if he can take the IV out of my wrist. "Oh my God, sure thing." For supper I have meatloaf with mashed potatoes, carrots, and peas. I don't feel like going down to the cafeteria. I look out the window: there's no projection on the courthouse wall tonight. I stay in bed, stare at my feet. All the scabs have gone from my heels. I open up my laptop, spend an hour and a half looking for a movie to watch. I settle on *The Devil Wears Prada*. I've never seen it. Funny enough, it's the only thing I can stand right now. Jean-Luc comes to hook me up. I am Matt Damon. I haven't heard from Amidala. I am Meryl Streep in a hospital gown. My antibiotic bag is empty. I press the buzzer. I am Anne Hathaway. Jean-Luc comes to unhook me and wishes me goodnight. "Thanks." I go put cream on my ass in the bathroom, wash my hands four times, and turn off the lights. I am Tom Hanks.

For once, I'm up before Willy comes by. I take out my phone, scroll through today's news, come across an article: "No More Wild Horses Left on Earth." That just gets me in a funk, so I go to Google and type, "How come roosters..." The results get off to a flying start with "How come roosters turn blue when they sit on a toaster?" I read on. "How come roosters crow and crows roost? How come roosters don't have any hands? How come roosters always look pissed off?" I laugh. I think about my breath; it must really stink. Nobody here could care less that I stink. A hospital is the only place on Earth where people are allowed to stink. To stink and die. Willy comes into my room. "Good morning, sir." "Hey there, Willy." Willy wants to see my butt, so I show him my butt. "Oh, it's much less red. That's good news." I'm relieved. I feel lighter already. I ask Willy if he ever takes time off. I can see him smiling behind his mask as he taps away at the machine on my pole. "I'll be off soon, sir." Willy is imperturbable, a gladiator of modern times. "Anyway, I'll miss you, Willy, when I get outta here." He doesn't answer. "I'll miss you," I say, "but not this bed." Willy chuckles behind his mask. You have to laugh in hospital. You have to laugh and stink if you ever want to get out. I go back on Google while he hooks up my antibiotics. Breakfast arrives earlier than usual, which is a nice surprise. I take the cover off the plate—muffins! They're warm. I cut them in two, put some butter inside. So good, so satisfying. Hospital muffins turn me on. The day flies by. I listen to relaxing music on the Internet. Sounds of nature. I listen to birds, insects, the wind, the sound of a distant river. My hospital bed is a national park. I'm Canada's leading tourist attraction. They line up outside my hospital room just to see my ass.

In the early afternoon, a red-haired, middle-aged lady pushes a wheelchair into my room and says I'm off to the allergy department. She warns me right away that it's a bit of a schlep, that we'll have to take a few different elevators to get there. I ask if I can listen to music on my headphones while she pushes me. "No problem."

I sit there and try not to get a hard-on. I listen to nature sounds. I close my eyes. The orderly pushing me isn't messing about, and it feels like we're flying along the hallways. It's nice. I can feel the insects against my face. I open my eyes. We pass by the burn unit, take the elevator. People stare at me in my wheelchair; I try to strangle them using the power of my mind, but it doesn't work. The orderly opens the big, grey automatic doors with her black pass. We go past Respiratory Therapy, get to Pavilion D, take another elevator, go through more doors—the sound of the birds smells like grey doors—head towards Occupational Therapy, more doors, right, right again, a covered glass walkway with big grey panels that have thousands of little holes in them. The daylight shines through each hole, leaving patterns of light on the floor. It looks nice, I think. I wish I had the Ring that would make me invisible and I'd spend all day lying there on the floor. I hear the wings of an insect, we go through Pavilion C then F. We're in the basement. It's really hot. There are pipes running along the ceiling. The orderly touches me on the shoulder; I take out an earbud, and she says it's like Cuba in here. I laugh even though it's not funny. We take another elevator, arrive at the allergy department. There are butterflies there. Everyone's allergic to butterflies; it's a crying shame. I turn off the music and sit in a big padded armchair, surrounded by people taking allergy tests. A woman beside me wearing a silk scarf is holding her left arm out straight. Her arm is covered with numbers written in blue ink. There are tiny drops of fish on her skin, lined up on top of each little numbered prick. She seems nervous. She tells the nurse, "It stings. It really stings." The nurse has a Russian accent. I try not to get a hard-on. "It's only been two minutes," she says. "You have to wait another three, OK?" The woman looks at the waiting-room clock every ten seconds. I rejoice in her pain. I'd like to stick little bits of salmon on her heart. I don't want her to die; I just want her whole body to sting a little more. I'd like everyone on Earth to come down with baboon syndrome for twenty-four hours. We could celebrate Baboon Syndrome Day. Right after New Year's, to get the year off to a good start. I am a dangerous psychopath. The Russian nurse gets a call, answers it, looks at me, asks me my name, hangs up. She says I'm to go to Room 7. I get up. "Thank you." I'm not hard. The allergist smiles and asks how I'm feeling today. I don't answer, I just show him my ass. I never want to speak again. I never want to form another sentence. I just want to show my butt by way of an answer to every question the world throws at me. This is how I'm feeling: look at my ass. He says, "Wow, that's marvelous!" I wonder what's so marvelous about it. It's the first time I've ever shown my butt to someone and they've said it's marvelous. But I'm pleased with his reaction, all the same. My ass is Machu Picchu. "The redness is almost entirely gone. This is very good news." "What now?" "Well, I'd have no issue letting you go home today. Now we know that you're allergic to ceftazidime." He thinks for a moment.

"Usually you do your own IV treatments at home and go to the clinic to get your dressings changed, right?" "Yes." "It'll depend on your respirologist, but I have no problem with that at all. I'll call him and let him know. He should come by to see you sometime later today." "Thanks." I want to thank absolutely everyone, even people who don't like me. A different orderly comes to get me, and he pushes me back to my room in my wheelchair. I feel like kissing everyone I meet on the way back. I feel like kissing everyone who's being pushed around like I am in a wheelchair. French kissing. I feel like starting up a wheelchair book club. We'd have muffins and all get hard-ons. I start fantasizing about Dagobah, about my bed. I'm a cat that's all worked up, a cat that's gotten its claws back and can go play outside. I wipe my eyes. I'm crying. I'm not sad. The sun is green inside my room. I sit in my fake leather armchair and look out at the clouds. Patience is my middle name. I wait for the respirologist. He's late; I start to get worried. The sun is green. The doctor arrives at the same time as lunch. I'm hungry. It's going to get cold. But at the same time, I couldn't really care less. A doctor is a sunset you get to see for four minutes a day. My respirologist is the X-wing pilot I saw the last time. He asks me how I am. "Great." My eyes are watery; there's a lump in my throat. I don't know why I'm sad. "I think you're good to go," the doctor says. "I'll have to let them know. It'll take a little while. We'll have to give you your meropenem at two o'clock, but after that you can go. That sound OK?"

I nod. "Anything else I can do for you?" Silence. "Do you want to see the social worker?" I nod. I'm a four-year-old kid. "OK. I'll give her a call, and she'll come see you." With superhuman effort, I say, "Thank you." The bread in my hot chicken sandwich is soggy. I take a few bites, but I'm not hungry anymore. The sun is still green. I try to write a poem about depression and hot chicken, but I can't. The nurse arrives a little before two and gets my meds ready. The social worker comes at the same time, asks me how things are. "I don't really know." She asks me if I want to talk about it. I don't know where to start. I tell her about Super C, Norm, Amidala, the anemia I had a couple of months back. Don't ask me why I brought up my anemia. She concludes that I've become detached from everything around me in order to pro-tect myself. "Right now, it's like you're up in space and don't know how to come back down to Earth. You've forgotten how to reconnect with yourself." I don't say anything. She hands me a leaflet, a special program that pays for psychological support for people with cystic fibrosis. She tells me to find a psychologist online and to stay clear of anyone who's into psychodynamics. "Oh, OK." "A more cognitive behavioural approach is what's going to help you." "Oh, OK." She talks some more, goes on and on. She says I can call her anytime. "Oh, OK." I do a Google search for "an astronaut." "An astronaut in sheep's clothing, an astronaut on the moon throws a wrench, an astronaut screams for nine minutes." I am an astronaut who's been screaming for thirty-one years.

By the time I get out of the hospital, I'm starving. I head to the closest McDonald's. I think about what I'm going to order. Decisions, decisions. Maybe a McChicken, maybe a Big Mac, maybe a Quarter Pounder with Cheese, maybe I should switch the fries for poutine. My legs feel weak. I haven't walked any further than the cafeteria for a whole week. I think I'll get a Big Mac, with two cheeseburgers and a poutine. There's a homeless guy on his knees on the sidewalk. He wants me to give him some money. I tell him I don't have any. "Sorry." "S'ok." I don't tell him, but I take a moment to give him my one and only power: the power to strangle people using only my mind. I keep walking north, passing by one building after another. The city is one big, open-air hospital. Everyone's a little sick. Everyone's dragging their own little invisible wheelchair. I turn right. It's so bright out. The daylight makes me feel like drinking Chemineaud. I stare at the sun. I try to make myself go blind, but it doesn't work. The sun is still green, and my erection's gone.

I sit in Norm's kitchen drinking coffee. I hooked up my IV antibiotics at six o'clock this morning. My meds are taking up all the space in the fridge. Norm says, "No worries, son. Take all the space you need." He laughs, "I'm gonna sell 'em on the black market." He laughs and slaps his knees. I'm sitting at my laptop, answering my publisher's emails about the poetry collection. I take out forty-odd pages and write a few new poems. I think

208

they're good. I'm feeling in good shape. I approve the cover. My PICC line patch is itchy. I apply cold compresses to my bicep, but it doesn't make much difference. I've got an appointment at the clinic at one o'clock. I make myself a couple of slices of toast with peanut butter, but I'm still hungry. I've got a craving for pancakes. I feel like drinking a gallon of maple syrup. I open a file on my computer and start reading: "The days are long." Maybe I could write about my job at the tourist information office. I think my story about that time I went around killing the flies one by one is funny enough to write about. I write for a couple of hours. I check the time: it's past one o'clock. "Shit." I throw on my coat, jump in the car, and drive to the clinic ten minutes from my place. I manage to hit every single red light on the way there. In the waiting room, there are only half-mummies, just alive enough so as not to be in hospital. I could embark on a high-flying career as an Egyptologist. The nurse calls my name. She seems frazzled. She tells me I'm late. I sit down on a stool on wheels. She puts on a mask and takes off my dressing. "Eww... I can't put anything on top of that. It's all infected. Look at that pus and the redness!" I look at my arm. "It's not that bad." "You must be kidding! You're allergic to Tegaderm." Great! The fun never stops. She takes a closer look at my arm, says she's never seen the likes of it. "I'm allergic to Tegawhat?" "Tegaderm. The dressing." "OK." A silence falls over the little room. "So, what do I do?" "You should probably get your PICC line taken out." I start to stress out. I don't want to go back to eating hot chicken at the hospital. "No, no... There must be something else we can do?" "Look, I can't put anything on top of that." I hold my head in my hands and scratch furiously at my scalp. She can tell I'm starting to panic. "Listen, I can put on a clean dressing... I'll wrap some gauze around your arm... To try and dry the infected area. But you're going to have to come back and see me again tomorrow." "OK." She rolls the gauze around my bicep, mummifying my arm. As I leave the room, I feel like flashing a peace sign at my fellow mummies sitting in the waiting room, but I don't. I feel depressed the whole way home. I put on *Fell in Love With a Girl* in the car. I scream. My head's been buried in the sand since I was four. An old guy in a Hyundai cuts me off. "Old fart in a Hyundai!" I cough. I can't stop coughing. I turn into a parking lot and turn off the engine. I try to calm down, try to breathe slowly. I'm in a supermarket parking lot, but it's not the Super C. I decide to go inside, just to distract myself. I walk up and down the aisles, not looking at anything in particular. I start over again from the first aisle, stop in front of the soup. There's a special on cans of Habitant soup. I grab four. My arms are full of soup, and I head for the checkout line. As I'm putting the cans in the trunk of the car, I have a craving for something sweet. I go back into the store and head for the frozen foods section, where I pick up a tub of Coaticook chocolate ice cream. As I walk past the freezer full of waffles, I see they've got big boxes of forty-eight Eggo waffles. A big box for twelve bucks. Wow! Ever since I got out of hospital, I've had wicked sugar cravings. Not sure why. I ditch the ice cream and grab the box of waffles and four cans of maple syrup. I avoid looking the cashier in the eye as I pay. Back in the car, I chuckle to myself. My day's not a write-off, after all. I can't wait to eat my forty-eight waffles. I don't feel like writing anymore; I just want to eat. I just want to enjoy my newfound passion for waffles. I check the time on my car radio. It's past two o'clock. I'm late for my afternoon dose. "Shit." I go straight home. I gently set down my box of waffles and my cans on the lawn. I unlock the front door, head for the fridge, and unwrap a bottle of meds. I disinfect the tip of my PICC line, I flush out the tube with NaCl, then I hook up my baby bottle of antibiotics to my line. I sit down on the sofa. I'm tired. I stretch out and snooze for an hour. The first thing I think about when I wake up is my box of waffles sitting in the front yard. "Shit." I rush to the front door, forgetting that my arm's hooked up to the bottle. I drag the plastic bottle after me for a few feet, like a dog on its leash. My heart stops beating. I stare at my arm. The vein doesn't seem to have torn open. Phew. Everything's OK. The bottle's empty; the drug's now running through my veins. There are two things I have to remember when I'm hooked up: not to get tangled up in door handles, and not to drag my antibiotics behind me like a dog on a leash. I unhook my bottle, flush out the line with a syringe of NaCl, then with another of heparin, so it doesn't get blocked. The box of waffles is still there.

I stack the bags of waffles in the freezer. There's one last bag of eight that won't fit. Norm's freezer is completely full. I don't want my eight waffles to go to waste, so I open Google to see if you can keep frozen waffles in the fridge. I type, "Can you leave..." and all kinds of stuff appears. I laugh out loud as I stand there in the kitchen. Can you leave a dog in the car? Can you leave a splinter in? Can you leave a cruise ship early? Can you leave apple pie out overnight? Can you leave North Korea? Can you leave the country while on EI? I hesitate to type in, "Can you leave eight frozen waffles in the fridge?" I don't want to add to the stupid questions. I decide to eat eight waffles for supper instead. I end up slathering on too much butter and syrup, and I'm feeling sick to my stomach by the seventh. I go onto the website of the Quebec psychologists' association. I type in my postal code and scroll down the list of psychologists in my neighbourhood. I see a Mario who's not too far away. I call him up. He doesn't answer, so I leave a message. Get back to me, Mario. Save me, Mario, save me! Save me from eating this eighth waffle and descending into madness. I laugh and eat my last waffle. I feel like puking, but I manage to keep it down. Success! I try hard not to scratch at my bandage. I stare out the window. Norm still hasn't taken down his Christmas decorations. I stare at the big black hole in the middle of the Christmas tree lights. I open a file on my computer and read back through everything I wrote today. I'm thinking about writing a novel where the action all takes place in a single day, a kind of poor guy's 24 where all the main character does is kill flies all day at the tourist office where he works. When Norm gets home from work, I'm still sitting at my computer in the kitchen. "Jesus, did you move at all today?" "Yeah, I went to the clinic." I show him the big bandage wrapped around my arm. Norm doesn't say anything. He takes off his coat and boots. He opens the fridge, cracks open a beer, and sits down at the table. He stares at my bandage. "Does it hurt?" "It's as itchy as hell." "Oh yeah?" "The nurse wanted to take it off. She said it's infected." "You've gotta be the unluckiest guy in the world, y'know that?" He takes a long swig of Molson Export and stares at my bandage some more. "I broke my arm once when I was a kid. All my buddies on my street signed my cast to bring me luck." "Luck for what?" "I dunno, just for whatever..." "OK." "D'you want me to sign it?" I think about it for a moment. "I'm not sure. It's not a cast." "Doesn't matter." "Yeah, OK then." My bandage is so thick I don't really mind. Norm gets up to find a black marker. "Write on the outside of my arm, OK? I don't want to get ink in the needle hole." Norm laughs. His breath already smells of stale beer. He moves closer and puts on his glasses. He takes his time. "There ya go!" I look at what he wrote, reading it upside down: Hang in there. The words are crooked, as if they were written by a six-year-old. I smile. "Thanks." "It'll bring you luck." I get up from the table. "I'm going to bed. I bought waffles, if you want some..." Norm says he can't stand the things. "I'll pay the rent soon." "Hey, I told you not to worry about that, kid." I go down to Dagobah. It's cold. I don't bother turning on the lights. I have the eyes of a cat. I pull down the bedcovers, get undressed, and stretch out under my blanket. I'm still in my old hospital routine: I stare at the doorway for a long time, waiting for Willy to appear. He doesn't come. I look at my phone: no missed calls, no messages. I stare at my arm. I hold my phone up so the light shines on my bandage. I recite the higgledy-piggledy message on my bandage like an age-old prayer. I think about the black hole in front of the house. I wonder how many black holes I'd be able to eat. I'm sure I could knock back at least eight. Eight black holes with syrup.

I get up around five. I'm not tired. I get dressed, make myself a coffee, make a coffee for Norm. I eat two waffles, get syrup all over the table, clean it up with a damp cloth. I'm so tired. I hook up my antibiotics, stuff my bottle into the pocket of my jeans. I don't really know what to do with my day. I wander around the house. I don't feel like writing. Norm heads out to work, and I can't seem to tear myself away from the living-room window. I go down to Dagobah, tidy up a little, throw lots of stuff out, and wash my bedroom floor. I want to scream. I couldn't shout at my old place: the neighbours would have called the police, and I'd have been locked up. I shout, "MY ROOM IS TIDY!" I listen to the silence of the walls. I shout again, "MY ROOM IS TIDY AS SHIT!" I go up into the kitchen and scroll through the classified ads online. I'm not looking to buy or sell anything in particular. Just for the hell of it, I look up how much I could get for my car. I eat another couple of waffles, pouring my maple syrup carefully this time. I don't spill any: I am a world-class maple syrup–pouring champion. I take a two-hour nap before going over to the clinic, where I get all stressed out in the parking lot. I repeat the mantra on my arm. I stay in the car and open up Google Translate. I type in "Hang in there." It's fascinating: *halte durch* in German, *håll ut* in Swedish, *hangai ma laila* in Hawaiian. In Burmese, all I see are lots of round squiggles, all lined up and stacked on top of each other. Talk about an alien language. In another life, I live on Tatouine and I'm from Burma. "Everything's just fine!" I shout to myself in my car. "I'm not going to get my PICC line out!" I shout to myself. I get out of the car. "Fuck the hospital, fuck soggy hot chicken sandwiches!" I don't even have to sit down in the waiting room. The nurse sees me when I come in and tells me to go straight to Room 3. She cuts off my bandage with a little pair of scissors. I don't look. I wait to see how she reacts instead. She says, "OK, that's better." I feel like laughing my head off. "HA! HA! HA! TAKE THAT, YA STUPID HOT CHICKEN!" But all I say is, "OK." The nurse tells me I'm to go to the clinic every other day to get my dressing changed. "No problem." "Buy an over-the-counter cortisone cream from the pharmacy, and we'll put some on the next time." "I already have some. The really strong stuff, for my baboon syndrome." "No! NOT THAT! All you need is a little over-the-counter cream." "OK." Back in my car, I shout, "I'M GOING TO THE PHARMACY!" There are seventeen pharmacies in Repentigny. I decide to go to Pharmaprix, the one right next to the Super C. I go in, buy my cream, leave, and walk over to the Super C. I don't dare go inside. I think back to all the times I had to push the shopping carts across the parking lot in the snow. It seems like ages ago. All the snow from the snowstorm has been cleared away. The parking lot is down to bare asphalt; I'm impressed. It makes me feel completely useless. I wouldn't have been much help clearing away the snow. I don't have a snowplow, don't even have a license to drive one. I'd have waited for the snow to melt in the spring, flashing peace signs to the customers all the while. I tap my foot against the asphalt. A car suddenly zooms out of nowhere and honks at me. The driver waves his arms in the air, so that I can see how annoyed he is. I do the same, and stare right back at him. He looks nasty; I hope he doesn't get out of his car and beat me up. All I have to defend myself with is my over-the-counter cortisone cream. I picture myself squirting cream in his eyes. He veers around me and disappears off behind a sea of cars. I recognize Akim by the entrance. He's stacking his carts. I go over to see him. He has his back to me, and I say, "Hi there, my friend." He turns around with a grin and gives me a hug. He's wearing a tattered safety vest over his winter coat. He asks how I am. "OK. You?" "Ah, not bad, not bad.

Keeping busy." I nod, and he says, "Are you coming back to work?" "No, I just wanted to see you." "Ah! That's nice, my friend... What you gonna do now?" "I don't really know." An old lady walks between us, tugging at one of those little shopping baskets on wheels. "I might go live in Tunisia." I laugh. That makes Akim laugh. I ask if Amidala's working today. He's surprised. "She doesn't work here anymore. I thought you knew." "Oh, OK... No, I didn't know." Amidala hasn't been in touch since the hospital. Akim notices my face drop. To change the subject, he says, "We should go for a beer sometime." "Sure thing." We hear an ambulance coming. It flashes past, crazy loud. I'd like to be in that ambulance. I'd like to be lying dead in that ambulance. I keep my eyes glued to it, watch it disappear as it turns onto Iberville. "I'll let you get back to work, then," I say. "Talk soon, my friend." Akim gives me an enormous smile. We shake hands, and I go back to my car. I think about Amidala in her hospital getup. I listen to the thrum of my car. Maybe Amidala is scared of me, scared of the living dead that I embody. Being ill isn't the most romantic thing in the world. I feel like crying, but I manage to hold it all in. "DON'T CRY, YOU MUMMY!" I shout. No sooner am I out of the parking lot than I hit a red light. I stare it down, still thinking of Amidala. I'm glad she's left the supermarket. I hope she's happy, I hope she's laughing right now. I connect my phone to the radio and try to find a song. A horn blares behind me: the light's turned green. I stay right where I am. I can hear the horns

217

blaring, but I don't care. I manage to find the song, turn up the sound, sing over the music coming out of the speakers. I turn off the engine right in the middle of my lane, leaving the battery on to listen to my music. I get out of the car, pretend there's something wrong with the engine. The cars behind me are starting to swerve around the Mazda, glaring at me like I'm a murderer. I open the hood, fold half of my body inside. I scream over the engine. I'm warm, and the engine's super warm. I scream as loud as I can. I want to lose my voice, lose my mind. "Don't let me down! Don't let me down!" I sing. "Don't let me down, you fucker!" I'm calmer now. I close the hood, start the engine. The light's red again. I feel like doing it all over, again and again. I'd keep going until I ran out of gas. I'd camp out in front of the lights, live right there. I'd move into my car. I'd cook Sidekicks on top of it on my camping stove. I'd grow my hair long, with a bushy beard. People'd call me the Baboon at the Lights on Iberville. Maybe I'd be happy living like that. I'm sure I could be. The light turns green.

I feel a small electric shock in my neck. Every time I get an electric shock, I'm afraid I'll go up in smoke. Two hundred pounds of smoke. Lying on my sofa, I hear the ceiling creak. I wonder if it's Mr. Jingles. I listen hard, but I can't hear it anymore. I'm disappointed. I feel like I've just come out of a coma. The soldiers on TV are jumping out of a plane. I watch the bubbles travelling up from my bottle and into my arm. They want me to join

218

the Canadian Armed Forces. I can just picture the scene: me in the trenches with my PICC line. "Hold my gun for a sec," I'd tell my fellow soldiers. "Just need to keep my PICC line open." I'd be the world's worst soldier. There'd be nothing for it but to stick me in the kitchen, only I'd eat all the desserts. I hear a snowplow pass by the house. Mario the psychologist never called me back. Two days later, I stop by his office. It's a dental practice. I ask the secretary if I can speak to Mario. "There's no Mario here." "You're sure? Mario, Suite 200, the psychologist." She stares at me like a statue. Her unease is palpable. "There are no psychologists here, sir." "Oh, sorry." I check the address again on the website, but it's the right one. "Stupid, shithead Mario," I say to myself all the way home. Still. I go back and lie down in front of the TV. I get another shock from the sofa, but I don't go up in smoke. I'm still alive. Once my treatment's over, I unhook myself, flush; I am a robot. I pick up the phone, call two more psychologists: Sylvie and Marielle. Neither picks up, so I leave both a message. I'm on hold. My life is a voice in an inbox somewhere. "I can't take this anymore." I go outside; I'm going for a walk. I feel like having a hot dog. I walk for forty-five minutes before I find one. The guy behind the cash looks at me through closed eyes. He's had enough, too. I'd like to ask him if he wants to come to Tatouine with me. I'd make him a little bedroom in the house I'd build with my bare hands. In return for my hospitality, he'd have to make me hot dogs every day. On the way home, I notice I have a missed call. I listen to the voice message. It's Sylvie telling me she can't take me on, that she's no longer accepting new patients. "Great... That's just swell... Come on, Marielle, get off your ass and answer the phone, Marielle. You can do it, Marielle!" I look at the time; I'm feeling a bit disheartened. I decide not to wait for Marielle to call. I phone every psychologist in Repentigny, leave a message for every one of them. I have a message, at last. My heart's off to the races. It's my sister Cammy. I'm a little disappointed. She's sent me a photo of a pair of socks she saw at a store. They have Freddy Krueger on them, with long blades where his fingers should be, and Jason Voorhees, the serial killer from *Friday the 13th*. "Cool," I write back, with a smiley face in case she thinks I could care less. She says that Aaron is trying to learn French. He's reading *The Deserts and Mountains of Cystic Fibrosis* in the original. "Does he understand any of it?" "Not a damned thing, but he likes looking at the pictures." I'm not in the mood. There's a ball of anxiety on my tongue. I look up flights to Tunisia. It's become a bit of an obsession of mine. I want to go visit Tataouine. I check the price. It's not all that expensive. I stare at the page of flights for a good hour. I scroll down as though I'll be able to teleport my way there. We should all be able to teleport. There should be free and universal teleportation for everyone on the planet who's sick. If I were a politician, that would be one of my election promises. I could go to Tunisia for five minutes then come back then leave again and come back again. I am

Captain James Kirk. I go to the bathroom. My cough is stubborn and throaty. I cough up big, solid gobs into the sink. I lean down and realize they're grey. I wonder in all seriousness if I've coughed up part of my lungs. I cough some more, try to catch my breath. I cough up some blood, my heart stops. It's the first time I've coughed up blood during an IV session. I'm hot. I give my temples a rub. Seriously? I come out of the bathroom, lie down on my bed, and listen to the bubbles in my throat. I stare at the ceiling. It just won't end. I try to clear my head, try to forget about it, try to go back to space. My social worker wouldn't be happy with me drifting off like this again. I look back up at the ceiling, realize I'm blinking. Every time I realize that, I stop, and now my eyes are stinging. I make myself blink again. It's not easy.

I suddenly jump up and start taking photos of my bed, my car, and my bookshelf. I go onto a classified ads site and create an account. I can't figure it out; it takes me an hour. I finally manage to post all the stuff I own. Ten minutes later, Josée wants to buy my bookshelf, for half the asking price. I wonder if she's a psychologist: she's quick to reply and seems efficient. I'd like to tell her about the ball of anxiety perched on my tongue. Without giving it a second thought, I write back: "Deal!" I've never been much good at haggling. I really couldn't care less. All I want is to make enough money to pay for my rent and a flight to Tunisia. I picture the *USS Enterprise* in my mind's eye. I can't see any further than the end of my nose. I don't have a nose anymore. I am Captain James Kirk with no nose.

I'm wearing a Guns N' Roses shirt at the hospital. The respiratory therapist says he hasn't listened to them for ages. "Me neither," I reply. He goes on about the Montreal Canadiens and how it's time they got rid of their coach. I couldn't care less. "Yeah, no kidding." I step onto the scales. I weigh a bit more than usual. "Gained a bit of weight, have we?" "I eat too many waffles." "Oh yeah, me too. Ever tried drinking a shot of maple syrup, then downing a glass of milk right after?" "No." "It's soo good." "That'd be great for my diabetes, eh?" "Err, no, maybe not." We go back to Room 4, and I blow into the machine. "44%," he says. I blow three more times. I ask him if I can try it standing up, but there's nothing doing: the result is exactly the same. "OK then." I feel spent. The respiratory therapist says something, but I don't understand. I just reply with a matter-of-fact "Yeah." He leaves the room with his wheely cart and little machine. I glance at my phone. Someone wants to buy the bedroom set I got at Structube. Gaétan (that's his name) is willing to pay the price I posted. He doesn't even try to work me down. I'm relieved. We arrange to meet the next morning. The doctor walks in, it's the X-wing pilot. He asks how I'm doing. "I'm good." "Your lung function doesn't appear to have improved... that's kind of strange. But you say you're feeling good, that you're feeling back to normal. "Yes," I lie. I don't tell him about the blood I spit up yesterday. My rebel days are behind me. I work for the Empire now. I'm done working with X-wing pilots, done working with doctors, done working with the enemy. I am Anakin Skywalker on Mustafar: I'm losing control, fading away, charred from head to toe. I've lost my lightsaber duel with Obi-Wan. Yeah, whatever. The doctor types on his keyboard, looks something up. "Well, if I look back at your earlier lung function results, your normal values are around 48%." "OK." "The difference is pretty slim. I'd be fine with you getting the PICC line removed today, but you're going to have to come back to the hospital in a month so we can see how things are looking." "OK, no problem." The doctor flashes me a rebel pilot smile and leaves the room. A nurse comes in looking rushed. She reminds me of Frances McDormand. She cuts off my bandage and stitches with a pair of scissors. "When I say so, you're going to take a deep breath and you're going to strain like you're having a bowel movement, OK?" "OK." I know the drill by heart. It's been embedded in my life for years. My life is but a series of déjà-vus, one "I'll hold my breath like I'm having a bowel movement" after another. She stands next to my outstretched arm and says, "OK, here we go." I take a deep breath. I watch her pull on the line. I can feel it sliding out of my arm. It takes forever. I watch her pulling on the never-ending tube. I'm almost out of breath. "OK! All done." I breathe in. I feel her hand pressing down on the hole in my bicep. She's holding a thick square bandage to stop the blood escaping from my arm. I remember the time the nurse didn't push down on my arm for long enough, and the blood shot three feet in the air. Frances McDormand holds my arm for five minutes before taping the bandage in place. She leaves the room and I'm alone again, just me and my arm. The skin is all red because of my allergy to Tegaderm. The social worker appears in the doorway and asks if I found a psychologist. "Yes," I lie. I am Anakin Skywalker on Mustafar. Not a single one of the psychologists returned my call. "That's good news. Let me know how it goes, if you like. We're putting together a list of psychologists here, and if you're happy with yours, if you enjoy your experience, we can refer other patients to them, too." "Yeah, sure." I'll be able to recommend my imaginary psychologist. I'll invent one. My dream shrink would be like Robin Williams in *Good Will Hunting*. I'd be Matt Damon, only not so intelligent. I'd still be useless at math. But I'd be able to name all the planets in *Star Wars*, and my shrink would be seriously impressed. He'd say, "You can do anything you want in life, Will." That's not my name, but during our sessions, I'd want him to call me Will. I'd tell him I accepted the offer from NASA, and we'd hug and laugh.

I leave the hospital and I take the metro, then the bus. I go back to Repentigny. I'm a free man, a free man who's going to live life as a free man in Repentigny. By the time I step off the bus, I have transformed completely into Darth Vader. I decide to walk around a bit. I want my fellow citizens to fear my presence. I walk, I breathe heavily, I cough. There's not a soul in the streets, and it really pisses me off. I walk for a long time. I finally spot an old guy shovelling his driveway. I try to strangle him using my mental powers, to show him who's boss around here. It doesn't work. I'm the one who chokes, I'm the one who feels like I'm being strangled. I have a coughing fit and have to stop, propping my hands on my knees and horking up an enormous gob of yellow mucus flecked with blood into the snow. The guy with the shovel asks if I'm OK. "Yeah, thanks." I turn back. I'm starting to feel tired. I turn right, right again, walk past the old guy with the shovel again. I'm lost. I've walked around the block without realizing it. I've never seen these streets before. I take out my phone and go to Google Maps. I enter my route. I turn right, go straight, turn left. I look at my phone: I'm lost again. I managed to get lost even with a GPS. I eventually make it back to Norm's house. I eat two waffles, drink a glass of orange juice, and turn on my computer. I check the price of flights to Tunisia and let out a little "Wha!?" They've dropped big time. I blink a few times and refresh the page to make sure I'm not hallucinating. I could buy a return ticket for next to nothing. I'm shaking a little, which makes me feel like an idiot. I buy the ticket. I eat six waffles with way too much butter. I touch my bicep, touch my bandage with my fingertips. I press lightly on it. I wish I could talk with Robin Williams and that he could tell me that everything's going to be OK, that this trip is going to help clear my mind and all that. I'd tell him that I don't want to clear my mind; I want to fill it with the things around me. I am Anakin on Mustafar, I am Darth Vader in Repentigny, I am Will Hunting in Tunisia.

Norm knocks on my bedroom door. It's really early. I wake up, jump out of bed, and throw on some underwear. I open the door. He says someone's here to see me about a bed. "Oh shit, that's right. I'm selling my bed." I pull on a sweater and go upstairs. There's a guy standing there. He smells like aftershave. He's wearing a gold watch. "Hi, I'm Gaétan. I've come about the bed and the bedside tables." "Yes, come on in. They're downstairs." Norm is sitting at the kitchen table reading the paper, his legs crossed, his glasses perched on the end of his nose. He gives me a look, question marks in his eyes. I go downstairs with Gaétan and show him the bed and the bedside tables. "Oh, you haven't taken the bed apart?" "Err, no." "You're gonna have to... I don't have a delivery truck, and it's a queen..." "Yeah." I feel pathetic in my underwear and my Mickey Mouse sweater. "You got a screwdriver at least, cause it's not gonna come apart on its own?" I break out in a sweat. I don't have a tool to my name, and I've never unscrewed a thing in my life. To reassure myself that I'm not entirely useless, I mentally run over the things I'm good at. Nothing comes to mind. Gaétan stares at me. He looks kind of disappointed in me. I think to myself: Well, I can recite all of Han Solo and Greedo's lines from the standoff scene at the Mos Eisley cantina. "So, about that screwdriver..." "I'll be right back." I go upstairs to find Norm. I feel like an eight-year-old kid. I ask him if he has a screwdriver. "Flat, Phillips, or Robertson?" I haven't the faintest idea. "One of each." He gets up and heads to the garage. He's wearing pyjama bottoms with the Incredible Hulk on them. He hands me the screwdrivers. "Thanks." Back on Dagobah, Gaétan is examining the bedside table. He hears me come in the room and turns around. "Where's the other table?" "In the closet... It wouldn't fit in the bedroom." He gives me a look, takes the screwdrivers, and gets to it. I'm relieved to see Gaétan taking matters in hand. I pitch in by stripping the sheets from the bed and pulling off the mattress. He hands me bits of bed as he goes. He starts with the headboard, then unscrews the legs one at a time. My bed is pretty basic. My life skills are pretty basic. I feel a little twinge of sorrow at the sight of my bed all in pieces. I hadn't really thought it through, and now I realize I no longer have a bed. I had to save up a long time to buy that bed, and it was kind of a point of pride. I just sold my pride to Gaétan. To console myself, I think about Tunisia. I help Gaétan carry the pieces of bed to his big, red Dodge Caravan. It's bright and shiny; it looks new enough to be this year's model. Gaétan pulls a wad of notes from his pocket. His watch glimmers in the winter sunlight. It's humid today, and it feels colder than usual. Gaétan counts out the bills with his fat fingers. "There you go, it's all there." "Yep."

He hands me the money and leaves without looking back. When I go back in the house, Norm asks what's going on. "I sold my bed." "I saw that... What for?" I stare at the floor, walk over to him, and sit down at the table. "I'm moving out." He sets his pencil down on his crossword. "You're moving out?" "Yeah, I wanted to tell you before that guy showed up this morning... Sorry." "Where're you moving to? You won't find anything cheaper... and you still owe me money." "Yeah, I know. I plan to sell my car, too." Norm stares at his newspaper in silence. "Where're you gonna live?" I don't know what to say. I don't feel like telling him I'm selling everything I own so I can go to Tunisia. I rack my brains, try to come up with a lie that doesn't sound obvious. The only one that comes to mind is Cammy. "I'm moving to New York to live with my sister for a while." He doesn't say anything. He picks up his pencil and makes a little X in the margin of his paper. "Oh," he says, looking up at me. "When are you leaving?" "This week... I found a last-minute flight." I can't bring myself to look him in the eye. I stare at a corner of the table. I wonder who might have sanded and varnished that table. Where are they now? Are they happy? Did they sell everything they owned, too, to go somewhere far away? Norm folds his paper, takes off his glasses, and sets them on the table. "OK, son." "Do you think I could sleep on the basement sofa until I leave?" "Sure." He gets up and walks out of the kitchen. I think I've hurt his feelings, and I feel bad. I go back down to Dagobah. I stuff all the clothes I never wear into garbage bags. I'll drop them off at the Saint Vincent de Paul before I go.

I check my phone: no messages. I sit down on the basement sofa with my laptop. I write in front of the turned-off TV. I keep fleshing out the story about the guy with the summer job in a tourist information office. It's dark, so I turn on the old floor lamp. I can hear Norm walking from the kitchen to the living room, then from the living room to his bedroom. I hear his door close. I yawn. I'm hungry, but I don't have the energy to make myself something to eat. I wouldn't know what to make anyway. My story ends in a McDonald's parking lot. I read it back through; it's no good. There's no rhythm to it, it's too repetitive, the main character is bland. Next time, I'll write about a diamond smuggler in Sierra Leone. All guns, death, and betrayal. People couldn't care less about some guy chasing flies around a tourist information office. I turn off my computer, lie down on the sofa, and think about what I'm going to do in Tunisia. I don't have a plan. I feel a bit like the character in that McDonald's parking lot. I yawn, roll over onto my side, and start to nod off. As I lie on the sofa, it feels like I'm in a little rowboat. I wonder what Tunisia's really like. I wonder if there are any McDonald's in Tunisia.

I dreamed I was going out with Armie Hammer. We were madly in love. We were at a hockey arena watching a game, taking selfies, eating hot dogs, taking more selfies, laughing and joking with the folks around us, kissing each other, our mouths full of hot dogs, only it wasn't disgusting. I type in "Tunisia is..." on Google and watch the answers come up. There are some good ones. I read, "Tunisia is finished, Tunisia is like a tub of harissa, Tunisia is ugly, Tunisia is so tiny..." If I were a country, I'd be Tunisia. I'm sitting in the vehicle registration office in Repentigny. I managed to get a good price for my car. In record time, too. A father and son have come to buy it. The dad's name is Martin. He reminds me a little of my own dad. He's a bit of a joker, laughs all the time. He seems happy to be buying his son his first car. When I turned the ignition to show that the Mazda's engine was still in good shape, the guitar from *Fell in Love With a Girl* blared out into the car. The dad jumped, and so did I. I dived to turn the radio down. "As you can see, the radio works great." The dad laughed. The kid didn't bat an eyelid. I have the sense of humour of a sixty-year-old dad. I feel a bit like I'm retired: no job to go to, off on my travels. I hand over my registration to the agent at the desk, and they refund me the four months I had left. I sign the paperwork and wait for a while in one of the green chairs while the dad sorts everything out. Back outside in the parking lot, I take off my license plate. I don't have a car anymore. Martin hands me a cheque that I deposit in the bank across the street right away, then he gives me a lift home, his son following behind us in my old car. I feel a little empty, like I've lost my bearings. I've set fire to every last bearing I had. All I have left are the waffles in Norm's freezer. I won't even have time to eat them all: I leave tomorrow. Martin pulls up in front of the house and says, "Well, thanks a lot. See you around." "Sure thing." We shake hands. I get out and watch my car pull away. I can hear loud rap music coming from the Mazda. Sadly, I don't think he's into the White Stripes. I watch the Mazda disappear. I can hear Jack White off in the distance, but that can't be real. It must be in my head. I think of Armie Hammer. It would be nice if he'd hold me in his arms on the sidewalk and tell me everything's going to be OK. I'd like to spend the rest of my days with Armie Hammer. I'd make him baloney and Sidekicks, and he'd think that was just the cutest thing. I go back inside, make myself a sandwich, watch TV. I try to talk to Norm, but he's acting a bit strange. Ever since I told him I was moving out, he's barely said a word. He's not avoiding me, but I think he's sad. Which makes me sad. I never thought I'd grow so fond of a landlord, especially one who looks like Joe Pesci and dresses up as Santa. I go down to Dagobah, look around the room. It's empty. The only thing left is my bookshelf and the books on it. I don't know what I'm going to do with them. Turns out, the woman who said she was interested never got back to me. I go upstairs to the kitchen, but Norm isn't there. I find him on the sofa, his head down. "You OK?" "Yeah, son. I'm fine." "OK... I emptied my room. There's just my bookshelf left. And the books. I wasn't able to sell the bookshelf. Do you want it? I'll give it to you for nothing." Norm turns a little and looks at me, his head hanging off to one side. "OK, son. Just leave it in your room. I'll keep it." "OK... Great... Thanks." I leave Norm in peace; I don't want to bother him anymore. I head back down to the sofa, lie on my back. Tomorrow I'll drop off two bags of my old clothes at the Saint Vincent de Paul. After that, I don't know. I'll just kill time, stare out the window, make waffles. I hear a creak on the stairs. I look up, stay where I am on the sofa, eyeing the stairs. I see Norm's legs slowly making their way downstairs. He comes over, asks if he can sit beside me. "Yeah." He sits down and looks at his hands. He's holding something. "Sorry, son. I haven't been feeling great lately. Your news really knocked the wind outta me." He stops talking, struggles to find his words. "I've grown real fond of you. I don't know, you remind me a bit of my son. It was nice having you about the place." "I like you too, Norm. You're the best landlord I ever had... No one ever made me a rigatoni cake before." He laughs, he laughs with his finest gap-toothed old guy laugh. "Forget about the rent. It doesn't matter. I'll take care of it." "No, no, Norm. Fair's fair, I'll pay you what I owe." "No, forget about it." He turns towards me and hands me an old coin, no bigger than a toonie. I take a closer look and recognize St. Christopher, the patron saint of travellers, though the coin's so worn, he's almost completely disappeared. "I found that on a fishing trip years ago," he says. "I thought it would be more use to you, seeing how you both have the same name and all."

I have a lump in my throat. There's a lot of warmth in Norm's eyes as he looks at me. He's an old fish that doesn't come around very often, the type you only catch once in a lifetime. An old fish that's not used to showing so much affection to another man. I feel lucky to be on the receiving end of so much affection. I don't really know what to make of it. I try not to cry. I don't want to ruin the moment. I take my time, making sure to keep my voice steady. "Thanks, Norm," I manage to say. "That's really nice of you." "You're welcome, son." He stands, doesn't look back, goes up the stairs one by one. He disappears slowly, then completely. I can't see him anymore, but I know he's still there, somewhere in my mind. He hasn't evaporated; he can't just run off up a set of creaking stairs. He's built himself a little fishing shack by the water somewhere inside my head. I know he's not going to budge from there. I know he'll wait for me, he won't leave me here by myself. I know he'll stay put in his shack until I'm ready to move on.

There's something mysterious about airports. They always remind me of my lung condition. I still don't understand how planes manage to fly. I mean, I get the concept of wings and the engine and all that. But, I don't know. See, if someone told me a bunch of aliens were going to wipe out all of humanity, and that they'd spare me so long as I explained how humanity evolved, I'd be in real trouble. I've forgotten everything I learned in history. I know a bit about the Big Bang, *Homo sapiens*,

Newton and his dumb apple, Darwin, and that kind of stuff. I don't know. If I tried to explain it, it'd come out all wrong. The aliens would ask me to build a toaster, a pyramid, a pen. And I'd tell them I'm no good at that kind of thing. They'd all give each other a look: What the fuck? All I'd be good for is writing them a poem or warming up some Sidekicks for them. The aliens would be so pissed off. I look around me. Everyone's on the move, everyone's doing something. There are bags everywhere. I'd like to open each one, find out what everyone's doing here, roast a big pig for everyone, and we could all chat about life for hours. Everyone has a kind of funny look about them, a language of their own. I keep an eye on them, watch the faces they make. I turn on my phone and head straight to Google: "Can a plane..." I've hit the jackpot, I think to myself. I read, "Can a plane hover in the sky? Can a plane stop in the air? Can a plane fly backwards? Can a plane fall from the sky? Can a plane take off by itself? Can a plane fly without an engine?" I chuckle to myself on my bench. I see a message pop up on my screen. It's Amidala. She writes, "Sorry, I was taking a break from my phone. How are you?" It's good to hear from her. I write back, "Good. And you?" "Great." "Glad to hear it." I wait for a while, but there's no answer. I write, "We should go for coffee sometime." I wait, still no answer. I watch a mom arguing with her daughter, telling her to stop fidgeting. The little girl huffs, her eyes full of tears. They call my flight. I stand up, walk over to the gate, and wait in line.

They let me through. I walk down the gangway and onto the plane. The flight attendant gives me a little smile, looks at my ticket, points me in the right direction. I put my bag in the overhead compartment and sit down. I have a window seat; I didn't even know. That's nice. I realize I don't have my big suitcase with me. My heart starts pounding, then I remember I gave it to a lady before going through preboarding. I'd forgotten already. My memory's not the best. My head's not the best. I am a goldfish. I glance at my phone. Amidala hasn't written back. I feel a bit depressed. I watch the people coming down the aisles, making their way to their seats. I write, "Look after yourself. Live life to the fullest, my little birdie." I turn off my phone and look out the window. Rain is falling in a fine mist. I've never seen such tiny raindrops. There's no snow that I can see on the runway. You'd think it was a dark day in August. I see a hand appear on the back of the seat in front of me. I peer around the seat, leaning into the window, and see a boy looking back. He's blond. He reminds me of young Anakin in *The Phantom Menace*. He sticks out his tongue and pulls a face. He hides behind his seat and pops in and out of his hiding place like a mouse going in and out of its hole. I make a face at him, and he laughs. I try to translate "little rascal" into Mandarin, but I still don't know how. I hide. I tuck my head between my knees, put my hands over my eyes. I feel myself disappearing. I feel the boy's fingers on my head. I feel myself disappearing into the seat.

QC FICTION

Current & Upcoming Books

01 *LIFE IN THE COURT OF MATANE*
by Eric Dupont
translated by Peter McCambridge

02 *THE UNKNOWN HUNTSMAN*
by Jean-Michel Fortier
translated by Katherine Hastings

03 *BROTHERS*
by David Clerson
translated by Katia Grubisic
Finalist, 2017 Governor General's Literary Award for Translation

04 *LISTENING FOR JUPITER*
by Pierre-Luc Landry
translated by Arielle Aaronson and Madeleine Stratford
Winner, 2017 Expozine Best Book Award

05 *I NEVER TALK ABOUT IT*
by Véronique Côté and Steve Gagnon
translated by 37 different translators

06 *BEHIND THE EYES WE MEET*
by Mélissa Verreault
translated by Arielle Aaronson

07 *SONGS FOR THE COLD OF HEART*
by Eric Dupont
translated by Peter McCambridge
Finalist, 2018 Scotiabank Giller Prize
Finalist, 2018 Governor General's Award
for Translation

08 *EXPLOSIONS: MICHAEL BAY AND THE PYROTECHNICS OF THE IMAGINATION*
by Mathieu Poulin
translated by Aleshia Jensen
Finalist, 2018 Governor General's Award
for Translation

09 *IN EVERY WAVE*
by Charles Quimper
translated by Guil Lefebvre

10 *IN THE END THEY TOLD THEM ALL TO GET LOST*
by Laurence Leduc-Primeau
translated by Natalia Hero

11 *PRAGUE*
by Maude Veilleux
translated by Aleshia Jensen & Aimee Wall

12 *THE LITTLE FOX OF MAYERVILLE*
by Éric Mathieu
translated by Peter McCambridge

13 *THE ART OF THE FALL*
by Véronique Coté, Jean-Michel Girouard,
Jean-Philippe Joubert, Simon Lepage, Danielle
Le Saux-Farmer, Marianne Marceau, Olivier Normand,
Pascale Renaud-Hébert
translated by Danielle Le Saux-Farmer

14 *THE ELECTRIC BATHS*
by Jean-Michel Fortier
translated by Katherine Hastings

15 *TATOUINE*
by Jean-Christophe Réhel
translated by Katherine Hastings & Peter McCambridge

Visit **qcfiction.com** for details and to subscribe
to a full season of QC Fiction titles.